OPERATION

ILKKA REMES

OPERATION OCEAN EMERALD

A LUKE BARON ADVENTURE

First published in 2010 by
Andersen Press Limited
20 Vauxhall Bridge Road
London SW1V 2SA
www.andersenpress.co.uk
www.lukebaron.com

British Library Cataloguing in Publication Data available.

ISBN 978 1 84939 058 3

Printed and bound in Great Britain by CPI Bookmarque, Croydon CR0 4TD

This story contains real clues you can
follow – if you dare…

PART
ONE

PART ONE

1

Luke was looking at the computer games and didn't notice a thing when Toni slipped the DVD into his shoulder bag. Shoplifting was a crime, Toni had told himself, but Luke was still only fourteen, so the police here in Finland couldn't touch him.

Toni then reached for another copy of the same DVD, showing it innocently to Luke. 'Bet your dad wouldn't like this. He's so uptight, it's a wonder you have a TV at all.'

'*The Butcher of the Bronx.*' Luke shook his head. 'Pathetic. It's not even Blu-ray.'

'What a snob,' Toni said, putting the DVD back.

'What are we doing here, anyway?' Luke asked. 'You don't have any money and nor do I.'

'That might change.' Toni took something from his breast pocket. 'If we sell *this.*'

The burgundy booklet in Toni's hand was the French passport the boys had found near a lay-by on the Helsinki motorway the day before. They'd taken Toni's car for a spin and had been stretching their legs at the lay-by when Luke spotted a slim hard-shell briefcase lying in the ditch. They'd forced it open and found the passport inside. Slipped between its pages was something very intriguing:

a boarding pass that looked like a credit card, with a photo of the passport-holder's face and a hologram of a ship, the *Ocean Emerald*. Tiny letters were printed on the back: *Property of Emerald Cruise Corporation, Miami, FL, U.S.A. Reward if found: US$100.*

'We should hand it in,' Luke said. 'The ship will be in Helsinki on Thursday. That's only an hour's drive. What do you say?'

'For one hundred dollars? It's an insult. The passport's worth at least a thousand on the black market, maybe more.'

Luke made a grab for the passport, but Toni didn't let go.

'She's not bad,' Toni said, grinning over the passport photo. 'Juliette du Pont,' he said, trying for a French accent. 'A bit like that actress in *Scream*, which of course you haven't seen.'

'Thankfully not.'

'I saw this TV series about a guy who sold EU passports to illegal immigrants,' Toni said, letting Luke take the documents. 'Criminals are always looking for new identities.'

'Go right ahead. I'll visit you in prison.'

Luke carefully slid the passport and boarding pass into the back pocket of his jeans. He followed his friend to the games section, where the manager was locking the glass cabinet containing PlayStations, Xboxes and Nintendos. The man was in his shirtsleeves and had massive sweat stains under his arms. He grunted something in Finnish and wagged his finger at Toni.

'What did he say?' Luke asked. He wasn't quite fluent in Finnish, his mother's language.

'They close in half an hour. And if we're not buying, we're welcome to leave right away.'

Luke expected Toni to answer back, or at least ignore the manager's words, but instead, he bowed his head, turned round and headed back towards the front of the shop. Luke hurried after him, between the shelves and towards the cash desks. Suddenly, he glimpsed a familiar face. Emma. Her parents were regular customers at Gran's antique shop. Her beautifully sculpted ponytail was held together by a black velvet scrunchie that gave her a sophisticated look. She sauntered towards him. Their eyes met and Luke felt the blood rushing to his cheeks.

'Luke!' Emma said.

'Hi,' was all he managed in reply.

Emma slowed her steps, then brushed past, stopping at the music section. She had looked surprised to see Luke, probably thinking he should have been back at school in whatever country he happened to be living in this year. Luke had lived in Switzerland until recently, but now he was based in Brussels, Belgium. His parents moved around a lot. Emma and he had known each other since they were in pushchairs, when their grannies used to take them to the playground here in Porvoo, on the southern coast of Finland. He had spent many summers here.

Luke stumbled past the cashier, feeling hot and clumsy. He glanced over his shoulder and saw Emma flicking through the CDs under a large poster of Amy Winehouse.

'Why are *you* so flustered?' Toni had caught up with Luke and was staring back at Emma. 'Oh, right... And what makes you think she'd go for a runt like you?'

Luke didn't bother to reply.

He stepped through the exit turnstile and jumped as the alarm burst into life and an orange light began to flash. The customers and cashiers turned to stare as the manager came striding from the shop and slapped his hand on Toni's shoulder.

The manager switched off the alarm and with visible relish began frisking Toni's pockets, then marched him back to the turnstile and told him to walk through again.

'Toni, what's going on?' Luke whispered, staring at his friend.

Toni had turned white.

Everyone else in the shop was just loving the show – except Emma. With a blast of shame, Luke met her eyes. He could barely breathe. Toni had embarrassed him before, but this went too far.

Toni stepped through the turnstile. Nothing happened.

With a sadistic frown, the man turned his attention to Luke. So did the customers. So did Emma.

'*Sinun vuorosi,*' the manager said.

'Your turn,' Toni said, blushing.

Luke swallowed. 'I haven't done anything.'

Luke could feel Emma's eyes on his back as he stepped through. At once, the alarm began to wail. The light pulsed. The manager took Luke to one side and asked to see his bag.

'You need to have that machine checked,' Luke said in English, but his voice came out weaker than he had hoped.

With shaking hands, he offered his bag. The manager pulled out a DVD: *The Butcher of the Bronx.*

'Do you have a receipt for this?' the manager said in heavily accented English.

'No, I don't...'

'Then follow me.'

'You creep,' Luke hissed at Toni. 'I can't believe this.'

'What shall I do?' Toni's fat cheeks were red. 'Should I come with you?'

'We don't need an audience,' the manager snapped. 'Move!'

Staring at the floor, Luke followed the manager into the office at the back.

Then Luke thought of something that made matters even worse. *He still had Juliette du Pont's passport and boarding pass in his pocket.* A stolen DVD was one thing, but what would the police say if they found him in possession of these documents? Cruises on the *Ocean Emerald* cost thousands of dollars, and a passport was a personal document. Nor did he fancy having to explain how he'd found the items.

He bowed his head. He felt totally miserable. Little did he know that a much worse nightmare lay ahead of him. One that would tear apart his summer holiday in Finland and terrorize thousands of innocent people.

2

Fifteen hundred kilometres from Luke, the *Ocean Emerald* was moored in the Port of Amsterdam. In a warehouse not far from the port, a minor delinquent named Ronny de Jong eased a plastic bag of explosives into the belly of a gutted swordfish.

He scooped crushed ice onto the fish and shook his freezing hands, cursing under his breath. Pulling a face, he reached for the massive, slimy octopus that lay on the stainless-steel work surface and slapped it into the polystyrene box, on top of the swordfish. Then he took a shrink-wrapped sub-machine-gun from his backpack on the floor and slid it inside the octopus

Ronny's breath steamed in the walk-in fridge, but he could feel sweat trickling under his shirt. A few more handfuls of ice, then the lid. He blew into his stinging hands, picked up a filleting knife and carefully marked both ends of the polystyrene box with a scratch. There were twenty boxes in all. Six were marked.

Ronny stepped into the sparsely furnished office and closed the door of the fridge behind him. He had packed all twenty boxes himself, after the rest of the staff had left. With numb hands, he printed out the invoice, folded it into his back pocket and stepped into the yard, where the delivery van was ready for loading. PIET HAARHUIS – FISH AND SEAFOOD was painted in Dutch on the sides and back of the van. Ten minutes later, the boxes were safely stacked inside and he was done.

Ronny swung the van onto Zuiderzeeweg and began to weave his way through the evening traffic towards the port. Explaining the assignment five months before, the Big Boss had told Ronny to get a job with Piet Haarhuis and to wait for further instructions. Having received them, Ronny had decided to execute his part like a real pro. That way, the Big Boss might give him an even better paid assignment next time.

As he approached the familiar port area on Java Island, Ronny switched his attention to his surroundings. The lights of the cranes and the customs houses shimmered in the thickening gloom. Suddenly, it hit home: *this wasn't a rehearsal any more.* The fish didn't contain metal bars. They were stuffed with powerful explosives, weapons and ammunition. Ronny's heart began to race. He reached into his pocket for the packet of chewing gum he'd brought specially and put a piece into his mouth.

Ronny flicked on the indicator and turned into Pana-maweg, which led into the port from the west. Most cruise ships docked at the passenger terminal near the city centre, within walking distance of Amsterdam's restaurants and museums, but the *Ocean Emerald* was simply too massive. So the world's most luxurious cruise ship had to find a berth here, among the humble tankers and container ships.

A gusty wind blew from the sea and the headlights of the oncoming traffic flashed in the puddles on the street. Lorries were returning from the port, having unloaded their innocent cargo into the cruise ship: provisions, clean laundry, spare parts and the luxuries sold in the duty-free shop, everything from gold watches to perfume.

The first gate was flanked by a small shelter for the security guards, who were drinking coffee inside. No one came out. With shaking hands, Ronny put two more pieces of gum into his mouth. The van's wipers laboured on the windscreen. At last the door opened and a guard stepped out into the rain. Ronny wound down his window.

'Piet Haarhuis, a consignment of fish for the *Ocean Emerald*.'

The guard yawned and waved his arm. Ronny passed through the gate and drove slowly into the brightly lit port.

Behind the warehouses and stacks of shipping containers, a majestic apparition towered against the night. It sparkled in the rain, a magic castle awash with light. The garland of electric bulbs decorating the funnel and the masts shone with festive brightness. The rows of balconies seemed to go on forever: two hundred and forty metres of luxury, forty-five thousand tonnes of extravagance, nine decks of privilege. Exotic cities, faraway lands, new continents... Voyages for the moneyed jet set. The *Ocean Emerald*, queen of the seven seas. This week, she would sail from Amsterdam to Helsinki, St Petersburg – and Hell.

Ronny suppressed an involuntary shiver and forced himself to focus on the task at hand. You had to take risks in life, if you wanted to get ahead. He'd never live on unemployment benefit again. The Big Boss paid well. Ronny would show him what he could do.

The long quay bustled with activity. Sewage was being pumped off the cruise ship, and rubbish truck after rubbish truck pulled up to receive the waste generated on board. Fresh water and tonnes of fuel flowed in the opposite direction, into the enormous tanks deep inside the ship.

A luxury bus had driven up to the *Ocean Emerald* and elderly tourists were shuffling onto the glass-walled gangway while their luggage was unloaded for security screening and delivery to the cabins. These passengers had flown into Schiphol airport in order to join the Baltic leg of the cruise in Amsterdam. They came from all over – the US, Asia, South Africa and South America – but they had one thing in common: they were rich.

The driver of the van in front of Ronny's hopped out into the rain and opened the back doors of his vehicle. Ronny swallowed as he watched the security guards wrench open one of the wooden wine crates. *A random check.*

The rain fell, heavier and heavier, engulfing the wipers.

Ronny rubbed his clammy palms against his thighs and forced himself to take deep breaths. Sheltering under a huge golf umbrella, one of the guards held a wine bottle against the light, mimed taking a swig, then handed it back to the driver. Maritime security had been tightened all over the world after 9/11, especially on cruise ships carrying a significant number of Americans – which meant *most* cruise ships.

Ronny released the clutch and eased the van up to the yellow line. He fought down the panic, trying desperately to focus on something innocent. For the first time, he regretted his greed.

* * *

A stack of CCTV screens filled a whole wall of the control room deep inside the *Ocean Emerald*. An alert pair of eyes darted from screen to screen, observing the stream of passengers passing under the chandelier in the ship's foyer. There were also cameras on the gangway, in the loading area on the quayside and above the airport-style conveyor belt that fed the luggage through the X-ray machine.

The head of security, former FBI agent Craig 'Coyote' Thomson, knew that the safety of one thousand passengers and six hundred crew depended on him. He liked his job and, being one of the world's finest security professionals, was proud of it, too.

He leaned closer to the topmost screen on the right. It showed a white delivery van marked PIET HAARHUIS – FISH AND SEAFOOD.

3

Luke glanced at Dad's strong hands on the wheel. The left one was bandaged: the tip of the little finger was missing. Luke had no idea what had happened to it and Dad refused to say. Something had gone wrong at work – and work was a topic Dad wouldn't discuss with Luke. What was the point of having a dad who worked for Europol if he never shared any stories with you?

'Looking on the bright side,' Luke said, 'you now have fewer fingernails to cut, and—'

'Were you alone in that shop?' Dad interrupted.

'Did you know that the longest fingernail ever grown measured 68.58 centimetres?'

'I asked you a question.'

Luke bit his lip. 'I was with Toni.'

Dad looked at him for the first time since they had got in the car. 'And did you tell the manager that?'

'The manager saw us together.'

The engine groaned as the old Volvo estate climbed a small cobbled street lined with cheerfully painted board fences and past the medieval church in the centre of Porvoo. Gnarled maples leaned over the dark river behind the old Finnish houses with their wooden porches. The lampposts cast a yellow glow against the black sky, reminding Luke of the gaslights in the old Sherlock Holmes films he used to watch as a little boy with his English grandfather in Dad's home in East Sussex.

Of course, Luke knew he had to cover for Toni. It was a question of honour: no matter what your friend did to you, telling tales was even worse. Revenge was another matter. Oh yes. Toni would pay for what he'd done. Luke would get hold of Toni's Visa card and use it to buy gambling tips online... He knew how easy this was, having borrowed his gran's credit card for the same purpose a couple of years ago, to his lingering shame. Gran, being a good sport, had never breathed a word to Mum and Dad, and Luke had sworn he would never do it again. But the promise only concerned *Gran's* card...

'Ring Toni and tell him to come over to Gran's.'

'Why?'

'Because I say so. Right now.'

Luke wriggled in his seat and extracted his mobile from his back pocket. Toni replied after a single ring.

'Dad wants to talk to you at Gran's,' Luke said.

'*I'm already here,*' Toni replied meekly.

'Right... Well, we're almost there.'

Luke cut the line. He felt much better. This was the best way out. He had done his utmost to protect Toni, but Dad had guessed everything, and Toni himself was clearly getting ready to own up to what he had done – which, in turn, would impress Dad.

'He's already there,' Luke said.

'Good. That's good.'

Luke knew exactly what to expect now: a calm, rational rebuke for Toni, and a lecture to Luke about the importance of choosing one's friends carefully. Tough words, but no shouting. Had it been Toni's dad, the shouting would have been the least of it. Dad slowed down and steered the Volvo through the narrow gate into Gran's yard.

Toni appeared from the shadows in his baggy jeans, black fleece and trainers. A dim bulb shone above the front door of the wooden house.

'You go in,' Dad told Luke. 'Toni and I will have a little word alone.'

Toni took Luke's place in the passenger seat, and avoiding his friend's eyes, Luke hurried across the yard and up the stone steps of Gran's little house.

'Luke, where have you been?' Mum asked.

'I'll explain . . .' Luke sidled past her, and went straight into the tiny box room, no larger than a walk-in wardrobe, which was reserved for him every summer.

'Luke, what is it? Where's Dad?'

'He's coming,' Luke called. 'He's in the car.'

Luke looked at the suitcases crammed into his room. Dad had just returned from Washington, and Mum was due to leave for a science conference the following week. Luke threw himself onto the bed and let out a deep sigh. He could smell pancakes – Dad must have been cooking dinner when he'd been called to the record shop. Once or twice each summer, Dad impressed Gran by making Finnish pancakes from scratch. She refused to eat pancakes made from a mix, or anything made from a mix, for that matter.

Luke turned onto his side, resting his cheek on his palm. He'd been looking forward to Dad's return, but what he wanted right now was to fall asleep for a week, until things had calmed down.

The small writing desk beside the bed was where he kept his treasures: a laser pointer, a compass and a pair of night-vision goggles. The items on the book shelf above the desk were even more interesting, especially the two books that Luke had recently ordered online: *Hostage Rescue* and *Covert Surveillance*. Dad had frowned when the parcel arrived, but that same day Luke had caught him reading *Hostage Rescue* in the kitchen. Luke had been thrilled: it made him feel mature in Dad's eyes. Maybe one day soon Dad would open up about his job with Europol.

Luke's bookshelf also contained four well-thumbed volumes of *The Guinness Book of World Records* and an embarrassing detective set that his own dad, of all people, had given him last summer, which contained a kit for collecting fingerprints, a magnifying glass and a fake nose with huge eyebrows attached. Under the writing desk was a powerful PC that Luke had assembled all by himself, using second-hand components harvested from junk shops and eBay. The plasma screen on the desk looked out of place against the faded floral wallpaper and the wooden window frame.

Gran used the PC to send Luke emails during the school year, and Luke was secretly designing a website for her as a birthday present. She could use it to market her antiques, if she wanted. Gran would be seventy this winter, but she still put in long hours in her small shop in Porvoo, a short walk from the house.

In former years, the family's summer routine had included swimming trips, picnics, berry-picking expeditions and of course bathing in the sauna on Saturdays. Their summer life in Finland was quiet. TV was rationed.

Loud music was forbidden altogether. The summer was supposed to be a time when Mum, Dad and Luke were all together, but last year, and again this year, Luke had spent most of July and August alone with Gran. Mum was writing a scientific paper that seemed to have taken over her entire holiday. Like Dad, she had an important job and loved what she did. Had it not been for Toni, Luke would have died of boredom.

The door opened. It was Mum, *The Journal of High-Energy Particle Physics* in hand.

'Luke, what's going on? Why is Dad talking to Toni in the car?'

'It's no big deal.' Luke bit his lip. 'By the way, if you have any more suitcases to store, there's plenty of room, for example, on my bed.'

'Sorry, darling. Peter just shoved his stuff in here when he arrived, and I'll be off in a few days, so it doesn't seem worth hauling them upstairs... Oh, you put it on the wall!'

'Yeah, it's cool. Thanks.'

Luke glanced at the huge, colourful poster representing a carbon atom. Mum had brought it back from a science symposium in Tokyo and Luke had pinned it above his bed at the beginning of the holiday. Mum had only just noticed. Next to the poster was a facsimile copy of an ancient star chart, which Dad had found in Krakow.

'Well, there's dinner when you're ready. Dad made pancakes. He's jet-lagged. I'm just going upstairs to do a tiny bit more work.'

Mum closed the door. Luke squeezed past the suitcases to the window just in time to see Toni solemnly shaking hands with his father, then skulking out of the gate. The front door opened and closed and Dad's footsteps went towards the kitchen.

Toni had confessed, Luke felt sure of it. He knew it would have been best to join his parents right away, so as to get the awkward discussion over with, but he couldn't face it. They'd lay into Toni as usual, and this time they had a reason. Luke rubbed his face. Toni was his best mate in this part of the world. Or had been, until tonight's incident.

Suddenly, his mobile vibrated. It was Toni. Luke hesitated, then took the call.

'*I've told your dad everything that happened.*'

'And that makes it OK, does it?'

'*Sorry, mate. Really.*'

Luke let out a sigh. 'Whatever.'

'*I was stupid. Look, about the passport... If you want to ask your dad what we should do, that's fine by me.*'

Luke hesitated. 'He doesn't need to know everything,' he finally said, keeping his voice down.

'*So the road trip to Helsinki is still on?*'

'Sure it's on.'

Toni was silent for a moment, then said, '*Excellent, Mr C.*'

'But after we've split the reward, I get ten per cent of your share.'

'*What for?*'

'For stress and aggravation caused. And this will be only the first instalment.'

'*In that case I want some money for the petrol.*'

'No way. See you on Thursday. Try not to get arrested before then.'

Luke cut the line, sat in front of his computer and nudged the mouse. He typed in the address of his blog, www.heliocentrist.net, and entered the password that was only known to his inner circle. Two hits and no replies. With a sigh, he clicked on his favourites, chose www.OceanEmeraldCruises.com, and the *Ocean Emerald*'s resplendent home page filled the screen. He took the Frenchwoman's passport and boarding pass from his pocket, preparing to continue his research into her identity, then rushed to hide them under his mattress when he heard Gran's footsteps behind his door. She knocked her discreet knock.

'Come in, Gran.'

Gran's eyes twinkled. She was clutching the straw hat she always wore when she read the newspaper on the garden swing. Luke saw from her expression that she knew he was in a spot of trouble and had come to show her support.

'Hungry?' she said.

'Starving.'

She slipped her hand under Luke's arm. 'Then let's go and see what your dad's pancakes are like.'

'How was business today, Gran?'

'Middling. I need to modernize! But how do you modernize an antique shop, tell me that?'

'I've told you, Gran. Go online.'

'Talking of which, when do I get my next computer lesson?'

'Whenever you like! Except on Thursday…'

'What are your rates again?' Gran said, pretending not to remember.

'Ten euros an hour.'

'That's the discounted family rate, isn't it?'

Luke laughed. 'Yes.'

'Sounds reasonable to me. What about right after dinner?'

'Sure, Gran. That sounds great.'

'Very good.' Gran pretended to be thinking hard. 'In fact, I might go for a double lesson this time. Twenty euros, very good...'

Screaming seagulls dipped in and out of the darkness as they circled the battery of floodlights over the quay. Ronny was grateful for the rain, which disguised the nervous sweat streaming down his face as he unloaded the van. He spat his gum onto the asphalt and dried his forehead on his sleeve. Glancing at the man inside the fork-lift truck, he lifted another polystyrene box onto the wooden pallet on the fork. The scratch at the end of the box was clearly visible.

From the corner of his eye, Ronny saw the approaching figure of yet another security guard, this one armed with a torch, which he swung like a truncheon. Bending inside the van, where several boxes still remained, Ronny chose one without a scratch mark, then changed his mind and took a scratched box instead. He walked back to the fork-lift truck, heaved the box onto the pallet and turned to face the security guard, who pointed his long torch inside the van. Ronny grabbed another box.

'Wait.'

'I'm late as it is,' Ronny said.

'Open it.'

The lid of the polystyrene box squeaked when Ronny removed it. The guard scrabbled at the crushed ice with his gloved hand, revealing the mottled skin of a large salmon. Ronny replaced the lid and put the box on the pallet, on top of the others. The guard didn't move. Ronny could feel his heart hammering inside his ribcage. The next box had a scratch on it. Inside the box was a swordfish, and inside the swordfish was a two-kilo packet of Semtex, one of the most powerful explosives available. The charge couldn't be detected by X-rays or electronic screening, and sniffer dogs would be thrown off by the stench of fish. An anti-explosive swab taken from the seal between the lid and the box would, however, give the game away, and of course the guard could detect the explosives with his own hands and eyes if he probed inside the fish. Ronny leaned into his van and reached for another box.

'Hang on,' the guard said. 'Step aside.'

Ronny put the box back down on the floor of the van. He could only pray that the numbing cold would account for the frozen expression on his face.

The guard leaned forward and pulled the box closer.

'Heavy, aren't they?' he said.

'Tell me about it,' Ronny said.

'What's in here? Stones?' The guard prised off the lid of the box, revealing the dull-eyed swordfish on its bed of ice.

The lorry behind Ronny's van hooted its horn.

'Come on, man,' Ronny said, tensing his muscles, ready to act. 'Can't they inspect them on board?'

'I'm only doing my job.' The guard gave the fish a shove with the end of his torch. 'OK, off you go.'

Ronny barely felt the weight of the remaining boxes as he carried them from the van. When the last box was safely loaded onto the pallet, he nodded at the operator of the fork-lift truck and hurried back to his driving seat. As he sped off, feeling completely drained, Ronny caught a glimpse of the passengers filing up the glass-walled gangway.

He felt a faint twinge of pity, but of course it was too late for that.

4

Four days later

A man in his forties leaned against the railing on the Promenade Deck of the *Ocean Emerald*. Deeply tanned, he had curly hair and tortoiseshell glasses and wore a silk scarf around his neck. His hair streamed in the wind. Behind the racing clouds, the sun shone like a ball of fire over the Helsinki skyline.

The man adjusted the scarf with his strong, calloused hand, hiding the scar he had incurred in Marseilles back in 1988. Three hostages had died when the armed robbery had turned into a police shoot-out, but Philippe Delacroix had got away and evaded all attempts to catch him, despite the serious wound to his neck. That had been his first big heist – ruthless, efficient and well planned. International jobs followed, and Delacroix had tried his hand at the art trade. Then he'd got out of crime for several years, lying low, doing construction work again while studying in the evenings.

Delacroix kept his eyes on the quay, where the buses were discharging their passengers after a half-day tour of Helsinki. A few new faces would also join the cruise in

Helsinki, some intending to continue on to the Mediterranean after the visit to St Petersburg.

Ronny had delivered the first consignment in Amsterdam and another lad had brought the rest of the hardware in Copenhagen. So far so good. Two key people would board in Helsinki. One was Delacroix's closest associate, a woman. The other was an old man, a famous billionaire who normally had round-the-clock protection, and who went on cruises to relax without the company of his bodyguards. This cruise would turn out to be different.

Like most of the ship, the deck was monitored by CCTV cameras 24/7, but Delacroix felt relaxed about the eyes that were watching. Leaning against the railing to enjoy the fresh air was the most normal thing you could do on a cruise ship. Cameras couldn't read the thoughts of the people they filmed.

Delacroix was starting to feel chilly when Juliette du Pont finally appeared at his side. That was not her real name, but Delacroix thought it suited an athletic French beauty. Her eyes burned with manic energy, and Delacroix knew he had all of that energy under his command. She rested her hands on the railing, gazing towards the whitewashed Lutheran cathedral in the heart of Helsinki's historic centre. Delacroix noted a warm current surging through his veins. It was here, at last – the biggest gamble of his life.

'They're forecasting heavy seas,' Juliette said quietly. 'Gale-force winds.'

'They'll have no idea how to measure the force of *this* storm,' Delacroix said, and walked off, resisting the urge to talk longer.

He was relieved to see Juliette safely on board. Only a

week before the operation, her false passport and genuine boarding card had been stolen in a chance robbery targeting an armoured courier van that had been transporting cash and valuables from St Petersburg to Helsinki, where Juliette was already waiting.

Delacroix had been beside himself with rage: some bunch of small-timers had almost ruined his operation before it had even started. According to media reports, a large amount of money taken by the robbers was still missing, but various other items had been recovered along the Porvoo-Helsinki motorway. He had no way of knowing what had happened to the hard-shell briefcase containing Juliette's original travel documents.

But she had found a simple solution when she successfully applied for an emergency passport under her false identity at the French Consulate in Helsinki. The boarding pass had been replaced for a small fee.

Delacroix glanced at his watch. Three and a half hours to go. There was no sign of the billionaire... He walked to the bow of the ship, took the lift to the eighth deck for his next rendezvous.

Emilio Fernández, who worked on the ship as a cleaner, arrived punctually at the agreed spot in the middle of the long corridor, pushing his trolley and pretending to read the print-out listing his cabins for the day. Delacroix glanced round instinctively. There was no one else about and he already knew that there were no cameras in this part of the vessel.

'Where?' Delacroix asked Emilio, resisting the powerful urge to look at the trolley. Somewhere under the linen and towels and miniature bottles of shampoo and shower gel, the detonator lay hidden.

'Deck Nine, Corridor One,' he whispered. 'The fuse box near the bridge.'

Again, Delacroix walked off as soon as he had made contact with his associate. The *Ocean Emerald*'s staff code was 'friendly but discreet' and it was unusual for a passenger to exchange more than just a few words with a cleaner. At this stage, he was taking no risks whatsoever.

5

Luke sat in the front passenger seat of Toni's Nissan, Juliette du Pont's passport and boarding card clutched in his hand. The shoplifting episode already seemed a distant memory. Dad had been very reasonable after Toni had confessed what he'd done.

'There it is,' Luke said, as the tall forecastle, radio antennae and funnel of the immense cruise ship came into view behind the waterfront apartment blocks of southern Helsinki.

'We'll be lucky if we get a single cent.' Toni drove past a red-brick warehouse, towards the quay where the *Ocean Emerald* was moored. 'They'll say "Thanks, boys", and that will be that.'

'I bet you ten euros we'll get more than a hundred if we hand in the passport as well,' Luke said.

'And I bet your gran wears woolly underwear in winter! You're addicted to betting.'

'You're addicted to splatter.'

'Which is worse? Gambling or watching films?'

'You sound like Dad. Investment betting isn't the same as playing the lottery. In fact, it's not betting at all.'

'You sound like my mum when she's explaining how her drinking isn't really drinking.'

Luke felt his cheeks go red – for once, Toni had him speechless.

'Let's at least *try* to sell the passport,' Toni continued. 'We can even do it online.'

'Too risky.' Luke wondered whether he should tell Toni what he had discovered about Juliette du Pont, or what he thought he had discovered, and decided against it. Toni would simply laugh at his suspicions.

'Maybe you should watch some real films,' Toni said. 'It might build up your tolerance to stress.'

'What do you recommend? *The Butcher of the Bronx*?'

'You're so funny.' Toni's face darkened. 'Look, I'm sorry about all that.'

'Did my dad give you a hard time?'

'No more than I deserved. Your dad's pretty cool, Luke.'

Luke grinned. 'Yeah.'

A car on the right hooted its horn and Toni had to swerve to avoid it. The man behind the wheel shook his fist and Luke decided it was best to let Toni concentrate on the driving. Mum and Dad hated the fact that Toni had his own car and they constantly quizzed Luke about his friend's driving skills. They had hang-ups about most things, but traffic was a subject they just loved to worry about. Leaving home earlier, Luke had simply said he was going out, without mentioning Toni, and least of all the ride to Helsinki in Toni's car.

Dozens of curious onlookers were strolling beside the *Ocean Emerald*, gazing up at its gleaming white bulk. Souvenir stands selling reindeer skins and postcards had sprung up near the passenger terminal, where flags fluttered in the wind. A police car crawled alongside the ship, patrolling the crowds.

'And where am I supposed to park?' Toni asked.

'Leave me at that gate,' Luke said. 'Then wait for my text.'

'I'm coming with you.'

'Suit yourself,' Luke said. 'But that's a police car and that's a No Parking sign.'

'You're right.' Toni glanced at the police car. 'Hop out, quick.'

Toni pulled up and Luke got out, passport in hand.

'Make sure they pay us extra for the passport, or you're walking home!'

Just inside the wire fence, passengers were getting off a bus with tinted windows, wandering towards the gangway with their shopping. Judging by the bags, many had opted for Finnish Marimekko textiles and delicacies from Stockmann, the best department store in Helsinki. The passengers reeked of wealth, but what Luke really envied was their air of freedom. The prospect of a cruise lasting several weeks, even months, was mind-blowing. In just a week, school would start again...

He headed for the gate by which the buses entered the quay and found his path blocked by a giant. The words VARTIJA-SECURITY were printed on his grey overalls. He'd shaved his head, and apparently polished it, too, and his wraparound sunglasses gave him an inhuman air.

'Hi,' Luke said in English, trying to make eye contact. 'Excuse me?'

'What do you want?' the man said.

'I found this.'

Luke handed the boarding pass to the guard. It was hard to tell whether he worked on the ship or was employed by the harbour authorities.

'So you want your hundred dollars?' The guard took off his shades and squinted at the text written on the back of the card and grinned. 'Hang on.'

Turning his back to Luke, he took his radio from his belt and said something that Luke couldn't hear.

'OK.' The security guard put his hand on Luke's shoulder. 'See that man in the white uniform?'

Luke saw a man greeting the passengers at the foot of the gangway. 'Yes.'

'Talk to him. I just told him you were coming.'

'Thanks!'

Congratulating himself on the good start, Luke strode off towards the *Ocean Emerald*. On the balconies, small tables and padded deckchairs waited for the returning passengers. As he came closer, the vessel looked like an enormous, flawlessly white wall. He tilted back his neck. The higher decks seemed lost in the clouds.

Emilio trundled his cleaning trolley along Corridor One, on the ninth deck. He knew there was a security camera hidden in the lighting fixture in front of cabin 9313. Corridor One was crucial as it was located right next to the bridge, the equivalent of the cockpit of a passenger jet.

Emilio's forehead was beaded with perspiration. The work of a cleaner had turned out to be an effective but exhausting cover. His first assignment had been to reconnoitre the on-board security system, including the precise location of all the security cameras. During the past three months, he'd familiarized himself one hundred per cent with the ship's layout.

He positioned his trolley between the camera and the fuse box mounted on the wall, preparing to open the box and hide the radio-controlled detonator inside. Like all the equipment that Helmut had given him, the device still smelled faintly of fish.

In the control room, Craig 'Coyote' Thomson was up to his ears in paperwork. But every minute or so, his eyes flicked across to the CCTV screens.

Five years before, the FBI had fired him on the grounds of 'negligence' during the course of a bungled joint operation with federal anti-narcotics agents, two of whom had been killed in the melee. The allegation of incompetence was intolerable to a man like Thomson, who'd always contested it. If the incident had scarred him, it had also redoubled his professional motivation, making him an even more relentless perfectionist.

Thomson fixed his gaze on the view from the camera on Deck Nine, Corridor One, not far from the armoured door leading to the bridge.

Why was a cleaner's trolley abandoned in the corridor at this time of day? It was too late for the morning clean, yet too early for the evening round when the staterooms were freshened up for the night. An abandoned trolley wasn't unheard of, but it was a lapse – and Thomson was trained to spot lapses.

He leaned closer. A male cleaner with a Hispanic complexion appeared, took something from the trolley and crouched down beside it. Thomson relaxed. The trolley hadn't been forgotten after all. The man was merely doing his job. Thomson watched as the cleaner stepped up to the fuse box on the wall. He was probably dusting it. Nevertheless, before turning his attention to the next screen, Thomson made sure he got a good look at the cleaner's face.

6

Luke shivered as he waited for his turn on the windy quay in Helsinki. The white-suited man stationed beside the gangway had a friendly word for every passenger. A lady in a fur coat and a pearl necklace was next in line. The man checked her boarding pass and quickly found her a porter, who took charge of her tiny shopping bag. The lady flashed Luke a friendly smile and began her slow climb up the gangway.

Observing how carefully the man checked the boarding passes before admitting the passengers onto the gangway, Luke felt his heart sink. Obviously, he wasn't going to be allowed any further than this.

'Excuse me?' Luke said.

The man looked amused. 'Yes, my young friend!'

Luke explained why he was there.

'I guess it's your lucky day.' The man winked and spoke into his phone. 'Carol? We have a young man here who has found a boarding pass.'

Luke prepared to hand over the card, but the man pointed at the gangway.

'Off you go.' He swung his arm, as if to chase Luke away.

'What?'

'You might as well see the ship since you're here, no?'

'Oh…' Luke smiled. 'Thanks!'

'They'll pay you the reward at the Reception desk. Don't get lost, now. We leave in two hours.'

'OK.' Luke put the boarding pass back between the pages of Juliette du Pont's passport, and trotted energetically up the gangway, which led to a spectacular atrium that was several decks high and spanned the width of the ship.

A young woman took Luke's jacket and put it through the airport-style X-ray machine. She idly picked up the passport and opened it, assuming it was Luke's, who blushed as he explained why he was on the ship without a passport of his own. For the first time since they'd set off from Porvoo in Toni's car, he wondered whether this was such a bright idea. But it was too late to turn back. With a racing heart, he passed through the metal detector. On the other side, a purser in a gleaming white uniform stood waiting for him.

'Hi there!' she said in an American accent. 'I'm Carol. How are you today?'

'I'm fine,' Luke said, deliberately omitting to smile. 'How are you?'

'Fine thanks!' the woman laughed. 'What's your name?'

Luke sighed – just like the guard, she was treating him like a kid. They were clearly mainly used to dealing with old people on this ship.

'Luke C. Baron,' he said firmly, offering his hand.

'What does the "C" stand for?' Carol said with an amused smile.

34

'I only use the initial.' Luke kept his middle name a secret, but he thought using the initial made him sound older.

'You want Lost and Found, don't you?'

'The Reception desk.'

'That's it. This way, please.'

Carol ushered Luke to the bank of lifts in the middle of the atrium. The thick, spongy carpet muffled their footsteps and the hum of air-conditioning was the only sound. Paintings in ornate frames hung from the cream-coloured walls. Carol paused to give an elderly couple directions to the spa, then led Luke into a gold-plated lift. Just as the sliding doors were closing, a woman in her mid-thirties and a much younger man shouldered their way in.

'Mind the doors, now,' Carol said cheerfully.

'Sorry!' the woman said, turning to admire her own reflection in the full-length mirror. She looked South American.

The man, who wore an American football shirt and Bermuda shorts, scratched at the stubble on his double chin, his face set in a sulky frown. They got off on the seventh deck and Luke heard them bickering about something to do with singing.

'They're from Miami,' Carol whispered conspiratorially, rolling her eyes. 'She's the third wife of the CEO of the Emerald Cruise Corporation.'

'And who was the guy in shorts?'

'The CEO's son from an earlier marriage. The current wife will be singing for us this evening. She thinks she's the next Jennifer Lopez.'

'Does anyone else agree?'

'Put it this way' – Carol prodded Luke's arm with her finger – 'if she's the new Jennifer Lopez, I'm the next Britney Spears.'

Luke laughed. Carol seemed really friendly.

He cast a furtive glance at his own reflection in the mirror. He was almost as tall as Carol, and there was nothing childish about the way he was dressed: jeans, trainers, black T-shirt and sober jacket. The wide belt with its large buckle was a recent acquisition – and only Luke and Luke alone knew that it contained a secret compartment. Even at this moment, he could feel the contents pressing against his back: a tiny notebook and a stub of pencil; a miniature compass; two fructose tablets in a flat, waterproof container; a fishing line and three hooks. When in funds, he sometimes also folded a banknote into the belt, but he always ended up using the money for something other than the emergency he imagined he might one day face. He varied the contents of his belt on a random basis, for his own private amusement, and would never have dreamed of telling anyone else about it, especially Toni or Dad. He usually also kept a tiny Swiss Army knife inside the belt, but had left it behind today. Lucky thing, too – it had spared him no end of trouble at the X-ray machine. Apparently the fish-hooks were small enough to slip through unremarked.

The lift stopped and Luke followed Carol past a large fountain and into a sunlit bar, where an Elvis impersonator sat tinkling the keys of an enormous grand piano.

'I see you've hired the King as well,' Luke said.

'You bet,' Carol laughed.

They came into a vast circular space lined with service

desks marked with large signs: RECEPTION, SHORE EXCURSIONS, INFORMATION... Opposite the Reception desk was a sweeping staircase flanked by a pair of panorama lifts. Luke had been in a five-star hotel once, in Geneva, when Mum had been speaking at a conference on elementary particles, but the *Ocean Emerald* was a hundred times more impressive. He felt as though he'd stepped into a magical world or a parallel universe in some cheesy science fiction film – only this was real.

Smiling clerks sat behind the long Reception desk, serving the passengers. On the wall behind, a row of clocks showed the time in New York, London, Moscow, Tokyo, Sydney and Los Angeles. As they made their way through the throng to the Reception desk, Luke heard snatches of some of the foreign languages he was familiar with: French, German, Italian...

Carol spoke to the clerk, a young man wearing a dark blazer and a beautifully knotted tie.

'Josh, this young gentleman wants to return a lost boarding pass.'

'So how come this is worth a hundred dollars?' Luke said, handing over the pass, but keeping the passport.

'We don't want them to get into the wrong hands. We've already issued a new boarding card for Miss du Pont, but it's good you brought this one back. Security hates it when we lose one. As you've seen, it has the passenger's photo on it. Whenever you board or disembark, you must insert the card in the reader. That way we can keep track of everyone.'

'And you can keep out the stowaways.'

'You got it.' Josh laughed. 'OK, kid, would you fill in this form, please?'

Luke's heart sank. *His name would be recorded.* He knew how data was used in modern police work: day and night, the data-mining supercomputers of various law enforcement organizations processed vast quantities of information, cross-referencing it, matching names, incidents and places. Once Luke's name was on file, there was no way he could sell the passport. He'd be the first suspect if the police happened to consult the ship's database.

'Here you go, Luke,' Josh said, placing a hundred-dollar note beside the form. 'Good job.'

'By the way, I also found this.' Luke slapped the passport onto the desk and began filling in the form, trying to hide his blushing cheeks.

'Well, Miss du Pont will be happy to have *that* back, I'm sure.' With a surprised frown, Josh took the passport and picked up a phone. 'Let me call her right away.'

Luke smiled and a wave of sweet relief passed through him. The whole idea of selling someone else's passport suddenly seemed stupid and sordid – a bit like shoplifting. He'd almost made a terrible mistake.

7

In Corridor One on the ninth deck, near the bridge, Emilio Fernández was still standing in front of the fuse box. He was furious, having just discovered that the door wouldn't close when the detonator was inside.

He cursed under his breath. The cleaner's uniform made him invisible to the passengers and most of the crew, but he knew that other eyes were watching. It was not for nothing that Craig Thomson was called 'Coyote'. The man was a born hunter, tirelessly alert. But surely even *he* couldn't track the movements of the entire crew? The *Ocean Emerald* employed an army of cleaners who spruced up all the cabins twice a day.

Emilio turned the detonator onto its side, but still the little metal door refused to shut. Sweat stung his eyes. He wondered how long it would take to find somewhere else to hide it. Delacroix would throw a fit if he discovered that Emilio hadn't even checked that the hiding place was big enough. Emilio made one last attempt, and finally discovered a position in which the detonator fitted inside, just. He closed the door and hastened away with his trolley.

***

At that moment, Craig Thomson wasn't, in fact, looking at the screens, but at the passenger list. That list was the most important tool at his disposal. The second most important tool was the personnel list, which contained the names of the ship's officers and crew. The security cameras only came third. Updated constantly, the lists recorded the names of all individuals on board the *Ocean Emerald*, and it was those people – some, of course, more than others – who were the source of almost all the potential security risks.

Drug mules sometimes used cruise ships to transport their wares. Common thieves were a pest. Cruise passengers, who were mostly old and wealthy, offered a sitting target for cheats, pickpockets and conmen, who could quickly destroy the reputation of a ship or a whole cruise brand. The last thing the Emerald Cruise Corporation wanted in the current economic climate was a damning report posted in one of the many chatrooms where cruise-goers compared experiences and swapped tips.

The risks came in all shapes and sizes: food poisoning, collisions, shipwrecks – yes, even pirates... Thomson knew that the notorious pirates off the coast of Somalia were a local threat restricted to the Arabian Sea, but that there were also other areas where piracy was making a comeback. Terrorism was the unthinkable, worldwide one-in-a-million mega-risk. It was rare, but could happen anywhere. When it did, you didn't want to be the head of security.

Thomson received regular risk assessments from his former FBI colleagues and other associates, as well as from the London-based private security firm in charge of the Emerald Cruise Corporation's security strategy. According to the latest bulletin, which had arrived in the form of an encrypted email that morning, neither al Qaeda nor any other known organization posed an imminent threat to cruise shipping.

However, Thomson feared it was only a matter of time before some terror organization somewhere struck one of the hundreds of cruise liners that plied the world's oceans. The size and passenger-load of a cruise ship made it a prestigious target. Then there was the novelty value. Planes had been attacked endless times before, but if a major cruise vessel were to be hit by terrorists, the world's media would have a field day.

Thomson studied the personal details of the three passengers who'd boarded in Helsinki: a retired Finnish IT engineer who had worked for Nokia, his wife, and a young French businesswoman based in Paris. Why Juliette du Pont had boarded in Helsinki the database didn't say, but the choice wasn't unusual in itself, as many tourists used Helsinki as a safe and practical bridgehead for visiting Russia. Perhaps she had a Finnish boyfriend – but if so, why was she listed as the sole occupant of her cabin?

Juliette du Pont was in suite 8062 on the eighth deck. She'd never travelled with Emerald Cruises before and had no criminal record. Nevertheless, Thomson entered an X beside her name before moving on to the next name. Naturally, the Emerald Cruise Corporation used an automated profiling system, as did all commercial airlines, but Thomson also made a point of personally reviewing the passenger list at each port of call. He earmarked a number of individuals, knowing that most of them would turn out to be perfectly harmless.

Besides seeking to identify potentially dangerous individuals, Thomson took a close interest in VIP passengers, such as David C. McMorgan, who owned one of the biggest construction companies on the east coast of America, and usually travelled with his personal bodyguard. On a cruise, even *he* could relax and enjoy some privacy. However, his VIP designation meant that special arrangements would be needed when McMorgan left the ship. For example, he would see St Petersburg through the windows of a limousine rather than a tour bus. That is, if he ever made it to St Petersburg – the billionaire had been due to board in Helsinki, but was about to miss the boat...

Leaning back in his chair in front of the computer, Thomson then called up the file on Philippe Delacroix, which had been bothering him. An entire dossier including a potted biography was devoted to this passenger, a one-time art dealer thought to have contacts with a gang that had smuggled artworks looted from Baghdad during the second Iraq war, but who had never been convicted. An oddball who seemed to have hovered between crime and respectability, he'd recently spent several years labouring on construction sites in southern France while studying part-time for degrees in art history and finance – degrees he never completed. Thomson had kept a close eye on Delacroix ever since he had boarded in Amsterdam. The previous April and May, Delacroix had voyaged from Buenos Aires to Genoa on the *Ocean Jewel*. The twenty-one day crossing in a cabin with a balcony had cost fifty-five thousand dollars.

The *Ocean Jewel* and the *Ocean Emerald* were identical vessels, twin flagships of the Emerald Cruise Corporation, and it was a little surprising that Delacroix was rich enough to afford cruises on both within the space of half a year, each time during the holiday season.

Thomson scrolled through the file. As on the previous cruise, Delacroix had treated himself to a suite with a balcony, this time paying forty thousand dollars for less than a fortnight. Did he have business in St Petersburg? If so, why didn't he fly there? Or was he smuggling something? Stolen artworks? Forgeries? The baggage allowance on a cruise ship was generous. Smugglers liked cruise ships because their schedules were known months and even years ahead. The exact berths in each port were also known – the same didn't apply to cargo ships.

Thomson decided to contact a former colleague at the FBI, requesting a data sweep on Delacroix. Such contacts were mutually beneficial: Thomson received fresh intelligence on certain individuals and his former associates got an update on those individuals' movements. Thomson also decided to alert the captain to Delacroix's presence on board. Finally, he memorized Delacroix's cabin number: 7039.

8

As the slim, athletic woman appeared from one of the panorama lifts facing the Reception desk, Luke immediately recognized her face from the passport and the boarding pass. Juliette du Pont had insisted on coming down herself when she heard that someone had handed in her documents. She could be a supermodel, Luke thought to himself as she approached, moving like a cat in her close-fitting black clothes. The running tights, halter top and marathon-grade running shoes spoke of a long session spent in the ship's gym. She pulled a black sweatband off her head and shook out her short hair.

'Miss du Pont,' Carol said, resting her hand on Luke's shoulder. 'This boy has done you a big favour.'

'I'm Juliette,' Juliette du Pont said in English. She smiled as she took the passport, but the look in her eyes was steely and probing. 'Thank you so much.'

'Hi, I'm Luke C. Baron.'

As they fumbled a handshake, Luke felt a hot blush spreading across his face.

'Bye then, Luke C.,' the woman said coldly, and immediately turned to go.

Luke knew this was his only chance to test the significance of his discovery.

'I tried to find you online,' he said, watching carefully for the woman's reaction. 'But all I found was a woman with your name and birthday, who drowned in Corsica last summer.'

Juliette turned back very suddenly and let out a laugh.

'Du Pont is a common French name.' She glanced at Carol. 'But it's a funny coincidence nonetheless.'

'I agree,' Luke said.

The Frenchwoman looked amused. 'You've gone to a lot of trouble for my sake. Would you like to see the ship?' She was smiling now, almost laughing, with an intense sparkle in her eyes. 'I'll buy you an ice cream on the Lido Deck.'

Luke felt like a fool. So much for his suspicions.

'Go for it!' Carol said, with a wink.

Luke glanced at his watch, trying to look busy and indifferent. An ice cream, he was thinking: pathetic. Toni would laugh all the way back to Porvoo. On the other hand, this might be a chance to negotiate a proper reward – and he was longing to explore the ship.

'Yes, please,' he said, more feebly than he intended.

'Would that be OK?' Juliette du Pont asked.

'No problem,' Carol said.

'Can I take photos?' Luke asked, showing his mobile. 'Sure.'

Josh printed off a badge that Carol clipped onto Luke's chest. It said LUKE BARON, VISITOR in red capital letters.

'Have fun, Luke!' Carol said. 'You must return the badge when you disembark, OK? We leave in one and a half hours.'

Luke wanted to thank Carol for her help, but Juliette was already leading him towards the lift. She was clutching his arm. Once they were inside, she let go.

'You sound English.' Once again, the smile was warm but the eyes were not.

'Yeah. I'm English, but my gran lives here in Finland. I'm just on holiday.'

'So, where did you find my passport?'

'In a briefcase on the side of the motorway between Helsinki and Porvoo.'

'How lucky for me. And were you alone?'

'I was with a friend. I'm afraid we broke the briefcase . . .'

'That's OK. What's your friend's name?'

'Toni.'

'Surname?'

'Virtanen.'

'Toni Virtanen . . . OK. And he saw my passport too?'

'Yes, is that a problem?'

'Of course not. You've done me a good turn.' The woman was looking at the badge on Luke's chest. 'Toni is Finnish?'

Luke nodded.

'Where is he now?'

Luke turned his eyes to the floor. The conversation had taken a weird direction. Even as she thanked him, the woman was somehow telling him off.

'Luke?' Her voice was sharp. 'Where is Toni Virtanen now?'

'He's waiting for me. We came in his car.'

The lift stopped on the seventh deck. Again Juliette took hold of Luke's arm and this time her grip was firmer.

46

She had the hard, well-defined arms of an Olympic athlete. He could see no sign of any cafeteria or ice-cream bar, just an endless row of cabin doors on either side of a long corridor. This part of the ship didn't look at all like the Lido Deck that Luke had studied on the *Ocean Emerald*'s website. But maybe the woman wanted to fetch money from her cabin, or something like that. He wasn't quite sure, but he thought they were heading in the direction of the ship's bow.

'You can't imagine how grateful I am,' Juliette said and smiled fractionally.

Luke wanted to ask how the briefcase had ended up where he and Toni had found it, but he decided to wait.

'Where do you live, Luke, when you're not on holiday in Finland?'

'Brussels. My dad works there.'

'Nice town. What does he do?'

'International relations,' Luke said. He wanted to add: 'In a secret Europol unit,' but Dad had told him never to reveal his job to strangers.

'International relations?' Juliette paused. 'And what's his special field?'

'I don't know. He goes to a lot of meetings.' Luke blushed again. 'Where are we going, by the way?'

'The Lido Deck. I thought you wanted an ice cream?'

'Yes, but ... Are we going the right way?'

Luke read the numbers on the cabin doors: 7047, 7045, 7043 ...

'What about your mum, Luke? What does she do?'

'She's a physicist.'

'Well, that's an achievement.'

It was obvious from Juliette du Pont's voice that she

thought Luke didn't understand what his mum actually did, so he continued.

'Mum has a PhD in particle physics. She's building a computer grid, a massive system that can handle a million gigabytes.'

Luke waited, expecting an admiring answer, but Juliette simply charged on. She had let go of his arm but the steely look had reappeared on her face. The corridor seemed to go on and on.

'Is it still a long way?'

'Almost there.'

Luke suddenly realized that he no longer cared whether he got a reward for the passport. He wasn't interested in seeing the ship, or in the promised ice cream, or even in the hundred dollars in his pocket. He just wanted to go home. Everything the woman had said had been kind and reasonable, but there was something terrifying in her eyes. He was about to turn on his heels when Juliette stopped in front of cabin number 7039 and knocked loudly.

The door opened at once and Juliette hustled Luke into the suite, then locked the door. The large suite consisted of a sitting room, a balcony and a separate bedroom.

'He knows I'm not the real Juliette du Pont,' Juliette said to a man who was standing in the middle of the sitting room. 'What shall we do?'

She had spoken in French. Luke pretended not to have understood. His heart was pounding in his ears. *He had to get out, now.*

The man was staring at him. Deeply tanned, he wore glasses and a silk scarf. Luke nodded, but the man didn't respond to the greeting in any way. Instead, he shot a commanding glance at Juliette, then stepped forward and put his calloused palm over Luke's mouth, using his other hand to grab the front of his shirt.

Juliette plucked the visitor's badge from Luke's chest.

'Sorry, Luke, but we have no other choice,' she said, fixing him with her powerful gaze. 'Do we, Delacroix?'

She took hold of Luke's ankles, and the man she had called Delacroix gripped his shoulders. Luke tried to squirm free, but it was no use. They dragged him through the sitting room into the bedroom and pressed him against the floor, on his stomach.

Luke tried to shout, but the man's palm was sealed firmly against his mouth. Luke's arms were wrenched behind his back. Then he felt handcuffs clasp around his wrists. The man was extraordinarily strong and his hands felt like sandpaper.

'The gym's pathetic. It's clearly designed with the older passenger in mind,' Juliette said to Delacroix, swigging water from a small bottle. 'But I managed five K on the running mat.'

'Good girl,' Delacroix said, brushing her cheek with the back of his knuckles. 'Sit-ups next.'

'I'll just take his badge back first,' Juliette said. '*A tout de suite.*'

Luke felt chilly panic spreading through his abdomen. They were already speaking as though he were no longer present – or no longer alive. He decided not to let on that he understood French.

9

'Could you stop that, please?' The new Jennifer Lopez was studying a sheet of paper in the Piano Bar of the *Ocean Emerald*. 'I can't concentrate.'

'You can't concentrate, you can't sing and you can't leave me in peace. Is there anything you *can* do?' Max Lownie Junior carried on drumming the tabletop with his plump fingers. He was younger and shorter than his companion, but had the same unnaturally deep tan. His flashy, loose-hanging clothes failed to disguise his excess weight. Half hidden under the overhanging belly, his belt was loaded with gadgets: two mobile phones, a miniature torch, a digital camera and an iPod. The music flooding from his earphones was Wagner's opera *Siegfried*.

He stuffed the remains of his burger into his mouth and rolled the wrapper into a ball between his fat hands. A lifelong fast-food addict with a growing list of health problems at the age of twenty-five, he detested the gourmet restaurants on his father's ships and just ate what he always had back in Miami.

A male waiter glided from somewhere and whisked away the wrapper and the plate.

'I'll never learn this song,' Gabriela sighed.

'Who cares?' Max put his knuckles to his lips and let out a burp. 'No one gives a damn about your songs. I don't. Dad doesn't. He just pretends, to make you happy.'

'It's no use trying to upset me. I'm a professional.'

'Yeah, right.' With a loud cackle, Max reached for his packet of cigarillos and pushed away the No Smoking sign.

'Now listen, Maximilian. You and I need to get on. Just like a mother and her son.'

'Firstly, it's Max,' Max said, blowing smoke straight into his stepmother's face. 'And secondly, you're not my mum. You're a gold-digger after my dad's fortune.'

'Excuse me, sir, but we do have a no smoking policy, and for the comfort of the other passengers—'

'We're just going,' Max interrupted the skinny waiter who had appeared at his side.

'You can smoke on deck, sir.'

'I'd leave the whole ship if we weren't stuck in this hell-hole of a city. I've had enough. I might jump overboard this evening if this fraud here starts to sing.'

Max struggled to his feet, almost knocking over his bar stool as he lumbered into the corridor. Breathing heavily, he hurried past the internet café and the library, towards the cigar club, which was adjacent to the casino. As he pushed open the shiny glass door, he almost crashed into a lithe young woman dressed in black.

'*Faites attention, Monsieur!*' she hissed and continued on her way.

Max turned to steal a glance at her slim figure, then waddled towards the humidors where the cigars were kept, hitching up his baggy shorts as he went.

* * *

As she neared the Reception desk, Juliette du Pont slowed her steps and recomposed her face, putting on a calm, friendly smile.

'Miss du Pont,' the purser on duty grinned, leaning over the Reception desk. 'I hear you got your passport back?'

'Our young English friend has left. I showed him out.' Juliette fluttered her eyelashes at the purser and handed him the visitor's badge.

The purser looked ready to keep chatting, but Juliette walked off. With a little luck, the ship would leave Helsinki before Luke Baron was missed. It was impossible to let the boy go, or he might alert the police before the operation had even started. She couldn't afford to be exposed – not yet. His friend Toni Virtanen unfortunately knew the name on her passport, but that couldn't be helped.

The boy's presence on the ship was a stressful complication, but Juliette was prepared for such contingencies. As for stress, she treated it as a drug. If you cared about fitness, as she certainly did, stress was a most valuable fuel.

Max Lownie Junior knocked on the tinted glass door of the casino. The place looked closed – it was too early in the day. He could see the shape of the roulette table, and behind it, a row of slot machines blinking in the gloom. Depending on the stakes you played for, the jackpots could reach tens of thousands of dollars. The sight of the casino filled him with a familiar, arousing hunger, the only thing that could dispel his otherwise perpetual bad mood.

He was about to leave when a croupier in black tie hurried from the cashier cage and opened the door.

'I'd like to play the fruit machines,' Max said in his friendliest voice.

'Mr Lownie, I'm afraid that's not allowed when we're in port, as I think you know, sir...'

'Come on, Brad. I'm bored witless.' Max slipped fifty dollars into the croupier's palm and tried to fold the man's fingers around the money. 'You don't need to switch on the lights. I'll take the one at the back. No one will see.'

'I apologize, Mr Lownie, but the rules—'

'Rules!' Max sneered, pushing his face close to the croupier's face. 'I make my own rules.'

Using his bulk, Max tried to ram the croupier out of his way.

'Mr Lownie, please leave, or I'll have to call security.'

'Fine!' Max stepped back, raising his arms. 'You call security, and I'll call Dad and you can talk to him about your future on this ship.'

Max hitched up his shorts and swayed into the foyer. He chose the larger of his two mobile phones and squinted at the display. The Iridium satellite phone worked everywhere on the planet, from the widest ocean to the remotest desert.

A mobile phone rang on a polished cherry-wood table in the home of the CEO of the Emerald Cruise Corporation in Coral Gables, Miami.

A short man in his sixties picked up the handset and smiled when he saw his son's name on the display.

'Max! How are you doing?'

'*Not great, Dad.*'

'What's wrong?' Max Lownie Senior sank into his desk

chair and glanced at the framed picture of Gabriela. His wife's youthful smile cheered him up. He had silver hair, and the hair on the back of his fingers was white against the deep tan.

'*Pretty much everything. Your ship's full of jerks. Now they won't even let me play the slot machines.*'

'Where are you?'

'*Hell-something.*'

'Helsinki. Come on, Max. They'll open the casino as soon as you're at sea.' Lownie watched the rain trickling down the window. High on the horizon, purple clouds were bearing down on the city. 'And don't forget what we agreed? No more than a hundred dollars a week. You gotta learn thrift if you're to succeed me in the cruise business.'

'*There's nothing else to do, Dad. Why does the* Ocean Emerald *even stop here? I'd never heard of Helsinki before and I never want to hear about it again.*'

'That's precisely why. Our customers have been everywhere and seen everything.' Lownie swiped dust off his knee. 'As for you, I advise you to view it as an education. If we Americans knew a little more about other countries, maybe we could figure out how to be hated a little less.'

'*Let them hate us, provided they also fear us.*'

Lownie closed his eyes and counted to ten. Slowly, the anger subsided. How had his son turned out to be such a moron?

'Is Gabriela with you?'

'*No, thank God,*' Max cackled. '*Get this – she's supposed to be performing this evening, and the old scarecrow doesn't even know the lyrics yet!*'

'Let that be the last time you speak of her in that tone.' Lownie stopped trying to control himself. 'It's time you shaped up, my son. You're arrogant, you're rude. You're a spoiled brat. If you drop out of college one more time, you drop out of my will, too. And now I must go. Unlike you, I have a busy day ahead of me.'

Lownie Senior felt like getting back into bed and burying his head under the pillow, but that was impossible. The future of the Emerald Cruise Corporation was looking even more dismal than the weather outside. The cruise industry had always been a cut-throat game, but things had now reached a point where it was unclear whether Lownie's company would survive at all. It no longer depended on him, but on the goodwill of the banks, the investors and the creditors.

10

In cabin number 7039, Luke was lying on the floor of the bedroom with his wrists handcuffed behind his back and attached to the steel bed frame. His heart was pounding violently. The cream-coloured carpet felt ticklish and unpleasantly hot against his cheek. Muted voices carried through the open door leading into the sitting room, but he couldn't make out what they were saying.

Through the door, he saw Juliette putting something into a brown shoulder bag. The Frenchman was out of sight, but his voice was audible. What were these people up to? Why was Juliette du Pont travelling on a false passport, as she obviously was? And why had he been so stupid as to reveal his suspicions? Because he hadn't trusted his own instincts until it was too late...

Suddenly Luke froze. His mobile was ringing somewhere in the sitting room, louder and louder. They'd taken his phone and were able to monitor the calls he received. Since last summer, when he'd discovered Emma's favourite band, he'd been using various Coldplay tunes as his ringtone. Now, when he knew he couldn't answer, 'Lovers in Japan' pierced him with regret and longing.

The tanned man in the silk scarf appeared in the doorway with Luke's mobile in his hand. He dropped to his knees and looked at the display, then turned the handset so that Luke could see who it was. The display said 'Shoplifter Virtanen'.

'Who's this?' Delacroix said in English.

'My wrists are hurting...'

'I said, who's this?'

Luke hesitated, then spoke. 'It's my dad. He's coming to pick me up.'

'Your dad is a shoplifter?'

'It's a family joke. Dad's coming to pick me up from the port.'

Juliette appeared from the sitting room, her bare feet silent on the carpet. She took the phone and looked at the display.

'He's lying. It's his friend. He already told me a friend called Toni Virtanen was waiting for him in his car. Isn't that right, Luke?'

'He'll be wondering where I am.'

'He can wonder a little longer.'

Juliette pressed a button on the handset and the ringing stopped. The look she gave Luke made his insides turn cold.

Beep... beep... beep...

Why wasn't Luke answering? Toni tossed his phone onto the passenger seat and reached into his bag of sweets. He was getting seriously bored. He'd parked the Nissan in a back street several blocks from the port and there was nothing interesting to look at. He hadn't driven all this way just to sit in his car like a prat.

Maybe Luke was on the ship negotiating the reward – but why was it taking so long? No, Luke had probably returned empty-handed and was now too ashamed to show his face. Toni kicked himself for having stayed behind. His experience and cold nerves might have saved the day.

With an unpleasant pang, Toni remembered the mortifying scene in Luke's father's car earlier in the week. For a moment there, the situation had looked pretty desperate, but fortunately Peter Baron had been man enough to talk things through. Maybe it was because he had a police background. Toni knew he had acted stupidly. What had come over him? Luke was a real friend; indeed, Toni's only bankable friend. The DVD had been a mistake, but he would make it up to Luke somehow.

Toni dug another sweet from his bag, picked up his phone once more and scrolled through the menu, trying to decide which game to play. Then he checked his messages again. Nothing. Had he dialled the right number? Of course he had. It was totally weird that Luke had neither answered his phone nor texted to explain why he was taking so long.

Philippe Delacroix gently lowered a towel onto the explosive charge hidden inside Juliette's shoulder bag. He pulled the zip straight and closed it with a slow, careful movement of his big hand. He didn't like his hands. They were not the hands of a cultivated man – in that sense, they were not his hands at all.

As soon as the *Ocean Emerald* was out of Finnish waters, they would begin. The presence of Luke Baron in the cabin was an unexpected nuisance, but Delacroix wasn't too concerned, as the boy was unlikely to be missed before the evening. However, when he *was* missed, the spotlight would fall on Juliette, and to be safe, Delacroix had therefore brought the start-time forward by one hour.

'Go,' he said.

Juliette immediately swung the bag onto her shoulder. Her cheeks were flushed, but Delacroix knew he could trust her. Long before teaming up with Delacroix, she had pulled off a series of bank jobs and armed robberies, each one more audacious than the last, without ever being caught or even named as a suspect. If she could do all that while addicted to drugs, she could do anything when she was clean, Delacroix had reasoned. Together, he and Juliette had stolen a succession of priceless artworks from some of the world's most closely guarded museums and private collections. They'd decided to strike twice a year at most, putting quality over quantity. To prepare for their greatest ever plan, they'd withdrawn from crime for several years, living mainly in Dijon. Juliette's sister, who had joined the team a few years ago, also had a role in the present operation, although she wasn't actually on board.

They exchanged a wordless nod as Juliette slipped into the corridor with her shoulder bag.

Craig Thomson cracked open a Coke and took a long swig, keeping his eyes on the CCTV screens. The service vehicles were pulling away from the quay and the gangway was about to be closed. The deck crew were preparing the *Ocean Emerald* for departure.

Thomson used a pen to tear open a large envelope addressed to him care of the vessel's agent in Helsinki. It contained a brochure outlining next season's itinerary for another cruise ship, the *Queen Mary II*, whose head of security was due to retire. Thomson had his eye on the job.

He flicked through the heavy, lavishly illustrated brochure. The *Queen Mary II* was popular among world-class celebrities and tycoons. Just like the transatlantic cruise liners of old, she catered only for the elite. Given the needs of the clientele, on-board protection was taken very, very seriously, a fact that was also reflected in the status and salary of the ship's security chief. Here on the *Ocean Emerald*, by contrast, Thomson was viewed as an unavoidable nuisance. He knew what this meant from a security point of view – dangerous complacency.

The brochure did justice to the opulence of the *Queen Mary II*. The largest staterooms were named after the residences of the British Royal family: Windsor, Sandringham, Balmoral, Buckingham. Some of the suites were arranged over two floors.

Thomson returned his attention to his CCTV screens. It was rush hour on board. Having returned from their shore excursions, the last passengers were making their way back to their cabins. He recognized the lone figure of Max Lownie Junior slumped on a sofa near the casino, waiting for the gaming to resume. On another screen, the catlike Frenchwoman who had boarded in Helsinki was striding down the corridor on the Sun Deck, heading for the gym with her shoulder bag.

Thomson's thoughts wandered back to his short-lived FBI career and the incident that had ended it, which had cost the lives of two anti-narcotics agents. The old bitterness swelled inside him. With a black mark like that in his book, he was lucky to be working where he was. He could have ended up in industrial security, or in the mindless role of a private bodyguard, a job that consisted mainly of waiting.

Suddenly he remembered the cleaner he needed to check up on, the one who'd been fiddling with the fuse box on Deck Nine. Thomson was proud of his memory. He was particularly good at faces.

He scrolled through the photos of the ship's cleaners. Many were Hispanic. There he was. Thomson had assumed the man was South American, but in fact he was a Filipino. His name was Emilio Fernández. He'd started work three months ago, having been hired through an agency in Manila.

The face was expressionless. Passport photos tended to be like that, yet there was something wilfully hard about the man's stare. Thomson finished his Coke and decided to take a closer look at the fuse box as soon as he got a chance.

The computer emitted a quiet *ping* and a window opened up. Thomson clicked on the email message. It was a reply from his FBI contact.

Good to hear from you, Coyote!
How's the cruising life? My heart bleeds for you.
Thanks for the tip – yes indeed, PD is on our surveillance lists. Former art dealer. Dubious contacts. In April he was in Buenos Aires, where he maybe met with someone who may or may not be bankrolling al Qaeda. Why? Your guess is as good as mine. Maybe they're using art and diamonds for collateral, what with all the frozen accounts and financial regulation.

Keep your eyes open – and enjoy the pool.

Regards, Y

Thomson bit his lip. Captain Bauer would think it excessive, but it was best to check Delacroix's cabin. Thomson welcomed the diversion this would bring. Life on a cruise ship was monotonous and sometimes you had to manufacture stimulation to keep alert. Besides, it was worth following up on fifty hunches if it let you neutralize one real concern.

Suddenly he felt a faint thrumming underfoot. The ship's engines had come to life. Thomson turned to the screens and watched the orderly routine of departure: the gangway was closed and the moorings were being released at stern and bow.

Thomson stood up and stretched his arms and neck. As he left the control room, he took one last look at the screens. Behind the row of exercise machines, he saw the Frenchwoman opening the door into the ladies' changing room. There were, of course, no security cameras in there.

Outside, on the quay alongside the *Ocean Emerald*, a large black Mercedes screeched to a halt between an empty tour bus and the closed gangway. The driver opened the door for the passenger in the back seat, whose personal assistant was already lifting a vast suitcase from the boot. A porter spotted the last-minute arrival and sprinted over with a luggage cart.

David C. McMorgan ran a hand over what little remained of his reddish hair, refused the arm offered by his assistant and hastened towards the gangway, which was reopened specially for him. He had a slight stoop. His mottled skull and freckled face and arms gave him the air of a man wearing camouflage. His assistant, who doubled as a bodyguard, stayed at his side until he was safely in the hands of the ship's crew. His mood lifted as he passed from the rainy port into the welcoming glow of the ship.

After check-in, every passenger, even a billionaire, had to pass through the metal detector before boarding the vessel. McMorgan accepted this indignity with good grace, knowing that it was for his own protection. It also gave him a chance to catch his breath.

A seasoned cruise-goer, he was looking forward to the round of cocktails, fine meals and entertainment on board. As soon as he reached the Reception area, he walked up to a group of elegantly dressed ladies half his age and gave an old-fashioned bow.

'Excuse me, girls, do you play bridge?'

'No, we don't.'

'Too bad,' McMorgan laughed. 'I wonder who could teach you?'

The ladies giggled. Others joined in the banter. Smiling to himself, McMorgan took the lift up to the Promenade Deck and hobbled over to the railing on his unsteady legs. He saw massive quantities of foam bubbling to the surface of the water far below, as the gigantic vessel began to inch away from the quay.

11

The ship's horn gave three long blasts. The *Ocean Emerald* was departing Helsinki.

By craning his neck, Luke could just see a small patch of the city skyline above the balcony railing outside the window. Slowly but surely, the glass-walled terminal buildings were drifting away.

Cursing the handcuffs that chained him to the leg of the bed, preventing him from standing up, he lay down once more on the carpeted floor and closed his eyes. His lip was quivering. Never in his life had he felt so alone. Desperate for reassurance, he again played out the likely sequence of events back at Gran's: when he failed to return, Mum and Dad would get worried, they'd phone Toni, and then Toni would tell them everything.

But what would happen before that?

Luke ordered himself to get a grip. What would Dad have done in a situation like this? He'd have kept calm, that was certain. He'd have fought down the panic. Luke took a series of deep breaths. He'd lost nothing so far, except his freedom. It might be possible to get it back. The main thing was to keep a clear head. He thought of the items hidden inside his belt and immediately felt worse. What good were fish-hooks or glucose tablets if you were kidnapped by professional criminals?

The door was ajar. Luke gave a start. Someone entered the sitting room from the corridor. The card key was slotted into place and the lights came on. Voices spoke – this time it was two men. Twisting his body, Luke lifted up his head and tried to see into the sitting room.

He saw a pair of hands easing a heavy-looking object into a brown shoulder bag on the floor. The bag was identical to the one that Juliette had packed earlier. Coloured wires dangled from the object.

An explosive charge.

Luke's mind was racing. Were they terrorists? What else could they be? If they were ready to kidnap a complete stranger in order to hide their tracks, it had to be something bad... Something terrible... Perhaps they were going to blow up the ship – and only he knew about it.

After a few minutes, the lights went off in the sitting room and the men left. A dim night-light glowed just above the skirting board. To the right of the king-size bed was a small dressing table. On the wall above the chest of drawers hung an imitation nautical lantern, reminding Luke of a real one in Gran's shop in Porvoo. Like most of Gran's stock, that lantern had probably been in the shop for most of its existence. Whenever one of the bigger objects was sold, which was not often, she asked Luke to help him rearrange the collection. He loved his gran, but hefting furniture in the dusty, cigarette-smelling shop was not his idea of a good time. At this moment, though, he longed for the shop and even its musty smell.

Luke could see two deckchairs and a table out on the balcony. The tops of pine trees and a church steeple slowly drifted past. Luke recognized the island fortress of Suomenlinna. In the distance, a blue-and-white Finnish flag snapped against its pole. The force of the wind seemed to increase as the ship approached the open sea. He was being carried from a foreign country into the total unknown...

Again, Luke made himself calm his breathing and tried to put some order into his thoughts. One thing was sure: Toni would tell Dad everything, sooner or later, and as long as Toni remembered Juliette du Pont's name, the trail leading to the cabin on the *Ocean Emerald* would be child's play for the police to follow, provided they could be bothered.

'*This is the steward speaking,*' a pleasant voice said over the speaker system. '*Welcome on board, ladies and gentlemen, and welcome back to those of you who have rejoined us after a day in Helsinki...*'

The sound was so clear that Luke felt as though someone was talking behind him.

'*We are now headed for St Petersburg, where our estimated time of arrival is eight o'clock tomorrow morning, local time. The time in Russia is one hour ahead of us and we will be adjusting the clocks on board at three o'clock in the morning. Please also remember to move your watches forward by one hour and to adjust the time on your mobile phones and other electronic appliances.*'

In a few hours, the ship would be in Russian waters... What could the Finnish police do for him then? Luke felt his heart lurch with dread, but he forced himself to keep thinking as logically as he could.

How could he ever stop the terrorists, or whoever they were? He couldn't even save himself... He couldn't even move. With every passing minute, the cruise ship, which had felt so exciting at first, carried him further from everything that was safe and familiar.

He thought about Mum and Dad getting dinner ready, Gran smoking on the porch, the suitcases in his empty room. His whole life seemed strangely distant, as though it were already lost. He cast about for a cheering thought or person... Toni? Toni the newly qualified driver at the wheel of his Nissan. Toni the mechanic with oil on his hands. Toni the master shoplifter. Toni and his endless action films. How, Luke wondered, would Toni cope if he was ever in a situation where real action was required? Despite his fear, Luke knew that this was also a chance to show Toni what he was made of, once and for all. He'd show Emma, too.

Luke remembered the dismayed look she had given him in the record shop. No doubt she still thought he was a shoplifter. But he had bigger worries now...

He'd show everyone, as soon as he figured out how...

12

When the casino doors were finally opened, Max Lownie Junior was the first inside. He ambled up to the fruit machines and began to feed them with coins.

Like a man hypnotized, he stared at the spinning reels. Every so often, his hand would leap onto the buttons to lock one or two of the symbols in place. When luck was on his side, the machines flashed and shuddered and winnings jingled into the bowl. Max had just bent over to scoop up the coins when a passer-by bumped into him with his shoulder bag.

'*Excusez-moi, Monsieur,*' said a man wearing glasses and a silk scarf.

'That's quite all right,' Max said in a mellow voice, filling his pockets, lost in pleasure. 'Quite all right...'

As he strolled towards the men's bathroom, Delacroix observed the familiar routine unfolding in the casino. The croupiers were preparing their tables and a few early customers were already buying gaming chips from the cashier.

The bathroom was luxuriously decorated with marble, ceramic tiles, spotlights and plants. Elgar's Cello Concerto flowed from the sound system. Delacroix smiled fractionally. Elgar was one of his favourite composers.

He stood at the sink for a moment, listening, until he was absolutely sure that he was alone. He could feel the tension throbbing deep inside his belly. It was a healthy sign.

The space was partitioned off into sections by ceramic walls. Delacroix crossed the tiled floor to the small palm tree in the corner of the bathroom and bent over the large pot. The healthy-looking plant with its shiny fronds was, in fact, totally synthetic and its pot was made of plastic. The corner in which he was standing could not be seen from the door, but Delacroix nevertheless put his comb on the floor. If someone happened to come in, he would pretend that he'd reached down to retrieve it.

Delacroix buried his hand in the light, dry granules that filled the pot and felt for the detonator, which Emilio had hidden there when he'd cleaned the bathroom on the previous day. *There it was.* Delacroix could feel the neatly folded wires through the plastic wrapping. He scooped out more granules, revealing the detonator, then took a lump of Semtex from his bag and carefully inserted the wires of the radio-controlled detonator into the explosive.

When he was ready, he buried the charge in the potting mix and smoothed the surface, picked up his comb and went back to the sink to wash his hands. There was a row of luxury toiletries beside the mirror, including a bottle of coconut hand cream. Enjoying the scent, Delacroix massaged his hands with the cream, then tugged his silk scarf into position. An orphan who had never forgotten the humiliations he suffered at the care institution where he grew up, he was proud to have reinvented himself and felt very much at home as a paying customer in this luxurious setting.

The location of the bomb he'd just planted had been carefully chosen. There were no security cameras in the bathroom, and a chute behind the wall housed the ship's most vital electric wiring and data cables, which would be ripped to pieces when the bomb went off.

Craig Thomson carried a universal key card in his wallet that opened every cabin on board. He tested the card on his own cabin door, then took the lift to the reception area on the fifth deck. It was best to take a peek at Delacroix's suite, just in case.

He phoned the suite on his mobile for a second time, to be sure that no one was in. There was no reply.

He stepped up to the Purser's desk. Carol was on duty.

'Do you mind paging for Philippe Delacroix and asking him to come here?'

'Have you phoned?'

'He's not in.' Thomson handed Carol an envelope addressed to Delacroix. 'Could you give him this?'

The envelope only contained routine information about the cruise.

Carol reached for her microphone.

'Hang on,' Thomson said with a wink. 'Give me five minutes.'

Carol gave him a surprised look, but said nothing. Coyote never asked for favours without a good reason.

Thomson strolled towards the lifts. Suddenly he saw a familiar face. It was the cleaner, Emilio Fernández, heading towards the Promenade Deck. He was wearing casual clothes, not his cleaner's uniform. What business could he possibly have on deck? Whenever their presence was not required, all crew and staff were supposed to keep away from the public areas.

The doors of the lift opened, but Thomson spun on his heel and followed the cleaner out onto the windy deck, maintaining a safe distance. The sea air was delicious. He felt a pleasant flutter in his stomach. Shadowing a man was more interesting than staring at the CCTV screens and he enjoyed using his operational training from long ago.

The cleaner walked to the stern and looked over the rail. Thomson moved a little closer, keeping behind a lifeboat. Over the horizon, dark clouds were assembling. Seagulls wheeled over the ship's wake, almost touching the grey waves. Down below, a yacht with bulging sails was speeding back towards the Finnish coast. The family on its tiny deck waved up at the *Ocean Emerald*.

'You boys really should have told me what you'd found.' Peter Baron stepped aside to let Toni into the house. 'You'd better come in. Luke's mum is beside herself with worry.'

Peter stepped back as his wife Hanna rushed forward and grasped Toni's hands. 'Toni, what's going on? Where's Luke?'

Toni repeated his story.

'Maybe Luke just decided to stay in Helsinki?' Peter said lamely, but he knew as well as the others that something must be seriously amiss if Luke wasn't answering his phone. It had been a busy summer professionally for both

Peter and Hanna and they'd left their son to his own devices during their holiday in Finland. At this moment, it felt like that had been a mistake.

To make matters worse, Peter had a killer headache, brought on by jet lag and worry.

'Try his mobile again.' Hanna's voice sounded unnaturally high-pitched.

'He knows I've been trying,' Peter said, but dialled the number once more.

'*Hi – this is Luke. Keep it short. Cheers.*'

Peter decided not to leave another message. He fixed Toni with a stern look.

'The *Ocean Emerald*, you said?'

'Yes.'

'And you still can't remember the name on the passport?'

'Julia or Juliette . . . A French name. I've got it! It was Juliette du Pont.'

'Great. Do you have a telephone number for the ship?'

'We can get it online . . . Well, Luke would find it in a flash . . .'

No doubt about that, Peter was thinking. Luke had an effortless mastery of all things IT. Not long ago, he'd had the bright idea of installing a keystroke recorder on the family PC at home in Brussels. The tiny device, which recorded all the keystrokes typed on the computer, had caused a frantic alert at Peter's workplace, Europol's secret anti-terrorism unit in Brussels. Peter had been assigned to the position by the UK government, having previously worked for MI6. When Luke's prank was discovered, the security people at Europol had initially thought Peter's personal computer had been targeted by hostile agents.

His colleagues had a good laugh when it turned out he'd been bugged by his own son.

Hanna was thumbing through the Helsinki phone book at the dining room table.

'Helsinki port authority,' she said, holding her finger on the number. 'Here, Peter.'

Having spoken to three different people, Peter was finally given the number of the ship's Reception desk. He dialled it calmly and tried to keep his expression neutral, but inside him, anxiety burned. He spoke to the purser, who introduced herself as Carol.

'*Sure, Mr Baron, your son was here,*' she said. '*Great kid – he came over specially to return some property belonging to one of our passengers. I'm sure she'd be happy to speak to you. She was really grateful . . . I'm putting you through now.*'

The phone began to ring, but there was no reply.

Peter shook his head and cut the line after ten rings. He looked first at his wife, who was staring into her laptop, then at his mother-in-law, who was smoking silently by the open window. Then he looked down at the wooden floor.

13

Philippe Delacroix went to check on the captive in the bedroom section of the cabin.

The boy lifted his head. 'They'll be looking for me already. If you think—'

'Shut up.' Delacroix turned and pulled the door shut. He glanced at his mobile. The mast icon was missing: no network. Then the icon reappeared. The coverage was patchy at best along the Finnish coast and would disappear altogether out on the open sea.

Delacroix took a deep breath. 'Number two?' he said quietly into his sleeve microphone.

'*OK*,' Emilio's voice replied through the button earphone.

Delacroix stepped up to the window. Dusk was falling over the turbulent sea and the low-hanging clouds had soaked up the red light of the setting sun.

'Number three?'

'*OK*,' Juliette said.

'Number four?'

'*OK*,' Helmut said. He worked in the ship's kitchens, but was currently off duty. It was he who had taken delivery of the fish consignment that was loaded in

Amsterdam and he was responsible for delivering the supplies to the team at agreed times...

Everything was going just right. The billionaire McMorgan had boarded in Helsinki as planned.

Delacroix rested his gaze on the sea. The wind moaned and whitecaps rose and fell in the thickening gloom, but the massive vessel powered ahead, solid as a train.

'Let's begin,' Delacroix said into his microphone. He turned round, strode out of the door and marched down the corridor to the main stairwell. He visualized himself as a figure in a slow-motion film, with rousing music in the background.

Long ago, as a cowering child at the orphanage near Marseilles, and for years thereafter, he had always been the one who obeyed orders. Eat this soup; wear these clothes; no, you can't have your own football boots; take this construction job; mix this cement... Even at night school he had been looked down upon and patronized, but he'd carried on with his studies until he had learned all he needed to know. Now, everyone did *his* bidding and he acted as he pleased and took what he wanted.

This was it. This was his moment. The realization filled his mind with a strange, sombre calm. Then a loud-speaker burst into life right above his head, shattering the magical moment.

'*Mr Philippe Delacroix, Mr Philippe Delacroix. Please come to the Reception desk on Deck Six. Mr Philippe Delacroix. Thank you.*'

What was this? The shock of the announcement was like scalding water poured over his body, but he concealed it. Without so much as breaking his stride, he stepped into the lift and pressed the button for Deck Six.

He joined the queue behind a lady whose face was taut from too much plastic surgery. The smiling purser handed her a guide to St Petersburg and the lady went teetering towards the lift, poodle in tow.

Delacroix stepped up to the desk and glanced at the name tag pinned to the purser's chest: Carol.

'I'm Philippe Delacroix. You paged me.'

The purser handed him a brown envelope, which he ripped open. It contained a copy of the cruise schedule: a completely inconsequential document. *Why had he been summoned to the Purser's desk just for this?*

Delacroix put the document on the desk and thought for a moment, then said: 'I'd like to speak to Captain Bauer, please.'

'What?' Carol gave a start, then recomposed her habitual smile. 'I'm sorry, sir, but the captain is always busy. Could someone else help you?'

'No. Please phone the captain for me. It's important.'

Delacroix sensed the purser's hesitation. He held her gaze, drawing on the mental strength he had been collecting during the months of preparation – during years spent improving himself. Carol picked up a cordless phone and moved away, turning her back to Delacroix. He could not hear what she was saying. A few moments later, she turned round and offered him the handset.

'Captain Bauer?' Delacroix said, moving to one side.

'*Speaking.*' The Captain had a German accent and sounded irritated.

'I need to speak to you urgently. May I come and see you on the bridge?'

'*What does the matter concern and who do I have the honour of speaking with?*'

'My name is Philippe Delacroix. It concerns a security threat. Meet me in the corridor outside the bridge. I'm coming up now.'

Delacroix cut the line and handed the phone back to Carol. He noticed the startled expression on her face, and knew that it would soon change to a look of terror.

Crouched behind one of the lifeboat davits at the back of the Promenade Deck, Thomson kept his gaze locked on the cleaner, Emilio Fernández, who was still standing at the windy railing, shifting his feet and glancing at his watch.

About half a dozen passengers were taking the air under the lowering sky. The wind came in sudden gusts and the passengers had to hold onto their hats and their hair.

Thomson was worried. He could have sworn he'd just seen Fernández speak into a sleeve microphone. It made no sense. He'd probably just been coughing, but Thomson had decided to watch a little longer.

His emergency response team, the Ferrum Group, maintained contact by radio, but Fernández was not a member – although, as it happened, according to the file that Thomson had read, the cleaner had applied to join. But Fernández had been passed over in favour of more long-serving members of the *Ocean Emerald*'s staff and crew, hand-picked men and women with expertise in different aspects of the day-to-day running of the ship. Thomson had christened the group himself. *Ferrum* was Latin for 'sword'.

Thomson's mobile vibrated in his waistband. He couldn't reply without being heard by Fernández, so he let voicemail take the call.

14

Karl-Heinz Bauer, the fifty-six-year-old captain of the *Ocean Emerald*, stood on the bridge with a phone pressed to his ear. Flummoxed by Delacroix's call, he had decided to ring Thomson, just in case. However, there was no reply, and Bauer hung up before reaching the end of the automated greeting inviting him to leave a message.

Philippe Delacroix... Bauer remembered that Coyote had singled out this passenger in one of his tedious routine security briefings, but he couldn't for the life of him remember why.

He put the phone down and gazed through the starboard window, squinting at the sun, which was about to be swallowed into a billowing mass of dark cloud. According to the weather forecast, a cold front was due to hit the Bay of Finland. Captain Bauer braced himself for a night of violent wind and rain. He loved the sea, but he was an essentially timid man, a trait that was becoming more pronounced with age. He came from a family of admirals and naval war heroes, but had chosen civilian work in the merchant navy instead, wanting a more quiet life. Sometimes he wondered whether the German Navy might not have been the calmer option after all.

At the sound of the buzzer, the third mate glanced up from the steering pulpit.

'I'll get it,' Bauer said.

The third mate returned his attention to the small dots of light and the ragged green contours of the Finnish coastline on the radar screen.

Bauer pressed the button that opened the first door. He stepped into the airlock, closed the first door, opened the second one, and hastened out into the corridor. The door closed behind him with a robust click.

The man standing in the corridor was rough-featured and deeply tanned, but he had the focused air of a surgeon or a pilot. He wore a silk scarf and glasses.

'Good evening, Captain,' the man said in a calm voice. 'I'm Philippe Delacroix.'

'Good evening, Mr Delacroix.' Captain Bauer said in English. He made no attempt to conceal his annoyance. 'How can I help you?'

'Let's talk inside.'

'Passengers aren't allowed onto the bridge.'

'Listen very carefully, Captain.' Delacroix took a step closer to Bauer. 'Your ship has been hijacked. Do exactly as I say, or the passengers will suffer. Now, open the door.'

'Mr Delacroix'— Bauer could feel his right eyelid beginning to twitch – 'I don't like your joke.'

'I have two kilograms of Semtex here.' Delacroix lifted the flap of his shoulder bag. 'We have hidden charges throughout the ship. We can sink this vessel at a moment's notice.'

Delacroix ripped the captain's ID card off its lanyard and slid it into the lock, which opened with a quiet whirr. Bauer felt a wave of panic and disbelief roar through him.

He let Delacroix push him through the door. The man was strong. Delacroix opened the second door and they were back on the bridge.

The third mate and the deck hand turned to look.

'Carry on,' Bauer said.

Delacroix walked over to the chart table. Bauer followed him. *This is not happening*, his brain was saying – but it *was* happening. He knew what his first priority was: to keep utterly calm, yet he could feel his self-control melting away. And where the hell was Coyote when he was needed, for once?

The hum of the navigation instruments seemed unnaturally loud. A needle-thin streak of lightning flashed on the horizon.

Bauer cleared his throat. 'Mr Delacroix,' he said in a firm voice. 'What the hell do you want?'

Delacroix slipped his hand into his pocket and held up a black object about the size of a mobile phone.

'This is a radio control that can blow up this ship in less than a second.'

Bauer stared into Delacroix's eyes. 'We have one thousand passengers on board and six hundred crew.'

'And they will all die unless you do exactly as I say.'

Bauer was still trying to establish whether Delacroix was just a mentally deranged intruder or a genuine threat. Had Thomson not briefed him earlier about Delacroix's background, Bauer would have chosen the first option. The Frenchman's expression was neutral, and his voice was almost mild, but his eyes burned like coals.

'Obviously, it's no use arresting or eliminating me,' Delacroix said. 'My partner has an identical device. If something happens to me, the ship goes down. Do you understand?'

Bauer nodded.

'Here are the rules. One. No one touches the GMDSS.'

Bauer nodded again. The man knew what he was doing. The Global Maritime Distress Safety System, or GMDSS, was a set of internationally agreed safety procedures, including a distress signal beamed out via radio beacon to indicate an endangered vessel's identity and location.

'Two. Take a course towards the northern tip of Gotska Sandö. Full steam ahead.'

'Hang on.' Bauer tried to play for time. 'Altering course will attract attention. The Finnish and Estonian coastguards will see immediately that we're no longer headed for Russia.'

'So what?' The hijacker spoke with calm certainty. 'By the time Kronstadt pilot station starts wondering where we are, we'll be miles away.'

Bauer swallowed.

'Change course,' Delacroix said, glancing at the device in his hand.

Bauer stared into Delacroix's eyes. The man's face was unnaturally still, like a death mask, and the insane threat he had uttered suddenly felt very real. Bauer swallowed. The other officers on the bridge were out of earshot and in any case, the decision was his.

He bent over the chart table and made some calculations with a pencil. Then he strode up to the steering pulpit with Delacroix at his heels and said, 'New course one-four-zero.'

'Excuse me, Captain?' The third mate turned in his chair, then got to his feet. 'That would take us south-west... St Petersburg is in the east.'

'Do as I say, Giordano.' Bauer felt like shouting, but his voice came out as a strangled whisper. 'One-four-zero. It's an order.'

'Yes, Captain.' Giordano switched off the autopilot, then grabbed 'the pod', the stick that controlled the propeller-rudder propulsion device. With a glance at Delacroix, he turned the stick a few degrees to the right.

The *Ocean Emerald* listed very slightly as it turned south. The red numbers glowing above the window behind the steering pulpit flashed to the rhythm of the spiral compass: 170... 160... 150... 140...

Once the manoeuvre was completed, the ticking stopped.

'Course one-four-zero, Captain.'

Bauer kept his eyes on Delacroix, who was watching as Giordano locked the pod in the middle position, then pushed the speed controls forward and down.

The lights under the compass indicator began to flash as the speed increased from fourteen to twenty-one knots.

'Full steam ahead, Captain.' Giordano's voice was quiet and anxious. He gestured with his small hands. 'Captain, I'm sorry, but what are we doing?'

'I'll explain,' Bauer said. 'That's all for now.'

15

Night was falling in the old quarter of Porvoo. Peter turned off the engine and sat in the dark car for a few moments, trying to gather his thoughts. The light from the small windows of the house cast a yellow glow into the yard. Luke's window was dark. Peter swallowed. The headache throbbed behind his eyes.

A bat flitted twice around the naked bulb over the front door, then went reeling towards the treetops. Inside the house, Luke's mother and grandmother would be sitting at the kitchen table, waiting for news.

With a sigh, Peter heaved himself out of the driver's seat and climbed the stone steps.

'What did Toni's parents say?' Hanna asked as Peter entered the warm kitchen.

'I just dropped him off without going in.' Peter ran himself a glass of water. 'There's no point getting him into trouble.'

'I don't see why not,' Hanna said. 'Toni's eighteen and should know better—'

'Luke should know better, too,' Peter said calmly. 'He can't just go off to Helsinki without telling us.'

Hanna put the kettle on and began scrubbing the

spotless sink. Gran was sitting by the window in her floral summer dress, stirring her coffee over and over again. There was a long silence. Peter put an aspirin into his mouth and rinsed it down with the water.

They'd taken turns to quiz Toni all evening, until the lad was white with worry and guilt. Peter knew Toni wasn't an ideal friend for Luke, but he also recognized that Luke wouldn't have put up with Toni's faults if there hadn't been more to him than met the eye. Earlier that summer, Toni had spent long days in the garden shed, patiently restoring Gran's old motorbike. He came from a disadvantaged family and Peter respected Luke for the loyalty he showed, even when Toni went too far, as he had so spectacularly done earlier in the week.

Luckily, when Peter had collected Luke, the manager of the record shop had decided to let the matter drop. He need never be told who the real culprit was. Toni was an adult and Peter knew that even a minor conviction would have wrecked his career prospects, such as they were.

'Luke's been obsessed with that cruise ship for days,' Gran said.

'How do you know?' Peter asked. Not for the first time that summer, he felt ashamed to realize that, in some ways, his mother-in-law knew Luke better than he did.

'He showed it to me on the computer.' Gran chuckled. 'I wouldn't mind a few weeks on that ship myself. Maybe he's decided to run away?'

'This is no laughing matter, Mother,' Hanna sighed, flinging her dish rag into the sink.

A sudden gust of wind bent the birch tree outside and set a branch tapping at the window. For the hundredth time that evening, Peter looked at his mobile phone. He had no missed calls and no messages.

'We should tell the police,' Hanna said.

'I agree,' Peter said. 'If he's not on the last bus from Helsinki, I'm calling them.'

'I am *so* angry with him,' Hanna suddenly burst out, springing up from her chair. 'What's the point of driving around looking for adventure, when we could all be having such a nice holiday together here at Gran's?'

'Now wait a minute, the two of you,' Gran said gently. 'Peter's been away for most of the summer, and you, my dear, have been working nonstop.'

Thomson was sure now. The cleaner Emilio Fernández was up to something. A few moments ago, he had unmistakably spoken into a sleeve microphone and then set off towards the stern.

Thomson followed, keeping a gap of twenty metres between himself and Fernández, who was moving briskly. Perhaps he was just exercising? It took several minutes to walk the length of the ship from bow to stern. They passed the motorized lifeboats, whose dual propellers were shiny and unused. The words *Ocean Emerald – Nassau* were stencilled onto each boat.

Then, with a jolt, Thomson understood that something else was wrong. The sun was still shining, but it was nowhere to be seen. Had the *Ocean Emerald* been travelling eastward as planned, the sun should have been in the west, right ahead of Thomson, at the rear end of the ship.

Thomson hurried down to the aft railing and looked over it, still keeping half an eye on Fernández to his left. The rich glow of the setting sun, or what could be seen of it under a vast cloud formation, was on his right. Then Thomson saw something that set his heart racing. The water in the ship's wake was so agitated that it foamed against the stern of the ship. This meant that the *Ocean Emerald* was travelling at maximum speed. When the vessel was travelling on a straight course, the two Rolls-Royce propulsion devices were normally in a V-position, so that the wake narrowed at the stern. When the cruise liner was travelling at normal speed, the wall of water formed a few metres behind. Only when it travelled at maximum speed did the wake actually touch the ship.

The distance between Helsinki and St Petersburg was so short that there was no need for the vessel to travel at its maximum speed of twenty-two knots. Quite the contrary: if the aim was to arrive the following morning, the ship would have to travel as slowly as it could.

Something was wrong – seriously wrong. Why had the captain changed course and speed so dramatically?

Thomson took his mobile from his waistband as he watched Fernández step back inside the vessel. He pressed the button that gave him a direct line to Captain Bauer.

Thomson listened to the rings at the other end. The bridge was also linked up to the two-way radio network that was used in emergencies. Although relations between the two men were strained, to his credit, Bauer always answered Coyote's calls promptly.

But now there was no reply.

Just as Thomson was about to put away his phone, the captain finally picked up.

'*Bauer.*'

'Thomson here. Listen, why are we—'

'*Sorry, Redwood. I'm a little busy. Can you call me back later?*'

Thomson froze.

'Redwood' was the code word that Thomson had chosen for the ship's emergency procedures, to be used whenever normal communication was impossible.

The phone was beeping in Thomson's hand: the captain had cut the line.

He rushed towards the doors through which Fernández had disappeared, then forced himself to slow his pace. It was vital now to avoid attracting attention. As he strode towards the lifts, he phoned the third purser, who was his deputy in the Ferrum Group.

'Josh, can you talk?'

'*Sure.*'

'Code Red. Ferrum Group onto maximum alert. Total secrecy. I'm locking myself into the control room.'

Captain Karl-Heinz Bauer's legs were shaking slightly, but he felt triumphant. What quick thinking! When the emergency procedures had been put in place and Coyote had made everyone memorize the code word 'Redwood', Bauer had never imagined for one second that he would have cause to use it.

The only sound in the oppressive silence on the bridge came from the navigator, which beeped occasionally. The sun was already halfway under the western horizon, and the clouds to the southwest were joined to the sea by a grey veil of rain. Without thinking, Bauer noted the rising wind that preceded a rain front. Some of the dark waves were crested with white.

'Kill the internet,' Delacroix ordered in a firm voice. 'And I mean throughout the ship.'

Bauer went to the control panel on the right. Delacroix watched his hand hovering over the multitude of instruments.

Bauer put his hand on a black lever.

'Stop,' Delacroix said. 'That's not the internet.'

'I know.' Bauer kept his hand where it was. 'With your permission, I'd like to seal the bulkheads. Just in case.'

'No. Your concern for the passengers is touching. But the best thing you can do for them is to obey me to the letter.'

Bauer moved to the row of computers at the back of the bridge. Delacroix followed close on his heels. Having successfully slipped the code word to Thomson, Bauer had felt his courage return. He was now determined to do more, no matter what it cost him.

The third mate had been silently watching the captain and the stranger. When their backs were turned, he quickly turned a switch on his own control panel, which had dual controls for the ship's most important functions.

The switch he had chosen closed the doors in the watertight bulkheads on the lower decks. As each bulkhead was sealed, a number lit up on the control panel.

Captain Bauer nudged the mouse and disconnected the ship's satellite-powered internet connection.

'And the backup connection as well,' Delacroix said.

Again, Bauer shuddered to see the hijackers' level of preparation. Perhaps they'd had access to a simulator at some maritime college.

Bauer felt a cold knot tighten in his stomach. He took a small step sideways, which brought him within reach of another panel, and inched his hand slowly towards a concealed button at the edge. Delacroix was still looking at the internet screen.

Despite his timidity, submission was not a reaction that came naturally to Bauer, so he did the exact opposite of what he had been told to do. With a deft flick of his hand, he set off the automatic distress signal, which automatically transmitted the ship's particulars and location to other vessels in the area. Through its powerful radio beacon, the GMDSS would beam the signal across a radius of hundreds of nautical miles.

'What did you press?' Delacroix's dark eyes flashed. 'Captain, that was a serious mistake.'

'Commander, a distress signal from the *Ocean Emerald*!'

The young marine offered a slip of paper to Jan van Heerevelt, the bored commander of the *Zeeland*, a frigate of the Royal Netherlands Navy. Following a tedious two-day visit to Tallinn in Estonia, the warship had set out onto the choppy sea at four in the afternoon. It was travelling at a speed of eighteen knots, on a westward course. Van Heerevelt yawned and wondered whether he should go and have a nap on his bunk. Computers took care of navigation and there were no naval battles to fight. This wasn't what he'd had in mind when, as a small boy, he'd dreamed of being a naval officer.

'Respond.' Van Heerevelt waved away his subordinate. 'Tell them we're on our way. Ask them what the problem is.'

The marine saluted his commanding officer and returned to the control room. The *Zeeland* was a De Zeven Provinciën-class frigate and the signal emitted by its Scout radar system was never stronger than a single watt, which meant that it could sneak up on another vessel without being easily detected, despite its size, a substantial 146 metres from bow to stern.

The *Zeeland* itself, however, was good at seeing others. Its air defence radar system could track up to a thousand targets at once and was capable of detecting an object the size of a tennis ball from a distance of sixty kilometres. If required, it could also react ferociously, being armed with anti-aircraft missiles and a twelve-centimetre cannon.

Van Heerevelt studied the print-out, still more annoyed than interested. The distressed vessel was approximately one hundred sea miles to the east. He was aware of the *Ocean Emerald*, a cruise ship with more than fifteen hundred persons aboard, including the crew. The GMDSS signal gave no details of the situation, but something serious had obviously happened. One of the worst possibilities was a fire on board, but it was probably something much less dramatic than that.

'New course zero-nine-zero, full steam ahead,' van Heerevelt said with another yawn, addressing the officer on duty. 'I'm going for a coffee.'

'New course zero-nine-zero, full steam ahead,' the watch officer repeated the command.

The *Zeeland* executed a wide eastward U-turn, its grey hull juddering on the waves. On the open sea, whitecaps flickered in the dusk. The exhaust fumes rising from the funnel streamed away into the wind as the Rolls-Royce Spey gas turbines throbbing in the engine room released their full power and the frigate built up momentum, soon reaching its maximum speed of thirty knots. The warship was now rapidly closing in on the cruise ship in distress.

PART TWO

16

The *Ocean Emerald* forged ahead through the gathering darkness, keeping its southward course across the Baltic. Hanko – the southernmost tip of the Finnish coast – was already far away. Behind the brightly lit cabin windows, the passengers were preparing for the evening's drinks, food and entertainment.

On the floor of the bedroom in cabin number 7039, Luke was trying to puzzle out a way to avert the impending terrorist attack, if that was what it was. Without help he would never escape. The only hope was to persuade his captors to free him. What if he feigned sickness? The plan was manifestly lame.

What would a British secret agent do in this situation? Luke didn't have the foggiest idea, because he'd rarely seen the kinds of films where agents set the world to rights. Even James Bond had been off limits for Luke until he reached the age of twelve, whereas his friends, it seemed, had discovered Bond as soon as they lost interest in the Teletubbies.

Luke's early years had been spent in England, but he'd started school in Geneva, after his mum got a job at CERN, the European Organization for Nuclear Research.

Some years later, Luke had moved to Brussels, where his father worked for Europol, as a British agent in a secret anti-terrorism unit. The Brussels unit was run with a very low profile and kept separate from the Europol head-quarters in The Hague. Mum visited at weekends and sometimes teleworked from Brussels.

Luke was often asked where his roots were. He always gave the same answer: Dad's childhood home in East Sussex. England was his homeland. But he could get by in the major European languages and was happy anywhere, provided he wasn't bored.

The reason why Dad was so uptight about screen violence, Luke understood, was somehow a result of the unpleasant things he saw in his job. Very occasionally, Dad had agreed to let Luke watch adventure films in the French version – it seemed anything was permitted in the name of language learning. Of his two parents, Mum was the more relaxed. When they'd lived in Geneva when Luke was little, she'd even bought him a PlayStation and a couple of shooting games. But one day Luke had over-heard Mum and Dad arguing and Dad had said the games were Mum's way of trying to compensate for the long hours she worked at CERN, leaving her son in the hands of the au pair. It had spoiled Luke's pleasure in the games.

Suddenly Luke remembered the full horror of his plight. Panic wasn't far away. No measure was too desper-ate now. He cleared his throat. He couldn't hear anyone out in the corridor. But maybe there was a ventilation shaft somewhere that could carry his voice to friendly ears?

He took an enormous breath and shouted at the top of his lungs. 'HELP! HELP!'

It was as though the thick carpet and soft furnishings had swallowed up the sound even as Luke produced it. He could feel his pulse racing from the exertion. Then the cabin door suddenly opened. Luke felt cold all over. Had his shout been heard by his kidnappers out in the corridor?

Through the half-open bedroom door, he saw Juliette du Pont enter the sitting room. He could not see what the woman was doing, but she moved about for a few minutes, then opened the door once more and left. She must have been right outside the cabin when he had shouted, yet she had not heard him, Luke reasoned with relief – and growing despair.

The radar screens glowed in the surveillance room of the Gulf of Finland Coastguard Station in Helsinki. Lieutenant Maria Vierto was tracking two points of light that were in fact colossal Baltic passenger ferries. The swift-moving *Viking Xpress* was about to overtake the *Tallink Romantika*. Her screen also showed several cargo ships, including a Russian oil tanker from Primorsk, travelling westward.

'Lieutenant, we have a distress signal from the *Ocean Emerald*.' The young duty officer's voice was taut. 'It's that cruise ship that embarked for St Petersburg from Helsinki this evening.'

'Radio them and request full details,' Maria Vierto said calmly. 'Prepare to launch a rescue operation.'

Maria knew better than most that time was of the essence when ships faced peril at sea. On the fateful night of 28 September 1994, her older brother had been a conscript at this very coastguard station when the *Estonia* ferry keeled over and sank, taking 852 men, women and children to the bottom of the sea. The events had marked her for life – but didn't stop her from deciding to build her own career in the coastguard. The night the *Estonia* sank, not much could be done for the victims because by the time the ship's officers called for help, the vessel was already listing badly and the violent storm had made conditions worse, a combination of factors that conspired to bring about a catastrophe of Biblical dimensions. Just as then, there were high winds on the Baltic tonight.

'*Finnish Coastguard calling* Ocean Emerald,' the duty officer said over the International Calling and Distress Channel, Channel 16.

When the duty officer turned to face Maria Vierto, he looked even more alarmed than before. 'No reply from the *Ocean Emerald*, Lieutenant.'

Maria nodded. She'd just noticed something strange. The *Ocean Emerald* was supposed to be on its way to St Petersburg, which was east of Helsinki, yet it was currently heading southwest.

Maria took the microphone from the duty officer and put on the headphones.

'Good evening, *Ocean Emerald*. You sent a distress signal over the GMDSS a few moments ago. What's wrong?'

There was a moment's silence. Maria could hear what sounded like heated voices in the background, but she couldn't make out the words. Then a man's voice spoke out clearly, in a German accent: '*This is the* Ocean Emerald. *The distress signal was transmitted by mistake. We're repairing the radio equipment and a technician made an error. We apologize.*'

The voice over the radio was calm and businesslike, yet Maria felt uneasy. Only an exceptionally careless technician would issue an emergency alert by mistake.

'You were supposed to be on the way to St Petersburg, but you're now southwest of Helsinki. May I ask why?'

'We... We had to change our itinerary... The company is facing financial difficulties. But I assure you that the ship, the passengers and the crew are safe and well. Everything is OK.'

'OK then. Thank you. Have a safe voyage.'

With a frown, Maria replaced the microphone in its stand. Never in her career had she come across a false alert quite like this one, and having a logical cast of mind, she very much doubted the explanation she had just heard.

She decided to report the incident to her superior.

17

'For your sake, let us hope that did the trick, Captain Bauer,' Philippe Delacroix said on the bridge of the *Ocean Emerald*. The floor rose and fell beneath him, as the vessel pitched and heaved in the rising swell.

'It is time to inform the passengers of the situation,' Delacroix continued in a quiet voice. 'After you have spoken, pass the microphone to me.'

Bauer said nothing. He was feeling shaky after his heroics. He was also desperate to use the lavatory, soon. For a fleeting moment he thought he might faint. He glanced at the third mate quietly manning the controls. Rain lashed at the windows. The multicoloured lights of the steering pulpit were reflected in the glass.

The intruder, Delacroix, stood by the office lamp over the chart table, a dark figure in a pool of light.

'I'd better tell our head of security, Mr Thomson, or he might do something you're not expecting.'

Delacroix seemed to be reflecting. 'OK then. But first tell me what you intend to say to him.'

Bauer explained and Delacroix nodded his assent.

Bauer had never imagined that the voice of Coyote could sound so sweet in his ears. He kept it short, so as not to arouse Delacroix's suspicions.

'Thomson, this is Captain Bauer. Listen carefully and don't interrupt. We've been hijacked. The leader of the hijackers, Mr Delacroix, is here on the bridge with me.' Bauer cleared his throat. 'There are radio-controlled explosives hidden throughout the vessel. Delacroix has one radio control, and another, unidentified hijacker has the other. We're co-operating with them. This is an order. Do you understand?'

'*I do. Can you—*'

At a signal from Delacroix, Bauer cut the line. He didn't want to endanger the lives of his passengers by crossing the hijacker again. Delacroix was not acting in the least bit like a fanatical terrorist and perhaps the safest thing was simply to obey him.

'Good. Now kindly describe the situation to the passengers in general terms as I have instructed. Then pass me the microphone.'

Bauer cleared his throat and took the microphone from its stand on the steering pulpit. His throat felt constricted, but he tried to keep his voice as calm as possible.

'Good evening, ladies and gentlemen. This is Captain Bauer speaking.' Bauer closed his eyes before continuing, saying exactly what Delacroix had told him to say. 'The ship has been hijacked. Do *not* use your mobile phone, even if you happen to get coverage. The hijackers have a scanner that will immediately reveal any calls made or received. I appeal for your full co-operation. Every passenger must obey the hijackers, or we will all suffer. Right now, we are OK, but I'm afraid we will not be able to reach St Petersburg tomorrow as planned. Thank you.'

Bauer handed the microphone to Delacroix.

'*Good evening from me as well. I have taken control of this ship...*'

Thomson had just locked himself in the control room on the sixth deck and was standing facing the stack of CCTV screens, out of breath, ears pricked. He listened to the unnaturally calm voice with a French accent that rang out over the speaker system.

'*As Captain Bauer just informed you, we will see immediately if one of you tries to use a mobile.*'

As he listened, Thomson switched on the two-way radio network, through which the members of the emergency response team, working in different parts of the ship, could maintain contact. Each member of the Ferrum Group had a discreet transmitter-receiver that was small enough to fit into a shirt pocket.

'*If someone attempts to use a mobile, we will kill one passenger at random.*'

Thomson narrowed his eyes. His face felt numb. He pressed the 'ALERT' button that sent all members of the group a vibrating signal.

'*The same applies if one of you tries to resist or capture us, or to affect the course of events in any other way.*'

Lying on the carpet, Luke listened to Delacroix's voice over the loudspeaker in the bedroom of cabin number 7039. He had a lump in his throat. As the situation became clearer, it also became more frightening.

'*If you co-operate one hundred per cent, no one will get hurt.*'

Or so you say, Luke was thinking. He had no faith whatsoever in Delacroix's words. He gritted his teeth. Could he have done something to thwart the hijacking? What if he'd taken the passport to the police as soon as he'd found it? Would it have helped? Perhaps he should have resisted harder when he was captured? Had he managed to escape, he could have rushed to the bridge to warn the captain. Or could he? What good was a fishing line when a forty-five-thousand-tonne cruise ship was hijacked?

He understood now how immature he'd been when he'd fantasized about becoming a private detective. The accessories hidden inside his belt wouldn't save anyone. Many things looked childish right now. Even his slight build irritated him more than ever. Why had he never taken the trouble to work out, like some of his body-building classmates?

At the family house in East Sussex, Luke slept in Dad's old room, where Dad's rusty old dumbbells still lay under the bed. Once or twice, Luke had tried to lift them, dreaming of a transformation such as he'd seen in the before and after photos of online ads, but these intentions were always short-lived. To Luke, surfing the web or reading a book was more appealing than exercise.

If you found yourself in real trouble, brute strength was useless and it was only brains that counted, Dad never tired of saying. And Dad knew what he was talking about. *Use your head*, Luke repeated to himself. *Use your head.*

Suddenly, the cabin door was wrenched open. Luke could feel his body tensing involuntarily. He struggled unsuccessfully to see who had come into the suite. For some time now, he had felt the need to use the toilet, and now he was getting desperate...

He heard rustling and small knocks from the sitting room, as though someone was packing their bags.

Then footsteps approached. What were they going to do to him?

Juliette du Pont appeared at the bedroom door. She had her customary fierce expression in her eyes, but she had changed out of her skin-tight sports attire into jeans and a grey rugby shirt. Luke barely recognized her. In her hand was a pistol. An inconspicuous earphone was hooked over one ear and there was a microphone on a slim swan-neck just under her mouth, which made her look like a stage entertainer.

Juliette slipped her hand into her pocket as she moved closer to Luke. He held his breath and felt his pulse shoot up.

'Turn onto your stomach,' Juliette ordered in a low, firm voice, pulling something from her pocket.

'What—'

'Turn over! Right now.'

The tone left no room for haggling. Luke rolled onto his belly. Juliette leaned over him, unlocked the handcuffs and freed him.

'Get up,' Juliette said.

Luke stumbled to his feet and had to grab hold of the bed frame to keep his balance. He could feel the blood rushing to his palms, which had gone completely white as he had lain immobilized on the floor. He got pins and needles all over his hands as circulation was restored.

Juliette pointed at the door. 'Go!'

Luke knew he was staring back with an idiotic look on his face, but he was too stunned to move.

'Go! You're still a hostage, just like everyone else on board, but you'll get no more special treatment.'

At that moment, Juliette's hand flew to her earphone, and turning her back to Luke, she said something into her microphone in a low voice.

Luke followed her into the sitting room and tried to snatch his mobile from the coffee table, but Juliette spun round just at the wrong moment and he retreated. Juliette continued whatever exchange she was having over the radiophone.

Luke quickly cast his gaze around the sitting room. Nothing revealed what its occupants had been up to. A few pieces of clothing lay on the sofa beside a shoulder bag and a sack of brown granules, like dog food. That was weird. Did the hijackers have a dog with them?

'I can't believe you're still here,' Juliette hissed from the bedroom door.

Luke opened the door that led into the corridor and slipped out, dreading that the woman might change her mind. Rubbing his wrists, he ran a few steps, then stopped beside a glass cabinet containing a fire extinguisher, wondering what to do next. The ship seemed deserted. Had the other passengers been locked in their cabins? Or had they been herded together somewhere for surveillance? Luke was travelling without a ticket, which meant that he had no cabin to go to.

He ran down the corridor towards the lifts, feeling dizzy with relief, although he knew that he was still a prisoner. His first instinct was to make contact with other human beings.

18

'*Frigate* Zeeland *of the Royal Netherlands Navy calling the* Ocean Emerald. *Over.*'

Leaning against the ledge in front of the large windows at the front of the bridge, Commander van Heerevelt watched as his subordinate attempted to contact the cruise ship. Outside, the waves heaved in huge mounds against the pitch-dark night. He could sense the chill of the stormy night behind him. The vibrations of the propeller travelled through the window ledge to his palms.

The *Zeeland* was pitching violently as the sea hammered its sides. Van Heerevelt needed another coffee. The digital log indicated the speed of the frigate in red: 32.9 knots kept changing to 33.0 knots and back again.

'*This is the* Ocean Emerald. *Over.*'

'We have received your distress signal. What is the matter?'

The silence that followed was broken only by the hiss of the air conditioning and the howl of the wind around the frigate's forecastle.

'*The signal was sent accidentally. We were repairing the radio. We are in no danger. Sorry.*'

There was a brief pause. Van Heerevelt went up to his subordinate and held out his hand. The officer gave him the microphone and van Heerevelt took a deep breath, pushing out his chest.

'Good evening, this is the commander of the *Zeeland*. You will forgive me for saying so, but I find it extremely disquieting that a GMDSS signal should accidentally be transmitted from a large passenger ship. Surely you understand that this can trigger a massive rescue operation?'

'*Good evening, Commander. This is Captain Bauer of the* Ocean Emerald. *I fully share your concern. We regret that this has happened. Please accept our sincere apologies...*'

Van Heerevelt thought there was an edge of distress in Bauer's voice, but maybe it was just embarrassment? The man had reason to fear for his job.

'OK then. Have a safe voyage.'

'*Thanks. The same to you.*'

Van Heerevelt put down the microphone. 'New course one-eight-zero, speed nineteen knots.'

'Course one-eight-zero, speed nineteen knots, sir.'

The turbines were switched off and the *Zeeland* switched back to diesel power. The frigate slowly turned onto a southward course, rolling a little as its side took the impact of the waves, then continued to fight its way through the shifting mountains of water. At regular intervals, the bow wave sent a copious spray arcing onto the bridge windows, as though a fire hose had been turned on them.

Van Heerevelt left the bridge. There was something odd about the incident, but he could not have said precisely what. He was already halfway to his cabin and the adventure novel on his bunk when he suddenly turned back, having decided to dispatch a report to the Navy Headquarters in Den Helder, just in case.

Although Luke had understood the gravity of the situation on board, it was not until he saw the reactions of his fellow passengers that he, too, began to fear for his life once more. It was a crazy sight. Mature, distinguished-looking men, many of them no doubt company executives and top lawyers, looked wild-eyed as they hastened to the seventh deck to surrender their mobile phones to the ship's crew, complying with the instructions they had just received over the speaker system. Not just all mobile phones, but all BlackBerries, personal organizers and laptops were to be handed over without delay.

He passed a small group of old ladies quietly murmuring among themselves. A young man hastening to hand in his iPad suddenly stopped dead in his tracks and vomited onto the floor. Was it seasickness? Or terror? Maybe both.

Luke knew he was the only passenger who had seen a glimpse of the hijackers' inner circle. He had quickly sketched a plan of action that was daring but entirely realistic. He hurried his steps. He was 'completely hyper', as Mum would have said, but for once, the situation justified it. It felt strange thinking about Mum and Dad, or even Toni. Everything he'd left behind when the ship sailed now felt like a distant dream. What must they all be thinking? Had Dad already understood that something was wrong?

Marshalling his thoughts, Luke weighed his fear of causing harm to the other passengers against the fear of not daring to try his utmost to help them. Having put himself in this situation by sneaking off to Helsinki, hoping to make money out of someone else's lost passport, he now felt he had to redeem himself in the eyes of his dad.

The first thing he needed to do was to get to the bridge, but where was it? The cruise ship was like a giant shopping centre laid out as a labyrinth.

As he passed the tinted glass doors of the casino, Luke was surprised to see a lonely gambler at the fruit machines. It felt good to find one person, at least, who was unfazed by the hijacking situation. Luke approached the portly figure. When he got close, he could hear classical music blaring from the man's earphones, until the sound was obliterated by the clatter of the fruit machine.

'That was lucky,' Luke said, impressed by the handfuls of coins that the fat man was scooping into the pockets of his shorts.

'There's luck, and there's skill, but not everyone can tell the difference,' the man said, reaching for the volume control that dangled on the cable of his earphones. He raised his chin and looked down at Luke. 'You don't know who I am, do you?'

Luke had in fact recognized him: it was the man from the lift earlier that day, the son of the CEO of the Emerald Cruise Corporation, whom Carol had pointed out. He only looked about ten years older than Luke, who felt like giving this oaf a lecture on the relative importance of luck and skill in gambling, but this was hardly the moment. His eyes were fixed on the mobile phones hanging from the fat man's belt.

'Have I seen you on TV?' Luke said, pretending to be impressed.

'It's possible.' The man's plump cheeks wobbled as his fat lips composed themselves into a self-satisfied smile. 'I'm Max Lownie Junior, owner of this ship. Well, my dad owns it, but it comes to the same thing. One day, Junior will become Senior.'

'I'm Luke C. Baron, an English stowaway.'

'What's that supposed to mean?'

'It's a long story and it's not important right now. I think we have a common problem,' Luke said in a serious voice.

'If you mean the hijackers, you can relax. There's a specially trained response team on board. And the head of security is a former FBI agent. They'll sort this out.'

Max sounded so certain that Luke, too, began to feel reassured. The man clearly knew what he was talking about. But ex-FBI or not, the head of security would surely want all the information he could lay his hands on about the hijackers – and Luke had no intention of dropping his own plan, either.

'Aren't you going to hand in your phones?' Luke said. 'And why do you have two?'

'Ever heard of SatPhones?' Max said with a look of infinite pity on his face. He took the bigger handset from its holster on his belt. 'Satellite phone. Works everywhere on the planet. I won't surrender this baby without a fight. The other one's useless out here at sea.'

The casino appeared to be deserted, yet Luke lowered his voice. 'Why don't we hide it somewhere?'

'Who's "we", missy? Leave this to the grown-ups, OK?'

Max set his phone down on a small drinks table and covered it with his baseball cap.

'Could you please tell me the way to the bridge?' Luke said.

'Take the lift to Deck Nine, then follow the starboard-side cabin corridor to the forward end. You'll then see a door on your left. Open it and take the stairs up,' Max said, wiping his sweaty brow. 'Alternatively, don't bother. The bridge is out of bounds to passengers, especially children.'

Suddenly, an anxious-looking woman with South American features appeared from somewhere. It was the would-be pop star that Carol had joked about.

'Max, I might have guessed you'd be here. We should stick together from now on. Have you had a call from your dad yet?'

'You heard what they said!' Max snapped back. 'We mustn't use the phones.'

'Oh God, I'm so scared,' Gabriela said.

Luke moved closer to Max's baseball cap.

'I've caught a stowaway. No wonder the hijackers got on board if a small kid like this can walk on board just like that.'

'Max, come on!' the woman said, grabbing her stepson by the elbow.

Max pulled himself free and reached for the rest of his winnings. As they scuffled, Luke slipped his hand under the baseball cap and put the satellite phone into his pocket. It reminded him of what Toni had done in the record shop. But this was different. This was an emergency.

'I'm going to find somewhere to hide,' Luke said. 'Until things settle down.' He hastened between the fruit machines and past the roulette table to the lifts, where yet more passengers were thronging with their phones, personal organizers and laptops.

Luke withdrew to the men's bathroom and locked himself in a cubicle. Having relieved himself, he turned his attention to the phone. The Iridium satellite phone featured an ordinary tri-band GSM, as well as standard camera and smartphone functions. It only took him a few minutes to master the commands he needed. His spirits sank when he realized that Max's phone wasn't configured to offer internet functions. It was a beautiful phone, yet the slob had probably been too lazy to learn how to use it. But Luke decided to work with what he had.

He took a test photo of the door handle and studied the result on the display. The quality wasn't that great, but it would have to do. He put the phone into his pocket and returned to the atrium and took the lift down to the sixth deck, where yet more crowds surged chaotically.

A Filipino man with a sub-machine-gun hanging across his chest was standing behind the Reception desk. Carol was nowhere to be seen.

'Let's have some order here!' the Filipino shouted. 'Everyone, wait for your turn!'

This had no effect whatsoever on the panic-stricken passengers. Juliette appeared beside the Filipino. Perfectly expressionless, she took the sub-machine-gun from him and climbed onto the Reception desk. Slipping behind a big-bellied Brit, Luke felt for Max Lownie Junior's satellite phone in his pocket. He pressed the button that activated the camera and moved closer to the Reception desk, trying to make sure that Juliette didn't see him. Then he pulled out the phone.

Without lifting it to his eye, Luke pointed the camera and took several pictures in quick succession of Juliette standing on the Reception desk, hoping that at least one of them would come out.

Suddenly there was a deafening burst of automatic fire. The rounds from Juliette's sub-machine-gun ripped into the ceiling and shards of mirror and bits of plaster rained down onto the screaming crowd. Luke threw himself onto the floor with everyone else. *Had he been seen?*

'Come forward one by one!' Juliette shouted, eyes blazing. 'It's not that difficult. Now let's try again.'

There were more screams, moans and sobs, but the passengers managed to form two exemplary queues. Panting for breath, Luke put the phone back into his pocket and stole away into the stairwell.

19

Craig Thomson had summoned all six members of his emergency response team to the control room, where they were standing in a semicircle, watching the chaotic scenes at the Reception desk on the CCTV screens. The members of the Ferrum Group, five men and one woman, all had previous experience in the security sector, although they also had real jobs on the cruise ship.

Thomson knew that his team was no match for a group of violent professionals, and at this moment, he wished he was already working for Cunard, whose security personnel largely consisted of ex-Gurkhas and other former soldiers of elite regiments. The ex-Gurkhas were utterly loyal to their superiors and would not hesitate to use their famous curved blades to defend the interests of their employer.

Thomson stood in front of his desk, with the CCTV screens behind him, and began the briefing.

'Explosive devices have been hidden on board and at least two of the hijackers have a radio control for detonating them.'

'Sorry, I have a question,' Carol interrupted almost immediately. Still dressed in her white purser's uniform, she looked and sounded like she was going to crack up.

'Yes, Carol,' Thomson said calmly.

'How many are they?'

'We don't know the number, but at least two have been identified. Philippe Delacroix, a French passenger, is apparently one of the leaders. Earlier this year he spent three weeks on the *Ocean Jewel,* which of course means that he also knows the layout of the *Ocean Emerald* perfectly. The other one is Emilio Fernández, a Filipino cleaner. I found him fiddling with the fuse box at the bow of the ship on Deck Nine earlier today. I meant to check the box, but didn't get the chance yet.'

'Why don't we arrest those two and get them to reveal the others?' John Curran said. A deck hand, he was dressed in blue overalls.

'John, I just said that at least two members of the group can set off the bombs. One of them is Delacroix. He says that if something happens to either of them, the other one will blow up the ship.'

'Bummer,' Curran said drily.

'Any more questions?' Thomson said, calmly soaking up the tension of his subordinates.

There was a brief pause. The members of the Ferrum Group kept their eyes on the CCTV screens behind Thomson's back. He knew what they were seeing: terrified passengers rushing around with no idea what to do.

'Panic is spreading,' Thomson said. 'The situation is about to get out of control. We need to act. Carol, you search for explosives in the public areas. John will assist you. I'll check the fuse box on Deck Nine. Brian and Josh, you take a look at the other fuse boxes. Then check the engine rooms and the crew and staff quarters, including the cabins. You'll be watched, so keep working at those cover jobs as well. Will and I will stay here for now.'

'What about the kitchen, the passenger cabins and the outside decks?' asked Brian Jones, one of the ship's electricians, who stood with his hands buried deep in the pockets of his white overalls.

'We'll search all the remaining areas during the second round. Both groups, report back one hour from now, at exactly—'

Thomson was cut short by a fierce knock at the door. A sheet of paper was swept off the desk as he swung round to look at the black-and-white CCTV screen that was connected to the camera in the corridor outside. No one said a word. There was more knocking, this time even louder. Standing behind the door of the control room were two hijackers armed with sub-machine-guns.

Thomson could see his own reflection on the convex surface of the screen.

Everyone in the room was waiting for his decision.

For a third time, the door shuddered as the violent knocking was repeated.

Curran pointed at the locked metal cupboard that contained the firearms for Thomson's team.

Thomson shook his head. 'We can't start a gun battle.'

'So what do you suggest? Let's offer them a cup of tea?'

'They want to take over the control room,' he said. 'They can have it.'

'If you say so, Coyote.'

'At least your captor is a beautiful young woman,' Thomson said with a glance at the CCTV screen.

'How consoling. But you know what they say,' Curran snarled. 'The female of the species is more deadly than the male.'

'Right, we're going in,' Juliette said and switched off her radiophone. As always, Delacroix's calm instructions had soothed her nerves.

'Get behind me,' she told Emilio in the corridor outside the control room, pointing the sub-machine-gun at the door, and listening. She could hear voices. She counted them calmly, and waited for the right moment.

Brought up with her sister by a single mother, who had been a minor French diplomat and major cocaine user, Juliette had passed from a privileged childhood to an unstable and eventually delinquent youth. She'd spent most of it in Italy, where her mother had been posted at the French Embassy. Academically talented, Juliette got a place at Rome University to study biology, wasted her chance through drug abuse and returned to France for treatment, which she soon gave up in favour of a violent crime spree to fund her addiction to heroin. Even as she prospered through crime, drugs ruled her life. That all changed on the day she met Delacroix.

It had been the day she reluctantly began a nursing course at night school, soon after she'd completed her third round of rehab. She still remembered the brooding figure at the coffee machine, a mature man who smiled at her, a paper cup like a thimble in his big, strong hand. Within a month they had been married. In Delacroix she had found the firm, paternal figure that had always been missing from her life. Delacroix supervised the fitness regime that helped her beat her drug habit. He even helped her choose her clothes. He took her to a Cézanne exhibition in Aix-en-Provence and surprised her with his love of art. Unlike her, Delacroix had been given precious few opportunities in life. It was he who planned the bold heists that would bring them the status they deserved. Juliette would do anything for Delacroix – and her sister felt the same way.

'Now,' Juliette said. Shots rang out in the narrow space, wood shattered and three hot cartridges fell onto the floor in a cloud of dust. Juliette kicked in the door and rushed through the bluish smoke. Emilio followed, sub-machine-gun at the ready, but no more shots were fired, as the occupants of the room had already taken refuge under a table and were waving their arms in a sign of surrender.

'Against the wall!' Juliette shouted. 'Turn your backs to me and keep your hands in the air.'

The sight of the helpless security team gave a special edge to Juliette's adrenaline rush – her new drug. She nodded at Emilio, who began frisking the prisoners for weapons.

'Who's the leader?'

'I am. The name's Craig Thomson.'

'Open the door of the data centre.' Juliette stared at Thomson, noting the strong build, the American accent and the intelligent eyes.

With a defiant glare at Juliette, Thomson calmly punched in the access code. Emilio entered the special air-conditioned room which housed the ship's central data processing units. He pulled out power cables and kicked over the main-frames, rapidly disabling the ship's nerve centre.

'Don't touch the CCTV.' Juliette's eyes were on Thomson's screens.

'OK,' she said to Thomson. 'Now get me a pair of scissors.'

Thomson turned round and narrowed his eyes.

'A pair of scissors!'

Thomson took a pair of scissors from a desk drawer and handed them to Juliette.

'On your knees.'

Thomson did as he was told. He tried to move out of the way when Juliette brought the scissors closer, so she grabbed his ear to hold him still.

'Just so we don't forget who you are,' she said, and began clipping at Thomson's hair until it was a crazy patchwork of tufts and bald skin, as though a drunken barber had been let loose on him.

Everyone got the same treatment, except for Curran, whose head was already shaved. Juliette used a can of spray paint to mark his scalp with a green stripe. She could sense the shame and fear of her captives and the fact that Thomson alone seemed in complete control of himself, but she wasn't scared of him. She'd kicked heroin. She loved her man. She wasn't scared of anyone.

'It's done,' she said into her radiophone.

'*Good girl...*' the voice of Philippe Delacroix immediately replied.

20

Luke fought his way through the disorientated crowds to the bridge on the ninth deck. In his hand was a scrunched-up towel, which he'd taken from the men's bathroom.

Someone had been taken ill and a doctor was being summoned over the loudspeaker. Around Luke, the distressed passengers argued and bickered and exchanged wild rumours. Incomprehensible voices in Russian, Japanese and Arabic alternated with the languages he could understand: English, French, Italian... But the note of uncertainty and terror was the same in all languages. In the snatches of conversation that he heard, any number of culprits were identified: al Qaeda, Chechens, Palestinians... But as far as he had seen, the hijackers were French.

Luke hastened down the main corridor on the ninth deck and took a right turn. A tall blond man with a neatly trimmed beard was doing something in front of a hatch on the wall.

'Excuse me,' Luke said. 'Could you tell me the way to the bridge?'

The man gave Luke a piercing look, measuring him from top to toe. 'Why do you ask?'

'Can you please just tell me where it is?'

'No idea,' the man said and turned to go, leaving Luke with the distinct impression that the man knew perfectly well, but preferred not to say.

Luke continued on his way until he met a dark-skinned young woman pushing a cleaning trolley, who told him without hesitation where the bridge was.

He followed her instructions and found an unmarked door. There was a card-reader next to the door and an ordinary-looking buzzer, which Luke pressed.

With a start, Delacroix looked up from the chart table.

'Someone's at the door,' Bauer said.

The buzzing stopped, then became continuous again.

'Go and see who it is,' Delacroix said.

Bauer stepped through the first of the airlock doors, and peeped through the spyhole before going further. A boy was standing in the corridor outside. He was in his early teens at best and had a slight build. Bauer opened the second door and stepped outside.

'What do you want?' Bauer said.

'Is Delacroix here?' the boy asked. He wore a towel like a bandage around his hand.

Bauer didn't even try to hide his surprise. 'Who are you and how do you know about Delacroix?'

'I can't explain right now. Is he here or not?'

'He is.'

'I want to speak to him.'

'I doubt he wants to speak to you.' Bauer couldn't suppress a slight smile. 'Off you go now.'

'Tell him Luke Baron is back.'

'How do you know him?' Bauer whispered. 'What's going on?'

'Please,' the boy said. 'It's important.'

Bauer and Delacroix met in the space between the double doors.

'Who's out there and what does he want?' Delacroix said.

'Some boy. Luke Baron. He asked for you by name.'

Delacroix brushed past Bauer and opened the armoured door a fraction.

'What is it?'

Bauer listened. He had no idea why the hijacker was speaking to the boy, or how he knew him.

'I wanted to ask, have you really thought this through?' the boy said in a precocious voice. 'This hijacking thing, I mean. If you stop now, you'll get off much more lightly—'

'Get out of here,' Delacroix said, slamming the door in the boy's face.

Congratulating himself, Luke scurried away from the door. Delacroix hadn't noticed a thing.

He hurried to the stairs and hid behind a vending machine. He unravelled the towel, took out the phone and checked what he had. His nervous fingers flew from key to key. The most difficult part had been positioning the tiny lens in such a way that it was not obscured by the fabric of the towel.

It had worked. Although the photo had been taken from a low angle, Delacroix was recognizable. He now had photos of both Juliette and Delacroix.

Luke put the phone into his belt, hiding it under his shirt. Then he headed towards one of the restaurants. The *Ristorante La Scala* was decorated in an Italian style, or what might pass for Italian on Miami's South Beach: paintings of classical ruins on the walls, a couple of replica Roman busts and designer furniture from Milan. The tables were laid with wine glasses, napkins and plates, and some meals had already been served, but there were no diners left in the restaurant. An eerie silence hung over the deserted scene.

Luke found a pen on the head waiter's desk and a sheet of paper with the Emerald Cruise Corporation logo on it.

'*Ladies and gentlemen, this is the new commander of this ship once more . . .*'

Luke froze at the sound of the loud announcement. He withdrew to a small table in the corridor and worked on his note as he listened.

'*Attention! All passengers must report to one of three different assembly points, in alphabetical order.*'

Restricting himself to as few words as possible, Luke recounted the events that had taken place on board. He described the hijackers, their weapons, and the orders they had given. He mentioned that Juliette du Pont was probably travelling under a false identity.

'*A to G: Passengers whose surnames begin with one of the letters A to G, assemble immediately in the Show Lounge. A to G: Show Lounge. H to O, assemble at the Purser's desk on Deck Six. H to O: Purser's desk. P to Z, assemble in the Cabaret Lounge on the seventh deck . . .*'

Luke folded the sheet of paper and put it in his pocket.

'*All passengers must bring their jewellery, their watches, their cash and their credit cards to the assembly point. Passengers who fail to bring these items will be punished.*'

Luke's heart missed a beat. So the hijackers weren't terrorists at all – they were pirates looting the ship! It seemed hard to believe. Was it all an elaborate smoke screen for something else? He took out the sheet of paper and recorded the latest announcement and the precise time.

Luke rushed through the saloon doors leading into the kitchen and walked straight into a shower of warm water. He stopped to wipe his stinging eyes and saw a foaming puddle and half a tomato on the floor.

'Sorry, I thought the hijackers were coming,' said a young woman and gave a bright laugh. 'You don't look like a hijacker.' She was little more than a girl, barely two or three years older than Luke.

'You think a bowl of dishwater will stop them?' Luke said, trying to recover his dignity.

'I said sorry.' The girl held out her hand. She had dark hair and eyes, and dimples on her thin cheeks. 'I'm Rosita.'

'Listen, I need your help,' Luke said, wiping his face. He glanced around in the huge, empty kitchen and lowered his voice. 'I need a large plastic container with a screw top. It has to be white. And I need a torch.'

Rosita looked surprised, but she set off at once. Luke followed the quick-moving girl into a storeroom. She was wearing a white kitchen tunic and a hairnet and had pink varnish on her nails. She handed Luke a torch.

'Great. Where do you keep the empty containers?'

'They're crushed for recycling the moment we're done with them.'

'Help me.' Luke pulled a ten-litre vinegar container from a shelf and dragged it across the threshold towards the dishwashers. He unscrewed the top and upended the container into the sink. A vile smell spread into the kitchen.

'How do I know you're not one of them?' Rosita suddenly said.

'You must be kidding. The ringleader is a French guy called Delacroix. This is what he looks like.' Luke displayed the photo on the camera. 'And that's Juliette, his creepy sidekick.'

Rosita handed back the camera, visibly impressed.

'I guess you might as well read this too.' He handed his note to Rosita. 'I've written down everything I've seen.'

While Rosita was reading the note, Luke typed a short text message on Max Lownie's satellite phone, and quickly found the timer function. He set the timer to send the message in half an hour. The stench of the vinegar almost made him retch.

The main thing was to get the photos to the authorities as fast as possible. As he couldn't email from Max's phone, the only option was to send a timed text message and hope that the phone could be traced.

Luke also longed to contact his family, to tell them he was all right. He quickly wrote two lines to Gran. It was just a few words, but at once his eyes started stinging. He looked up to see Rosita staring at him.

'Get me some plastic bags,' Luke said.

'Please,' Rosita said.

'Please. Transparent, and they have to be strong.'

In a flash, the girl was back with a roll of freezer bags. Luke put his note and Max's mobile into a bag and squeezed it into the container. It was not easy, and he had to force it.

Then he took the Maglite torch that Rosita had found him, switched it on, sealed it in a bag and put it, too, inside the container. Even in the brightly lit kitchen, the beam of the torch was clearly visible through the semi-transparent plastic. He replaced the screw top and glanced up at the round window set high in the kitchen wall, wondering whether the container would fit through it. It looked doable, provided he could reach that high.

Suddenly there was a noise at the door leading from the restaurant into the kitchen. Without a moment's hesitation, Rosita grabbed her mop, rushed towards the door, and began wiping up the water she had thrown at Luke. This gave Luke a second or two – just enough for him to slip out of view under the sink, container in hand. He was impressed by Rosita's quick thinking.

Clutching his container, Luke slithered behind a tall rubbish bin under the sink. Rosita carried on mopping. He peered out and saw Juliette appear. She slipped on the wet floor and swore at Rosita. Then there was the sound of a slap.

Startled, Luke jerked back and hit his head on something sharp. He felt with his hand: the tip of a screw protruded from the steel frame above him. He changed position and was now able to see both women clearly. Rosita was crying and holding her cheek. Then she released a volley of Spanish swear words. Juliette countered in French, tore the mop from Rosita's hands and sent it clattering across the floor.

'I need some rubbish sacks. You have some here, I am told.'

Rosita produced a roll of white sacks from a cupboard.

'More,' Juliette hissed.

Rosita handed her two more rolls and the hijacker left the kitchen. A few moments after the door into the restaurant had swung shut, Rosita rushed over to Luke, who came out with his container.

'Everyone's after bags, it seems,' she said. 'Did you see her eyes? Scary.'

'Are you OK?' Luke asked.

'It was just a slap. But you're bleeding!'

Luke touched his head and looked at the blood on his hand.

'It's nothing.'

'I'll find some disinfectant.'

'No! There's no time...'

But Rosita was already searching in a cabinet marked with a large red cross. Luke had never liked the sight of blood, but on this occasion, it somehow fed his determination. He felt like a hero. That, of course, was a childish idea and he dismissed it, or tried to.

'Keep still.' Rosita poured disinfectant into Luke's hair and dabbed it with a piece of bandage.

'Thanks,' Luke said. 'It's stopped bleeding... So you're a nurse on the side?' Luke smiled. 'Did you learn that in Spain?'

'Mexico. I have Aztec blood and Spanish blood.' Rosita's smile brought out her dimples. 'What's your name?'

'Luke C. Baron.'

'"C" for what?'

'Never mind.'

'Aren't we mysterious?'

'Listen, I need to get up to that window somehow.'

Rosita pointed at a stool. 'Help yourself.'

'I will.' Luke lifted the stool onto the table under the window. He put the container down beside the stool.

'Be careful,' Rosita said.

'Yes, Mum,' Luke shot back, climbing onto the stool, which felt none too steady. 'How do I open this thing?'

'Here.' Rosita passed him a small handle. 'Are you strong enough? The lock's quite tight.'

Without replying, Luke applied all his strength to the handle. At first, it wouldn't budge. Using both his hands, he managed to make it turn by tiny stages. After a gasping, embarrassing struggle, the window finally opened and a blast of sea air rushed into the kitchen. Luke leaped down from the stool, grabbed the container and climbed up again.

At that moment they heard more voices approaching from the restaurant.

Luke saw Rosita glance at the mop lying on the floor, but that ruse would not work a second time. He tried to push the container through, but the window was smaller than it had looked. He turned the container round and tried again. It went halfway, then would go no further.

'It's stuck now,' Luke said.

'Hide.' Rosita pointed under the sink. 'I've got an idea.'

Bending his head to avoid grazing himself on the screw again, Luke crawled back behind the bin under the sink. He saw Rosita grab a cast-iron frying pan, mount the stool and strike a fearsome blow at the container, which slipped through and disappeared into the dark night.

'There.' Rosita jumped to the floor and gave the stool a shove. It clattered to the floor just as one of the hijackers, the Filipino, appeared through the swinging doors.

'What's going on here?' He looked up at the open window.

Rosita gave the stool another kick, threw the frying pan into the sink and carried on in a similar vein, hurling things, stamping her foot and shrieking hysterically.

'Calm down!' the hijacker commanded.

Rosita stopped at once and stood rooted to the spot, breathing hard. The hijacker shook his head and turned to go.

Luke met Rosita's eyes and gave her an approving wink. The girl was brave and resourceful. They made a good team.

21

Standing under a street light at the bus station in Porvoo, Finland, umbrella in hand, Peter Baron scanned the passengers stepping off the Helsinki bus. His headache had gone, but he felt sick with worry. The wind drove sheets of rain from the dark sky into the light of the street lamps. The last passenger lifted his bag onto his shoulder and strode off into the night.

Still no sign of Luke. Even if he had lost his phone, there was no reason why he should have missed the last bus.

Peter crossed Mannerheim Street and walked briskly back towards Gran's house where Hanna waited for news, distraught. He tried Luke's number yet again. No reply.

He decided to quiz Toni again. The boy had been gutted by Luke's disappearance, but you never knew what information he might be holding back. Peter felt a burst of anger. He didn't trust Toni, not after the shoplifting episode. Maybe Hanna was right to be tough on Toni. An eighteen-year-old hiding a stolen DVD in the school bag of his younger friend – it was an ugly business, whichever way you looked at it.

Just as he passed the brightly lit newspaper kiosk, Peter's phone beeped. Without stopping, he read the message. The sender's number was unknown to him.

'*Dad, I'm on a hijacked ship. The* Ocean Emerald.'

Peter felt a huge wave of relief, then anger. What an irresponsible prank, even by Luke's standards! How could he be so thoughtless?

The message continued.

'*Trace this phone. It's in the sea, in a plastic container lit by a torch.*'

What an imagination, Peter thought to himself, as the relief got the better of his annoyance. A hijacked ship – whatever next? He continued walking, with a spring in his step. When Luke was eight years old and hooked on reading, he'd once hidden in the attic above the garden shed with a pile of Famous Five books and a supply of biscuits, and Hanna had looked for him all day before eventually phoning the police.

But why had Luke gone to the trouble of sending the message from a number other than his own? And why had Toni seemed so worried? He would surely have been in on Luke's practical joke.

Peter stopped and studied the message once more. Only now did he notice the unusual number of the sender, which began with the digits '445'. Peter's heart missed a beat. The message had been sent from a satellite phone.

How had Luke got hold of a satellite phone?

Without wasting another second, Peter dialled directory enquiries, but as he expected, they couldn't tell him who the satellite phone belonged to. Peter then asked for the number of the Finnish coastguard instead and was put through. He had to explain himself twice before his call was taken by the right person, a woman, Lieutenant Maria Vierto. He introduced himself, mentioning his work at Europol.

'Sorry to bother you, but I have a question about a cruise ship called the *Ocean Emerald*,' Peter said nervously.

'*What's your question?*'

The sharp tone of the woman's response caught Peter's attention.

'Is everything all right on the ship?'

'*Why are you asking this?*'

'My son found some documents that belonged to one of the passengers. He visited the ship when it was docked in Helsinki. We haven't seen him since. And ... Well ...'

'*Go on.*'

Peter had to force himself to continue. He suddenly felt certain again that Luke was simply clowning around as usual.

'I just received a text message from my son, in which he claims that the *Ocean Emerald* has been hijacked. I know I'm probably wasting your time. My son has a vivid imagination, and—'

'*Where are you ringing from? Can you please come over straight away?*'

'Yes, of course. I'm ringing from Porvoo.' Peter clutched the handset tightly. 'Why, is there some problem on board that ship?'

'*We received a distress signal from the* Ocean Emerald. *They said there had been a technical error, so let's hope it's nothing serious.*'

Peter began running towards the house and his car.

***

Cruising southwestward at maximum speed, the *Ocean Emerald* looked like a horizontal skyscraper with lights blazing in every window. Inside, the mood was sombre. Passengers jostled in front of the Purser's desk on the sixth deck. Among them stood a large man who had covered his messy haircut with a large hat.

Craig Thomson tried to keep out of sight of the hijackers as far as possible. He was trying to gauge the collective mood. What was the level of distress? Were the passengers paralysed by fear, or were they still operational? The hostages he was supposed to protect were a mixed lot, ranging from frail old ladies to cocksure young lawyers whose thoughts were written on their tanned faces: I can't wait to tell my friends in New York and London about this...

Yet even the faces of the young and resilient were marked with fear. Losing money or valuables was nothing. But the hijackers might have other motives. Everyone had the same unspoken fear: would this be another 9/11?

Thomson himself felt like a man trapped inside the nightmare he'd always dreaded, or looked forward to... Here was the chance of a lifetime to show himself and others that he could handle the pressure and save lives – instead of putting lives at risk, as the FBI had accused him of doing.

He'd ordered the members of the Ferrum Group to disperse among the crowd and pursue their cover jobs while in fact searching for the explosives and detonators. Their grotesque haircuts made them easy to identify, which was why each one had also been told by Thomson to recruit a trusted colleague to support their undercover work. But given the size of the ship, the search for the hidden explosives was an almost hopeless task.

'You can't treat us like this!' Max Lownie Junior bellowed, scratching himself through his football shirt. He was standing right next to Thomson.

'Shut up! You're drawing attention to us!' Gabriela hissed at her stepson, to Thomson's unspoken approval.

'SILENCE!' Juliette shouted into her microphone at the Purser's desk. 'I will now explain our demands in detail.'

The noisy crowd instantly froze. The tension was palpable.

'You are hostages. We could demand a ransom from each of your families, but that would be slow and risky. Instead, you'll pay the ransom yourselves. Each of you will hand over your credit card and we'll charge you a minimum of twenty thousand dollars. It's a tiny sum for you and your credit card companies. You'll also surrender all your valuables and your cash.'

Juliette put away the microphone and rolled her burning eyes at her terrified public. Thomson watched her. He was foxed. The more he thought about it, the more he admired the professionalism of the hijackers. They clearly knew that the credit card readers were hooked up to a satellite link and functioned in real time, independently of the internet connection that had been disrupted. Moreover, the financially beleaguered Emerald Cruise Corporation had made arrangements to ensure that credit card payments were cleared faster than usual and this would make matters even smoother for the hijackers. Did they have prior knowledge of everything?

If they really were after money – and it remained to be seen whether that was all there was to it – the plan was brilliant in its simplicity.

Thomson made a swift mental calculation. One thousand passengers multiplied by twenty thousand dollars made twenty million... plus diamonds and other valuables amounting to perhaps the same sum again... It was the kind of pay packet that might motivate the risk that the hijackers had taken, yet Thomson felt sure that there was more to the plot than cash alone.

Judging by their expressions, many passengers reacted with jubilation to the hijackers' latest instructions, thinking, so much the better if they could buy their way out of their ordeal by simply presenting their gold and platinum credit cards.

An aged couple stood at the head of the queue. The wife was stroking a diamond pinned to her breast. The husband spoke in a quiet voice.

'We are both ninety years old. My wife's brooch has only sentimental value—'

Juliette ripped off the diamond, leaving a long tear in the woman's dress.

Thomson moved away and fixed his eyes on a slim elderly man standing behind a pillar. It was David C. McMorgan, the richest man on board, whose security needs Thomson had discussed with him in person – persuading the construction tycoon that there was no need to bring his own bodyguard. As things stood, McMorgan was in no greater danger than anyone else and dealing with individuals was not Thomson's priority. He looked the other way, but it was too late: McMorgan grabbed his arm.

'Thomson, thank God,' McMorgan whispered. His face was pale under the freckles and his ring of reddish hair badly needed combing. 'There's no way I can give them my credit cards...'

'Yes, you can. It's only money, for God's sake.'

'And you're supposed to be protecting our security? You'll be hearing from me.' McMorgan shook his head and disappeared into the throng.

'MR MCMORGAN!' Juliette shouted from behind the desk. 'We want you over here.'

McMorgan froze.

'Come to the front of the queue.'

McMorgan shuffled over with the slow, heavy steps of a condemned man mounting a scaffold. He ran a small, freckled hand over his mottled skull. His lips looked blue, as though he might collapse from a heart attack at any moment.

Thomson took the lift to the ninth deck. Up here, the swaying of the ship was much more noticeable, and he had to support himself against the wall. He headed for Corridor One, where the fuse box was, careful not to glance up at the cameras and keeping his hat pulled over his brow. Undoubtedly, the hijackers were using the CCTV system to keep a close eye on the areas where the explosives were hidden.

Thomson opened the fuse box. It was empty. Whatever might have been hidden there was now gone.

22

A few metres from the fuse box, behind the airlock leading to the bridge, nerves were starting to fray. Although the ship's officers were still nominally exercising their duties, they were no longer in control.

Delacroix was sitting calmly at a round table placed on the left wing of the bridge. The radio control that could blow up the ship lay on the table in front of him. Every few seconds, a small red light flashed on the device. The only sounds were the quiet murmur of the navigation instruments and the regular thud of waves striking the ship's bow. Over the tossing sea, the wind was turning into a screaming gale. Delacroix was looking at the captain and the watch officer sitting silently at the steering pulpit.

'Ocean Emerald, Ocean Emerald, *this is the Finnish coastguard...*'

The female voice sounded metallic over the loudspeaker. Bauer looked up at Delacroix.

'Ocean Emerald, Ocean Emerald, *this is the Finnish coastguard...*'

Delacroix grabbed the radio control and jumped to his feet. He strode over to Bauer, who had dark rings round his eyes.

'I'll handle it.' Delacroix took the microphone from its stand. 'This is the *Ocean Emerald*, good evening.'

'*Good evening. This is Lieutenant Maria Vierto from the Finnish coastguard. Your next scheduled port of call was St Petersburg, but you are on a southwestward course. Can you please confirm that all is well on board?*'

Delacroix took a deep breath and leaned back for a second. He'd been expecting this moment, sooner or later. He was prepared, and yet he feared his voice would betray the turmoil inside him.

'This is the new master of the *Ocean Emerald* speaking. The vessel has been hijacked. Explosives have been placed in different parts of the ship, which I can detonate by remote control. Another member of my group is also in possession of a radio control and he will blow up the ship if something happens to me.'

There was a heavy silence at the other end.

'*Are the passengers and crew unharmed?*' Maria Vierto's English was impeccable and there was not the slightest trace of alarm in her voice.

'No one will be hurt, provided they do as I say. That includes you. If you disobey, we will blow up the ship and that unfortunately means a large number of fatalities.'

'*What are your demands?*' The woman sounded completely unmoved, totally in control.

Delacroix was holding the microphone in his right hand. As the bow plunged down after a big wave, he had to grab hold of the edge of the steering pulpit. 'Listen carefully, Lieutenant...'

'*Vierto.*'

'Lieutenant Vierto, no vessel or aircraft is to come within a three-mile radius of the *Ocean Emerald*. We're keeping a close eye on the radar. If a vessel or aircraft comes too near, we'll kill a passenger. May I just underline, Lieutenant, that I mean every word I say.'

The silence that followed seemed to go on for ever. Delacroix surmised that Vierto was consulting with her male superiors.

'*Very well. We'll transmit your orders to all ships in the area. With your permission, we'll also contact the Swedish, Estonian and Latvian authorities, to ensure that all players are aware of the situation.*'

'Excellent idea, Lieutenant.' Delacroix suppressed a smile. 'Go ahead.'

A black Lexus passed through a gate in a tall hedge and stopped in the yard of the Paxman Hotel in Miami. A valet in pressed trousers and a white linen shirt rushed over to park the car under the hotel.

Two men in dark suits rose from the Lexus and headed for the terrace perched on white pillars and lit by a vast overhead lamp that looked like an upended bucket. The porter opened the door as the men continued past the rattan furniture into the hotel reception.

'If all goes well, we'll pre-sell seventy per cent of the Caribbean season without discounts. Heck of a number, given the current market situation,' said Max Lownie Senior, leading the way down a long corridor lined by a series of tall columns and sheets of white fabric that extended from the floor to the ceiling. The place didn't do much for Lownie, but his wealthy, eccentric guests were into this kind of thing.

'We want cash flow, not speculation,' said Jeremy

Rosenblatt, director of Atlantic Bank. 'The *Ocean Emerald* is turning out to have been a purely speculative investment.'

Lownie's heart sank at the sound of Rosenblatt's chilly tone. Atlantic Bank was one of the main financers of the Emerald Cruise Corporation.

They arrived in the bar and Lownie ordered a beer for Rosenblatt and a mineral water for himself. There was a long silence. The drinks arrived.

'No one could have predicted the length and depth of the recession,' Lownie eventually pleaded in a quiet voice.

'Whatever, but from now on, I can't have you default on a single payment,' the banker said, and guzzled his beer in one go.

'The winter season is also selling very well—'

'That's great.' Rosenblatt placed his empty glass on the table, beside the flickering candle, and wiped his mouth. 'So was that. Sorry, Max. Nothing personal.'

Rosenblatt looked at his Rolex.

'Sure. There's no point falling out over a set of numbers,' Max Lownie Senior said, in the most cheerful voice he could muster. He glanced through the window at the nicely lit open-air restaurant on the veranda, where he would soon be pretending to enjoy a candle-lit dinner with a specialist cruise broker from San Diego and a group of travel journalists. The Paxman was pricey, but his guests were people the company depended on, who were used to being pampered with the finest luxuries, and it would have been suicide to disappoint them.

'How's Gabriela?' Rosenblatt asked, sounding almost friendly.

'Fine, fine... Actually, she's on the *Emerald* with my son.'

'Whereabouts?'

'On the way to St Petersburg. Excuse me...'

Lownie groped for his ringing mobile in his breast pocket. His secretary had activated the call screening function, which meant that only the most important calls came through.

'*Max, you won't believe this,*' said the director in charge of marine operations. '*The* Emerald *has been hijacked in the Baltic.*'

Lownie staggered to his feet and put his free hand to his silver hair. 'Say that again.'

23

Luke rinsed his face, filled his cupped palms with more cold water and slowly quenched his thirst, then reached for paper towels and dried his face and hands.

He caught his reflection in the large mirror in the men's bathroom at the forward end of the seventh deck of the *Ocean Emerald*. He was tall – but skinny. He crumpled up the luxuriously soft towel and tossed it towards the wastepaper basket, but it bounced off the rim onto the floor beside a potted plant.

Luke frowned. He was the worst basketball player at his school, if not the worst in Europe.

With a weary grunt, he bent down to pick up the towel. Then he froze. His gaze was fixed on the looping roots of the fake plant, which curved down into the brown granules that filled the pot. Where had he seen granules like that before?

With a satisfying jolt, the memory came back to him. *The sack of dog food – or what he'd mistaken for dog food – in Delacroix's cabin.* Potting mix – what could possibly explain the hijackers' interest in that? Why did they have a whole sack of potting mix in their cabin?

Nothing is important, except gardening, Luke recalled

the words of a Chinese proverb. *And even gardening isn't that important.*

Luke's gut told him he was onto something. But what? He had nothing concrete, just his gut feeling.

He bent closer to the pot and picked out a few of the almost weightless granules. Then he had it. *Eureka*, Archimedes had exclaimed, as he lay down in his bath and understood that his body displaced precisely its own volume of water.

Were the bombs hidden in one of the flowerpots? Luke dug deeper, then stopped. There were hundreds of plants on board and no doubt all of them stood in potting mix just like this one – besides, it might not be such a great idea to tamper with a bomb with his bare hands.

Luke stole into the corridor. He had no idea where Thomson was, so he decided to look for Carol. She wasn't easy to locate, but eventually one of her colleagues at the chaotic Purser's desk agreed to put his call through and Luke managed to persuade her to come and see him.

Carol pulled him to one side, away from the desk. She listened to his story, but didn't sound convinced. 'I'll alert the head of security and he'll decide what to do. He's called Thomson. In fact, you'd better tell him yourself.'

'Where is he?'

'The hijackers took over the control room, so we're using an empty bridal suite for our meetings.'

Carol escorted Luke to a cabin door and gave a patterned knock – probably an agreed code, Luke thought to himself. He felt immensely relieved to be with friendly adults. The head of security was surely the best man to talk to.

'Thomson will know what to do,' Carol said, as though reading his mind.

The man called Thomson appeared at the open door. 'Who's the kid?'

'He's called Luke. I think you should listen to him.'

'Get him out of here.' Thomson returned his attention to what looked like the ship's blueprint, which was spread over the enormous heart-shaped bed.

Luke's heart sank. He felt weird and disorientated. For some reason, everyone in the immense suite had a terrible haircut and one man had a green stripe painted onto his bald head. There were empty soft drink cans on top of the minibar. A pink chandelier hung from the ceiling and the cabin was furnished with what Luke immediately recognized as fake antiques – Gran had taught him a thing or two about genuine period furniture, and there was definitely none on this vessel.

'Hear the boy out,' Carol said. 'He might know something.'

Thomson didn't even look at her. 'Out, I said.'

'I know where the bomb is,' Luke said in a firm voice and paused for effect. 'Or one of them, at any rate.'

Now Thomson was listening. Everyone was.

'The bomb or bombs are hidden in the potted plants,' Luke said, blushing as all eyes turned to him.

'If so, keep your voice down,' said the man with the green head.

'Shut up, Curran.' Thomson was staring at Luke. 'What makes you think that, kid?'

Luke gave a short summary of what had happened to him: how he'd boarded the ship in order to return Juliette du Pont's belongings, and how he'd been taken captive, then let go.

'And in the hijackers' cabin, I saw a sack of potting mix exactly the same as in the flowerpots for the fake plants.'

Thomson seemed to be weighing Luke's story in his mind.

'Blimey,' Curran said, grinning. 'Smart kid.'

A hint of a smile played on Thomson's lips. 'Who looks after the greenery?'

'It's a Chinese crew member. I'll find him.'

'We must ask him for the precise location—'

'All the plants are listed in the furniture inventory.'

'Get me the inventory,' Thomson said. 'Now. And another thing.'

Luke watched Thomson fix his gaze on each of his subordinates in turn.

'We must find some way to contact the authorities without being detected by the hijackers – that means, without using a radio or a phone.'

'That's been taken care of,' Luke said, and again, all eyes turned to him.

He explained how he'd secretly photographed the hijackers with a camera phone, how he'd described the events on a sheet of paper, how he'd timed the text message to be sent later, how he'd put a torch inside an empty vinegar container, and thrown it into the sea.

As he spoke, the looks on the faces around him changed: there was less amusement and more respect.

'And where do you plan to work when you grow up?' Curran asked.

'Europol.'

'You took quite a risk, Luke,' Thomson said, folding away the blueprint. 'Well done.'

24

Thomson quietly chastised himself. Tactical breakthroughs often came from the most unexpected sources. He had learned that in his FBI days. It was *always* a mistake to underestimate a witness or collaborator, whatever their age or background. He'd tried to send the boy packing: a disastrous mistake. It was time to shape up and refocus.

'Before striking back, we must establish the location of the bombs and identify the second hijacker with a radio control.' He looked at his team. 'We're getting somewhere.'

The others nodded. Carol was grinning at Luke, ruffling his hair, and the boy was seething at this treatment. Curran chuckled to himself. For the first time that evening, Thomson saw an improvement in the Ferrum Group's morale. He opened the minibar and handed the boy a Coke.

A tanned bank clerk with big red glasses and lipstick sat in her cubicle at the High Street agency of the Hong Kong and Shanghai Banking Corporation in Georgetown, the capital of the Cayman Islands.

She stamped the completed transfer form, flicked it into the out-tray and reached for another in her in-tray. Her painted nails clicked on the keyboard. Oceanic Asset Management Limited was paying a diamond wholesaler in Antwerp US$19,850,000.

Tens and hundreds of millions were routine sums in this tax-free offshore banking centre and the clerk paid no particular attention to the transaction.

She typed in a few more details, pressed 'Enter', and moments later, the money was in the receiver's account in Antwerp. The clerk stamped the form and moved to the next transfer form.

Luke watched as Craig Thomson crouched down in front of the potted plant, crawling on all fours like some horticultural enthusiast at a flower show. The furniture inventory on the floor beside Thomson listed every single house plant on board, whether fake or living. Luke knew Thomson had so far only crossed ten plants off his share of the list, and that the impossible scale of the task was beginning to become apparent.

Thomson's floppy sun hat, borrowed from an American tourist, failed to cover his shorn head. Luke glanced around. If the hijackers caught them disobeying instructions like this, Luke would no doubt be killed along with the ship's head of security.

Thomson tapped the pot gently, but the sound gave nothing away.

'You sure that's a good idea?' Luke whispered. 'The bomb might go off.'

'If you want to help, here's how.' Thomson sounded

ready to snap. 'Keep your mouth shut. We don't even know if your theory's worth anything yet.'

'Got that.' Luke moved closer and watched Thomson's hands with apprehension, hoping the man had worked on bomb disposal jobs before.

'You're blocking out the light.'

Luke took a step back.

'Curran says this would have been a sweet spot.' Thomson knitted his brow. 'There's a bunch of sensitive wiring behind those tiles.'

Thomson raked his fingers softly through the light granules of the potting mix. Suddenly he froze.

'You found something?' Luke asked.

The only reply he received was a rolled eyeball. Thomson gently swept aside a few granules of potting mix.

'Malleable explosive . . .' Thomson's voice had faded to a strained whisper. 'Either C4 or Semtex.'

'Well, I'll just keep my mouth shut,' Luke said sarcastically, waiting to be thanked for his help in locating the first bomb.

Thomson said nothing to acknowledge Luke's role, but he shot him what could just possibly have been a grateful look.

'I wonder how many more there are?' Luke whispered.

'Each one is enough to sink the vessel and drown us all.'

Luke grimaced as a shiver travelled down his spine. He felt scared and thrilled at the same time, and the blend of sensations filled him with wild energy.

25

A group of worried men sat in the operation room at the Finnish National Bureau of Investigation (FNBI) in Vantaa, near Helsinki. Peter Baron was one of them.

The full horror of the situation had only just hit home. The hijackers had them over a barrel. For the time being, all they could do was let the *Ocean Emerald* continue on its course, towards an unknown destination; a vast fortress filled with explosives and hundreds of hostages. And what a fortress it was: easy to monitor, impossible to approach unseen, and ready to sink at a moment's notice, passengers and all.

The terrorists may well have been bluffing when they spoke of the bombs they would set off, but there was no way of being sure.

What made the situation especially hard to assess was the fact that no one knew who the hijackers were or what they wanted.

Peter had written a few words on the sheet of paper in front of him: *Ocean Emerald*, St Petersburg, Juliette du Pont...

He glanced at the sea chart on the wall, which showed a section of the Baltic Sea. A red pin marked the exact spot where the satellite phone floating in the plastic container had been at the moment when it sent the text message from Luke. Helicopters from the Finnish and Swedish coastguards were combing the area intensively, trying to locate the phone.

'Have you tried to contact the vessel?' Peter asked.

'Five minutes ago,' said one of the police officers.

'Not good enough. You must try *constantly*,' Peter said. He knew many of the officers present, having co-operated with the FNBI on several Europol investigations.

'What about the *Zeeland*?'

'They're shadowing the *Emerald* as closely as they can.'

'As long as they don't get too close.'

A round man with a bloated neck and stress-lined features appeared at the door. It was Mr Kanerva, the deputy director of the FNBI.

'Karhu's ready to go,' he said, referring to the 'Bear Squad', or the special unit of the Finnish police.

Peter fixed the man with a furious look. The agreement was that the special forces would only be deployed as a last resort.

'Let those boys get some sleep,' Peter said, forcing himself to speak in a measured tone. 'We won't be needing them for some time, if at all.'

'They need to be ready, surely you understand that?' Kanerva waddled up to Peter, pushing his face as close as he could without kissing him. 'I know you're worried for your son. It's OK by me if you'd rather step back and leave this to us.'

Peter bit his lip. Kanerva wanted him out the way.

'No,' Peter said in a hoarse voice.

'Fine, then.' Kanerva swayed back to his chair. 'Call Brussels. We need all the elite troops we can get, or we'll never sort this mess out. Start with the GSG-9 in Germany and the SAS in the UK. I want them both on high alert.'

Peter was suddenly overcome with pure and simple fear, but fear of such intensity that it swept away all other emotions.

There was no way they could resort to force. The risk was too great. All other means had to be tried first. But were there any other means?

Outside the window of the bridal suite on board the *Ocean Emerald*, the sea was wild and pitiless. Luke could feel the heart-shaped bed rising and falling under him. He closed his eyes, but couldn't sleep. He was exhausted, yet every sound made him jump: the tinkle of the chandelier, the closing of a door…

The whole ship was in the grip of insomnia. Luke could hear groups of passengers wandering the corridors, talking in muted voices. He couldn't make out any words, but the murmur was loud enough to keep him awake.

The passengers had been told not to move around without reason, but everyone was hungry for news, Luke included. Even lies and rumours were preferable to blind uncertainty. According to one persistent story, the hijackers intended to ram the cruise ship into the harbour in Copenhagen, in a maritime version of 9/11. Another rumour alleged that the Russians were involved in the hijacking, as in the case of the *Arctic Sea*. One thing Luke knew for sure: the members of the Ferrum Group had dispersed across the ship, hunting for the remaining bombs.

Suddenly Luke was startled by a knock at the door. He lay still, draped in a sheet, and listened.

There was a scraping sound as someone inserted the card key. The door slowly swung open. Holding his breath, Luke sat up on the bed, watching the shadow of a large hat that had appeared on the wall.

'Are you asleep?'

'The only answer ever given to that question is no,' Luke said. 'What's up?'

'We found another bomb,' Thomson whispered without warmth. 'We're trying to figure out how many more there are, and which of the other hijackers has the second radio control. If the situation gets too rough, we'll take them both out at once. Or try to. Are you sure you've told us everything you saw in Delacroix's cabin?'

'I thought I needed to keep my mouth shut,' Luke said defiantly and lay down again.

He felt Thomson's grip on his arm.

'I know you want a medal,' Thomson hissed into Luke's ear. 'But this isn't the moment.'

'I told you everything that was worth telling.' Luke sat up. 'But I can find out more, if you want.'

'What do you mean?'

'If you get me the key to Delacroix's cabin, I'll go and have a look around.'

'No way.'

'They'll recognize you and your men. As for me, they'll think I'm just a kid who's read too much Enid Blyton.'

Thomson was silent before answering. 'No. Too risky.'

'Compared with what? Sometimes you need to take small risks in order to neutralize big risks. In betting, if you want to optimize the risk—'

Thomson silenced Luke with a wave of his arm. 'I won't authorize anything like that.'

There was a pause.

'And what other options do we have?' Luke tried to muster the toughest voice he could. 'At least let me tell you what I have in mind.'

Thomson looked even more serious than before.

'Go on then,' he said at last.

'I need a card key and a guard posted on the corridor. It can't be any of your men, as they'll be recognized, but I know someone suitable, provided she agrees.' Luke was enjoying having Thomson's undivided attention. 'And I'll need a couple of two-way radios.'

'You must be dreaming,' Thomson's voice was annoyed, but a look of amusement played in his eyes. 'No. For this to work, we also need a man in the cabin above, who'll pull you to safety via the balcony if you're disturbed. How does that sound, chief?'

'Sounds good, Coyote,' Luke said, grinning. 'Now, I'd better go and talk to Rosita.'

The executive team of the Emerald Cruise Corporation had called an emergency meeting at the company head-quarters on Bricknell Avenue, Miami. The company occupied three of the glass skyscraper's forty floors, commanding a breathtaking view over central Miami.

'I've just been in touch with Helsinki. They have noth-ing new.' Max Lownie Senior was sweating profusely, despite the efficient air conditioning. He crossed his hands on the rectangular conference table and looked at the white hairs on the backs of his fingers. How had he got to be so old? 'As some of you may know, Gabriela and Max are among the passengers on the hijacked ship.'

The Deputy Director fiddled with his papers. He cleared his throat. 'It'll be OK, Max. The authorities won't risk putting the passengers in danger.'

There was a sudden knock at the door.

'Come in!' Lownie said.

His secretary stepped in, frowning. 'Mr Lownie, I've phoned six airlines and they all insist on cash payment for a ticket to Europe. It seems everyone's read the *Miami Herald*, so they know the sorry state of our company finances.'

'Is that so?' Lownie sprang to his feet and reached for his wallet. 'Here. Use my personal credit card. God damn it, I'm going to Helsinki, even if it costs me my last dime.'

26

The winds were rising in the eastern Baltic, where clouds shifting in dramatic formations had amassed across the night sky, blotting out the stars and the moon. Heavy rain doused the large windows of the bridge of the *Ocean Emerald*. It was just after midnight.

Captain Bauer felt dead with exhaustion, but he refused to leave his seat beside the second mate, who was manning the steering pulpit. The immense ship was heaving more and more violently in the heavy seas, and every now and then, a big wave would smash over the bow, sending foamy water swirling across the deck.

As he kept his silent watch, Bauer tried to analyse the situation. Piracy wasn't rare, nor was hostage-taking, and there had even been hijacking incidents in the Baltic in recent years. But the targets were always cargo ships.

Cargo ships were big, unwieldy and unprotected – so pirates preyed on them, striking every day in some part of the world or other. Bauer knew that piracy caused the shipping industry losses totalling twenty-five billion euros each year. Raiding a ship, it seemed, was less risky than robbing an old lady on dry land.

The most perilous waters were off the coasts of Somalia, India and Nigeria, around Indonesia, and in the Strait of Malacca, where disciplined groups using speedboats would creep up on a vessel under cover of darkness, approaching from the direction of the radar's blind sector, then holding the captain at gunpoint and forcing him to open the ship's safe.

The worst nightmare was the seizure of entire vessels by gangs targeting ships with cargoes that were easy to sell – fuel, coconut oil or aluminium. Bauer knew the blood-curdling stories all too well from the years he'd spent captaining an oil tanker. First, the crew of the vessel would be killed. Then the ship would be repainted, re-registered, and given a new crew, before being sent out to transport arms, drugs or illegal migrants. Awful crimes were committed at sea.

Bauer found himself thinking of his old uncle who'd fled abroad as a child when the Nazis came to power and ended up joining the US Navy in the Second World War, and who had almost drowned in a torpedo attack somewhere in the Pacific. Bauer came from a family of heroes, and this was his chance to be one, too. But as he dragged his mind back to the present, he again found himself in the grip of horrible, suffocating fear. Hijacking a cargo ship made sense, but targeting a cruise ship was a crazy idea. If the hijackers weren't pirates, what were they? Terrorists? If they were, nothing but death and carnage would satisfy them.

'New destination, Kaliningrad.' Delacroix's voice was still cold and businesslike. 'First mate, please take a course towards the Bay of Gdansk.'

Bauer's mouth felt dry. He shot a look at Delacroix. Kaliningrad was an isolated piece of Russian territory nestled between Poland and Lithuania. Bauer stepped up behind the first mate and studied the radar screen. The echo that had been six miles behind the *Ocean Emerald* appeared to have gained speed and moved to the vessel's right.

'First mate, you heard my instructions,' Delacroix said in a voice that was calm but firm.

'I only take orders from Captain Bauer.'

The first mate glanced at Bauer. After a short silence, Bauer nodded, without saying anything.

The first mate went over to the chart table to make the calculations and to mark the chart. Then he returned to the steering pulpit and entered the new course into the autopilot. Digital numbers began to flash over the middle window. The figure displayed became smaller as the ship turned, reaching 180 where it stopped. Having tilted slightly during the manoeuvre, the vessel returned to an even keel.

The second mate entered, reporting for his watch. He pointedly refused to look at Delacroix, who sat still at his station at the round table by the engine and thruster control pulpit on the bridge's left wing, with the flashing radio control on the table in front of him.

With unsteady hands, Bauer quickly reset the radar on the steering pulpit, increasing the radius to twelve miles. The vessel that was quietly shadowing the *Ocean Emerald* had appeared from the southwest, which was now to the front and left of its current course. It meticulously maintained a distance of six miles, as it had done since it began shadowing the *Emerald*.

Bauer took a deep breath, then reached for a yellow Post-it note from the set of stationery beside the radar and nodded at the first mate who had completed his watch and was leaving the bridge.

Bauer's heart hammered inside his chest as he wrote a few words on the note: '*Use an Aldis lamp to signal our destination to the ship that's following us. No radio.*'

He stepped back and the first mate glanced at the note as he passed. Five minutes later, a series of flashes was beamed out into the stormy night from a secluded spot under the ship's funnel, on the aft deck.

27

A dented old red Alfa Romeo crawled along Leopold-straat, a dimly lit street in northeastern Antwerp. Pallid moonlight touched the brickwork of the ornate gables of the narrow Flemish townhouses. The street was lined with small businesses and workshops, their windows unlit at this late hour. The car swung onto Orgelstraat, a dank side alley that seldom saw a ray of sun. It was hard to believe that these nondescript streets were the very heart of the world's diamond trade.

The Alfa Romeo continued its slow advance and pulled up at number 71.

The driver switched off the headlights, but stayed at his wheel while the woman in the passenger seat got out and hastened to the massive oak door. The shop front was in a wretched state. What had once been its display window was now covered with an armed metal blind so rusty it looked like it would never be raised again. The driver watched from the car as the woman rang the doorbell.

Eva fixed her gaze at the peephole, knowing full well that another human eye was staring at her from the other side. There was no business plaque on the door, just a small nameplate, clearly legible by the light of the moon: Ariel Halevi.

Suddenly there was a succession of clicks and a long rasping sound as a series of locks were opened and a heavy steel bolt was pulled aside.

'*Shalom*,' said the grey-bearded old man in a soft voice, beckoning Eva to step inside, and locking the door behind her.

The man had the black clothes and hanging side locks of an Orthodox Jew.

The dusty entrance hall was sparsely furnished with just a few chairs, a simple table and a stack of dark wooden trays the size of chocolate boxes. The corners of the trays were worn almost round by years of service. Perched on top of a bookshelf at the back of the room, a stuffed owl with extended wings seemed ready to swoop down.

'Your friend will wait in the car?'

'He'll make sure we're not disturbed.'

The stooped old man gave a nervous laugh and pulled aside a faded velvet curtain that had once been bottle green, gesturing for Eva to follow. The corners of the back room were dark, but the lamp on the work desk cast a hard-edged beam of light. Arranged on a threadbare dark-green cloth under the lamp were diamond-encrusted rings, earrings and necklaces.

Blinking, Eva quickly cast her gaze around the room. The light was reflected from the cracked mirror in a chipped gilded frame. With a gasp, she suddenly noticed a young woman dressed in black standing in the corner of the room, staring blankly in front of her.

'Miriam's my great niece. She's an ex-Israeli army officer.'

Eva nodded fractionally at the stranger, who nodded back. It was no surprise to Eva that Ariel Halevi had taken security measures before the meeting – it was unlikely he'd ever done a deal on this scale before. He, or indeed anyone else in the business.

'Did you come straight from Rome?' the old man asked.

Eva disliked Halevi's questions, even though she understood his curiosity, given the circumstances. She'd told him she was from Rome, which wasn't completely untrue, as she'd lived there for some years with her sister when their mother – a French diplomat – had been posted in Italy.

The said sister was the one who'd lined up the deal that was about to be concluded. She'd been working for her husband, a man called Philippe Delacroix, for several years now. She changed aliases regularly and was currently working under the name Juliette du Pont. They made a good couple, despite the age difference, Delacroix being forty-five to Juliette's thirty-three. Eva knew Delacroix was just the kind of strong, protective man Juliette needed.

'I suggest we proceed,' Eva said, glancing at the female bodyguard, who had neither moved nor spoken.

As the old man nudged up his thick-framed glasses, Eva saw that his hand was shaking slightly.

'You are surprised to see a woman protecting me?' Halevi shuffled up to the only painting in the room. 'Now you're probably wondering why I have a picture of the crucifixion on my wall. I am a broad-minded old man. Many of my customers are Christian.'

The old man lifted the ancient picture, revealing a small modern safe embedded in the wall. He stood in such a way that his back blocked Eva's view of his hands as he entered the code. 'You know, I have a dear cousin in Rome. He has an antique shop on the Via Giulia. You should go and see him. Send my regards.'

'Excuse me, but I'm in a hurry.'

'It's right next to the Piazza Campo dei Fiori. You probably know the flower market?'

'Do you have the quantity we agreed?'

The old man paused in what he was doing, then replied in a quiet voice: 'We diamond dealers keep our word.'

'Sorry. It's just that I'm in a hurry, as I said.'

'Open Sesame, as our Arab brothers would say.' Halevi opened the thick door of the safe a little way.

Eva tried to peer round his shoulder, but he'd already re-closed the safe and was wheeling round to face her. In his hand was a cheap teddy bear, like a prize at a fairground. One of its ears was folded, which gave it a comical air.

'We've fattened him up, as agreed.' Halevi offered the bear to Eva.

Eva pulled the zipper sewn into the teddy bear's belly and revealed a grey bag made of Kevlar fibre. She took out a single diamond, reached for the loupe in her pocket and went over to the work desk, examining the stone for several minutes under its bright lamp. Yes, all was as it should be. The stone was a colourless, loupe-clean, IF-class specimen, polished to a dazzling brilliance.

Meanwhile, Halevi had phoned his bank. He replaced the handset on the desk, a relieved grin on his face.

'All is in order,' he said. 'The goods and the payment have changed hands.'

Eva slipped the diamond back into the bag and put the bag back inside the teddy bear.

The first consignment had been safely procured. Four more were waiting with other merchants in the same neighbourhood. The money to pay for them had been dispatched from the Cayman Islands, through a complicated chain of transactions, whose initiator was untraceable.

Luke felt the ship lunge downwards and had to steady himself against the wall of the cabin corridor.

'Quietly!' Rosita turned to hiss at him. She looked even nicer in her jeans, sandals and rose-embroidered cotton shirt, and without the hairnet that had earlier imprisoned her glossy dark locks.

Each time the storm-battered *Ocean Emerald* listed to one side, Luke felt his innards lurch. He thought of *Titanic*, which he'd seen three times. The *Titanic* had sunk after hitting an iceberg, due to human error. The hijackers on board the *Ocean Emerald* didn't intend to commit errors – but they'd sink the cruise ship deliberately, if they so wished.

'Are you sure we're going the right way?' he whispered.

'Too many questions,' Rosita scoffed in reply. 'Just follow me.'

Luke didn't like the bossy air that Rosita had put on, which reminded him of Thomson's style of speaking. It seemed everyone on this ship took him for a child. Hadn't he helped to uncover the bombs, or at least some of them? But this wasn't the moment to be touchy. Lives were at stake, his own included. At any second, a hijacker might appear, putting an early end to the gamble he and Rosita were taking. For a moment, Luke wondered to himself what had made him suggest it.

Rosita stopped, turned and looked Luke in the eye. 'Behind that corner.'

Luke tensed and felt instinctively for his pocket. The key card was still there. 'There's nowhere for you to hide,' he said.

'Yes, there is. That's a broom cupboard.'

She pointed at a small unmarked door between two cabins, painted the same colour as the walls.

'Right then,' Luke said through clenched teeth.

'Are you sure you know what you're doing?' Rosita said.

'Of course,' Luke lied. 'Trust me.'

'Maybe I should come with you?'

'And leave no one on guard?' Luke whispered in a mocking voice. 'You do know how to use the two-way radio if someone comes, don't you?'

Rosita pulled the radio from her pocket and stared at it.

'Of course,' she said.

'Good. I'll be off then.'

Rosita smiled. 'For all your faults, you're quite a plucky boy.'

Blushing with pleasure, Luke slipped round the corner and came into another deserted stretch of corridor. With a pounding heart, he stopped at the door of Delacroix's cabin, glanced around and knocked on the door. No one answered.

Luke slid the card into the lock. There was a quiet click and a small green light came on. Knowing he could never explain his presence there if he was caught, Luke stepped into the cabin.

28

'Your *diary?*' Emilio Fernández stared at Delacroix in disbelief on the bridge. 'Are you kidding?'

'It's in my cabin,' Delacroix said. 'Fetch it for me, now.'

Emilio left the bridge and Delacroix sank into his thoughts. The captain had retreated to his cabin for a rest and the second mate and a few other officers were manning the bridge. The first mate would soon return for his next shift. Delacroix could feel the force of their contempt, although nothing was said aloud.

He didn't let it bother him. These men were simpletons, unaware of the true nature of his work. Any brainless gangster could commit acts of violence and cruelty, but what Delacroix was engaged in was a cultural enterprise involving intelligence and creativity. He despised small-time criminals with no higher values. For him, violence was purely a means to an end. He sometimes felt like a theatre director or a conductor leading a spectacular artistic performance.

He avoided murder if he could – so messy – but he had no problem whatsoever with breaking the law. Quite the contrary. Crime was the ultimate form of independence, freedom from all rules. The perfect crime remained a secret, like a masterpiece that a painter never showed to the public. That was why Delacroix kept a diary. He didn't intend to show his greatest work during his lifetime, but after he died his notes would be published and bring him the fame he deserved.

Delacroix smiled inwardly. No doubt Emilio would try to sneak a peek at the mysterious diary, but the poor cretin lacked the education to decode the words. They were composed in Latin, using mirror writing exactly as Leonardo da Vinci had done in his notebooks. Delacroix had an immense admiration for Leonardo. That was why his second passport – an Argentine one – was in the name of Vincent Leonard.

At that very moment, Luke was in Delacroix's cabin, leafing through a black leather notebook. The ornate letters scratched with a fountain pen looked distorted, until Luke realized that they were in mirror writing. He couldn't decipher the Latin words, but it was obvious that something important was written on these pages.

Was it a secret diary? He'd found it right at the bottom of one of the bags in the cabin. He glanced towards the balcony, above which Thomson's men were waiting with the rope ladder in case he had to make a rapid exit. Rosita was in the corridor, ready to warn him if she saw someone approaching.

A muted thud from the corridor made Luke give a start. He stood stock-still for a few seconds, preparing to rush out onto the balcony, but he heard no footsteps approaching. He stuffed the diary into his waistband and studied his surroundings. Then he reached for the blue sports bag in which he'd found the diary, and zipped it up.

Rosita picked the two-way radio off the floor, examining it for damage, and cursing her clumsiness. Fortunately, Luke hadn't seen her inept performance. Never entirely sure she'd know how to operate the device, she now had reason to doubt whether it worked at all.

She gave the device a good shake and switched on the power. There was a hissing sound. That presumably was normal. Just as she was about to try one of the buttons, she heard the sound of brisk footsteps in the corridor behind her.

Rosita rushed into the broom cupboard. She held her breath as the footsteps came tramping past and turned round the corner. Panicking, she pressed the keys of the radio, which only beeped and squealed in protest. Why had she been too proud to admit to Luke that she didn't even know which way round to hold a two-way radio handset? She'd thought it would be self-explanatory and that she'd have plenty of time to work it out, but now it seemed the hijackers were back already and she hadn't warned Luke...

Luke was sure the footsteps in the corridor outside the cabin belonged to a man. Their tread was too heavy to be Rosita's. They stopped right outside the cabin door.

Luke steadied himself against the cabin wall as the ship heaved under him once more. His heart was racing wildly. In his hand was an extract of the ship's furniture inventory, which listed all the plants on board. He'd found it inside the sports bag. Someone had written notes on it. It might lead them to the other bombs. Crunching the photocopy in his hand, he took the card key from its slot, switching off the lights. He bounded across to the balcony door, but it was locked. He could see the rope ladder outside, but it was too late. Cursing himself for not having checked the balcony door when he first entered, he rushed into the bedroom and slithered under the bed – a pitifully obvious place to hide, but there was no other choice.

With a buzz, the cabin door opened. Footsteps crossed the living room. Luke could feel dust tickling in his nose. Holding his breath, he fought the need to sneeze, pressing his palm to his mouth and nose. He saw a pair of shiny black shoes. They stopped right beside the bed.

The crackle of a radiophone broke the unbearable silence.

'Number one?' the man said. 'I'm in your cabin now. Which bag did you say your diary was in?'

Luke let out a quiet sigh. The hijacker would simply retrieve what he was looking for, then leave. He would hardly look for the diary under the bed. Then Luke felt the blood rushing to his head. The diary *was* under the bed, in Luke's waistband. He couldn't replace it in the bag without being seen. Nor would the hijacker leave before he'd found what he was looking for.

Through the open door, Luke could see the blue sports bag lying on the floor of the living room and the crouched figure of the hijacker, who was rummaging inside it. Delacroix, presumably, had explained where he had left the diary, and as soon as the hijacker realized it wasn't in its proper place, a thorough search would begin. Luke watched as the man rose to his feet, strode into the bedroom and up-ended the bag onto the dressing table in one last attempt to find what he was looking for. Then he gave up, staggering out of the bedroom, supporting himself against the door frame.

Luke pulled the diary from his waistband. He knew he'd only get one shot at this . . .

He squirmed along the floor under the bed and quickly slipped the diary among the jumble of clothes on the dressing table. At that moment the hijacker returned. His radiophone burst into life.

'Well, it's *not* in the blue bag!' The man exclaimed, tugging at the clothes on the table. 'Could it be somewhere else? Hold it . . . sorry, I think I've just found it.'

The solution that Luke had improvised had worked! He shuddered to think what would have happened if the hijacker had seen him.

The man continued talking. 'Helmut? He's off duty. I just saw him among the passengers. No one seems to have noticed. OK . . . I know he has the other one! OK, I'll pass the order on to him.'

The lights turned off and the door clicked shut. Luke scrambled out from under the bed and waited, breathing hard, until he thought it was safe to open the door. He peered out. The coast was clear.

He crept round the corner and saw Rosita, who had an odd expression on her face. Why hadn't she warned him about the intruder? He was about to give her an earful when someone stepped into view from behind the next turn in the corridor. It was the Filipino hijacker. He was carrying a gun. Rosita was his prisoner.

'Where have you been, boy?' Emilio Fernández said, pointing his gun at him and Rosita in turn.

'Me?' Luke said innocently. 'I just got lost in these endless corridors.'

'That so?' Emilio said. 'You know what happens to little liars?'

'I guess they get no Christmas presents,' Luke said, but his voice sounded thin. 'And maybe they do all kinds of stupid stuff when they grow up, and then they go to prison.'

'I see we have the original Smart Alec on board,' Emilio snarled. 'I promise you one thing: I'll wipe that cheeky grin off your face.'

The area around the lifeboats had been lit up with special floodlights. A few dozen passengers summoned on deck by the hijackers stood shivering in the wind, Max Lownie Junior among them. His face betrayed a hungry interest in what he was about to see. Luke could feel the strength draining from his legs. The stage was bathed in light, the audience was ready, and the show was about to start.

'Come over here,' Delacroix demanded, quietly adjusting his tortoiseshell glasses.

Luke didn't move. He glanced at Thomson, who was standing to one side with a few crew members, but what could Thomson do to help him?

'I said, come here!' Delacroix didn't raise his voice, but he stared straight into Luke's eyes. '*I* am the boss here. Who sent you?'

'No one did. We got lost.'

'Carrying two-way radios? And I suppose you found this just by chance?' Delacroix brandished the photocopy of the plant inventory that Luke had found in the blue sports bag in the cabin. 'We now have no option but to show you what happens when you cross us.'

The serious expression on Delacroix's face added to Luke's dread. The danger he was in, which he'd managed to forget for a while, was suddenly all too real.

'If we don't react, we'll lose our grip on the officers.' Delacroix paused to direct a hard glance at Thomson. 'We'll now give you a lesson you'll never forget.'

As he took in these words, Luke felt a wave of relief travel through him: they didn't plan to kill him... It made no sense to speak of a dead person never forgetting a lesson.

'Your little helper will pay the price for your stupidity.'

Luke looked on helplessly as the hijackers blindfolded Rosita with a scarf.

'No...' he mumbled.

Emilio led the struggling girl towards the wet railing, which glittered in the bright glow of the floodlights. The ship pitched and heaved, and far below, the waves crashed against its sides.

There were gates in the railing for launching the lifeboats and Delacroix opened the nearest one, revealing a sheer drop into the black waves.

Without thinking, Luke threw himself towards Emilio. Delacroix made a grab for him at the edge of the gate. Dropping his shoulder, and mustering all his strength for the tackle, Luke shoved him aside.

'Watch out!' Emilio yelled at his boss.

Clutching Luke's arm with one of his big hands,

Delacroix fumbled for the railing with the other, but it was slippery with brine. Luke realized that Delacroix had lost his footing and his grip and was falling into the darkness – without letting go of him.

It was like a dive off the roof of an apartment building. Yelling out in terror, Luke plunged through the air towards the black waves below.

29

'Men overboard!' Thomson shouted. 'John, help me!'

A man with a stripe of green spray paint across his head was sprinting aft of the boat deck, carrying several orange life buoys in his hands.

'LUKE!' Rosita screamed with tears in her eyes, staring down over the railing at the surging waves below. 'He tried to save me...' Her voice cracked.

John Curran swung out his arm in a huge arc to hurl a life buoy into the darkness, followed by a second, a third and a fourth.

'You better get Delacroix back on board,' Juliette screamed in a falsetto, 'or we'll dunk in the captain to keep him company.'

Thomson pressed a button on his radiophone, which gave him a direct line to the bridge. 'Bauer, stop the ship. Men overboard.' There was no response. 'Bauer? Are you there? Damn it, answer me!'

'*This is Bauer. We're stopping the engines. Deploy the Fast Rescue Boat.*'

A member of the crew was already racing to the control panel on the boat deck, to lower the rescue boat into the water. This speedboat, a seven-metre dinghy made of fibreglass-reinforced plastic and powered by a 145 HP Mercury inboard engine with waterjet propulsion, was an obligatory piece of safety equipment on all passenger vessels, designed specially for cases where someone fell overboard.

'Hurry up!' Juliette's voice was thin with distress. 'Save Delacroix!'

'Stop screaming and hold this lever until you see a red light,' Thomson said, his voice angry but calm. He joined Curran in the Fast Rescue Boat. A shrill wind whistled in the cables. As the *Emerald* stopped, it had immediately begun to pitch and heave erratically.

A deck hand trained in launching the lifeboats came running.

'OK, off you go!' the man hollered. 'Hold on tight!'

Hanging from the davit, the boat cleared the railing, then began its rapid descent towards the sea. It was lowered by means of a single cable, a nimble operation compared with the launch of the ordinary lifeboats that had a cable at both bow and stern.

Before they were even near the surface of the water, Curran had started the huge black engine. Thomson held onto the safety hand grabs on either side of the boat and braced himself for a rough ride. The waves tossed the boat like a chip of wood, but it was, for now, partly sheltered by the cruise ship, which Bauer had turned against the wind.

As the boat made contact with the water, a huge wave swelled up, tossing the dinghy against the side of the *Emerald*, where it bobbed like a cork. The yellow light that gleamed from the long line of portholes seemed to dissolve in the inky darkness of the sea.

The two men's faces were drenched by the hard spray as they waited for the right moment to release the cable that still attached them to the ship. At last, when the Fast Rescue Boat seemed to settle for a few seconds, Curran quickly detached the lock and Thomson reached for the thermal camera in the box at the foot of the windscreen in front of the wheel.

Luke couldn't see a thing, hear a thing or, in fact, feel a thing, as he channelled all his strength into the task of staying afloat. He tried to do breaststroke as he rose and fell with the waves, but the best he could manage was a desperate doggy paddle. For the first time since he'd fallen overboard, he caught a glimpse of the *Ocean Emerald*'s lights and was horrified to see that the vessel was already several hundred metres away. His limbs were beginning to stiffen in the freezing water. He gagged and coughed, fighting to keep his head above the surface – and to keep from surrendering to panic.

He suddenly remembered his first swimming lessons as a little boy at a friend's pool in East Sussex, when Mum had held him with her safe, firm hands. He saw her face as it had been then, her encouraging smile beaming in the sun. Then a massive wave sucked Luke under and the bright image vanished into blackness. He felt the pain he would cause Mum, Dad, Gran and all his loved ones if he gave up now.

Kicking and squirming, Luke struggled to raise his head above the water. Now he saw Mum's face again... It gave him a boost of energy. Drops of water glittered in her eyelashes, but they suddenly looked like tears.

Another wave approached, towering over Luke, and Mum's face was filled with distress and pain. Again Luke felt the mass of water slamming over him. He battled with every muscle to stay afloat and suck air into his lungs. He understood clearly now that he might never return to Mum and Dad.

Bouncing and leaping wildly on the waves, the Fast Rescue Boat sped northwards, retracing the route of the *Ocean Emerald*. Clutching the thermal camera, Thomson clung onto the steering pulpit with his other hand. It was an acrobatic struggle to keep upright in the violently tossing boat, amid the rain and the flying spray. On Thomson's right, Curran looked like he was floating in the air as he calmly adjusted his weight to the erratic dance of the dinghy.

Thomson glanced back at the *Ocean Emerald*, which looked warm, safe and bright. In the darkness ahead lurked certain death. Similar thoughts had perhaps gone through the heads of the passengers of the *Titanic* when they crammed into the lifeboats on that fateful night in April 1912.

Thomson returned his attention to the green glow of the thermal camera's viewer. Suddenly, he saw a fleck of white.

A person.

'Over there!' Thomson pointed into the darkness, to the left of the bow.

As the boat turned, it bucked over a huge wave, then slid down into the hollow on the other side, like a sleigh speeding into a valley. For the first time in his life,

Thomson felt seasick. He vomited, but his eyes never left the small screen on the thermal camera. There were now two flecks, at opposite ends of the screen.

Curran adjusted one of the powerful searchlights mounted on the rollbar above his head. He wiped his face, peering into the agitated waves.

At the same moment, Thomson and Curran saw the small dark figure in the beam of the searchlight.

The boy.

As Thomson turned to look at the other blurry shape on the viewer, the storm inside his mind was even wilder than the ocean around him. Two people were in imminent danger of drowning. Neither could survive in the freezing water for more than a few minutes. If they tried to save the boy, Delacroix might drown – and vice versa. Of the two, Delacroix was further out. Who should they pick up first? The hijacker, whose death might be avenged by other deaths? Or the innocent boy, who also happened to be closer?

30

The light beaming through the darkness dazzled Luke's eyes. In his mind, he thought he saw the sun streaming from an English summer sky. He knew he was sinking and tried desperately to grasp hold of his mother, but she disappeared and all that was left was water, and a taste of brine, and his heavy limbs, hanging down with no strength left in them.

But the beam didn't disappear. It leaped and dipped with the waves.

A searchlight.

Luke tried to raise his arm, but he began sinking as soon as he did so. *He didn't even have the strength to wave.*

Worse, his limbs were now so numb he could barely feel them. His last strength was ebbing out of him as the boat pulled away. Was this what dying felt like? He tried to scream, but only managed a spluttering cough. His teeth were chattering so hard he thought they might break.

Out in the darkness, the boat was turning in a wide arc. It didn't go away, but came speeding towards him.

***

Thomson tried to hold the beam of the searchlight on the boy. He'd been both shocked and moved by Luke's brave attempt to save the girl and could only pray the boy's courage would hold out until he could be hauled from the water.

Curran reduced speed and neatly steered the dinghy towards the small figure that was being tossed like a rag doll, slapped onto the crest of a wave, then sent plummeting between the heaving masses of water once more. When the boat was almost on top of Luke, Thomson threw the life buoy that was attached to the boat with a strong rope.

The boy raised a hand to clutch at the red-and-white ring, but it slipped out of his reach. He didn't have the strength to save himself.

'I'll dive in for him if I have to,' Thomson shouted at Curran through the howling wind.

He looped a white rope around his waist, but it was painfully slow work with cold and numb fingers.

'Move to the stern!' Curran hollered, turning the dinghy's bow in the direction of the waves. 'And keep that damned rope well away from the propeller.'

The Fast Rescue Boat almost capsized as a giant wave struck its bow, hurling the dinghy upwards, then sending it flying backwards into a bottomless pit. Thomson used another rope to fasten himself to the boat and crawled with difficulty to the stern, clinging onto the hand grabs on the side of the boat. He could only hope that Delacroix had more stamina than the boy.

Curran swivelled the searchlight, directing it behind the boat. Thomson leaned over the side and tried to slip his hands under the boy's arms. Ice-cold water drenched his chest and legs. At last he got hold of the boy's jacket and was able to pull him towards him, but a colossal wave smacked against the dinghy and Thomson lost his grip. He swallowed salt water and began coughing violently.

Curran battled to keep the boat still – an impossible task. Again, Thomson tried to reach Luke. He'd learned something. This time, when he managed to grab hold of the boy, he waited until the side of the boat dipped, which meant the boy came closer. At exactly the right moment, he yanked with all his might, hauling Luke's upper body over the side of the boat.

By now, a large quantity of water was sloshing inside the boat, so Thomson sat on the thwart holding the shaking boy in his arms. The boy put his arms around his neck, which allowed Thomson to reach for the thermal camera with his free hands.

Curran's searchlight cut a swathe of brightness over the foaming waves, probing in all directions, but Delacroix was nowhere to be seen.

The hijacker had sunk under the surface.

'Let's go, or the boy won't make it,' Thomson shouted.

He felt not an ounce of pity for the hijacker, but the welcome they'd receive from the other hijackers already filled him with dread.

Curran accelerated and the dinghy shot forward, towards the bright lights of the *Ocean Emerald*.

Back at the police headquarters in Finland, Peter Baron stared at the glowing white container that the helicopter crewman placed in front of him on the rain-swept yard. The clamour of the rotors was deafening, yet Peter heard nothing. His entire attention was focused on the object in front of him. Then he looked up at the men around him.

'Thanks, guys,' he called out. He had a lump in his throat. The lights of the helicopter blazed against the night sky, stinging his eyes.

Peter shook the container. Something rattled inside.

'Let's get out of the rain,' said the superintendent, reaching to grab the container.

Peter snatched it from under the man's nose and rushed into the soulless white building.

He set the container down on the concrete floor of a lab-like room inside and was immediately surrounded by half a dozen curious men. He pulled on a pair of latex gloves and unscrewed the thick black plastic top. He tilted the container and a small torch clattered onto the floor. He tried to ease out the satellite phone, but the mouth of the container was too small.

'Get me a knife,' he grunted.

Someone handed him an orange box cutter, which he used to slice open the container. He put the phone into the rubber-gloved hands of his colleague and turned his attention to the neatly folded sheet of paper.

'AT 15.30, I BOARDED THE OCEAN EMERALD TO RETURN JULIETTE DU PONT'S BOARDING PASS AND PASSPORT...'

The sight of Luke's scrawly handwriting almost brought tears rushing into Peter Baron's eyes.

Luke had described everything concisely and with exemplary clarity.

181

The man who'd bent over to examine the phone straightened his back and said: 'Quite a son you've got there. He's taken photos of the hijackers and of the situation on board.'

Peter felt his chest swell up with pride – then the dread came crowding into his mind again.

31

Soaked to the skin, Thomson climbed from the Fast Rescue Boat onto the deck of the *Ocean Emerald*, still holding Luke in his arms. Rosita sprinted forward to meet them and pressed a blanket over Luke, whose skin was a shade between white and grey, and whose vacant stare suggested he was oblivious to everything around him.

He whimpered something and Thomson brought his ear close to the boy's mouth. 'Did you know who holds... the world record... for surviving in the sea? It's a Brazilian fisherman called Juan... I don't remember the surname...'

Juliette came closer, glaring, sub-machine-gun in hand. 'I see you chose the kid?'

'There wasn't any choice,' Thomson said coldly, carrying Luke towards the door. 'It's lucky we even found one.'

Juliette blocked their way, her wet, pallid face glistening in the deck lights.

'Don't forget what I said,' she yelled in a thin, high-pitched voice, eyes burning with anger. 'If my husband has drowned, your captain drowns as well!'

A husband and wife team? Thomson calmly registered

the information as he brushed past and reached for the door handle.

'That's right, you take the brat inside, then come and face the consequences.'

Just before the heavy iron door closed behind him, Thomson heard the hysterical-sounding command that Juliette hissed into her radiophone. 'Emilio, bring the captain out onto the boat deck.'

Three nautical miles from the *Ocean Emerald*, the *Zeeland* was waiting, with its lights dimmed. Commander van Heerevelt stood on the warship's boat deck, onto which an electric winch was pulling the vessel's lifeboat. Fired up by the extraordinary events of this stormy night, he wasn't bored any more.

Van Heerevelt wiped the spray from his face and stared at the dripping figure being helped to its feet by a Dutch marine dressed in a glistening black wetsuit. The weight of the water pulled down the man's sodden clothes, and van Heerevelt noticed that he had an ugly scar on the side of his neck.

Aldis lamp signals beamed from the *Ocean Emerald* had told them that two men had fallen overboard. The message had been cut short, but van Heerevelt had ordered the frigate's lifeboat to be deployed – a fortunate decision. The passenger plucked from the waves by the marine would otherwise not have survived. The hijackers had apparently flung the poor man into the sea.

'*Dieu merci*,' the man kept saying, over and over again. 'Get him some dry clothes, then put him in my cabin,' van Heerevelt said. He was dying to hear what was happening on the cruise ship.

Moments later, Delacroix was pulling fresh clothes on in the frigate's sick room, pretending to be even more shocked and exhausted than he was. He'd lost his silk scarf and his glasses. The glasses didn't matter. He only wore them in order to give an educated impression – he had 20/20 vision.

Much worse was the fact that he'd lost the radio control that could detonate the bombs. It was at the bottom of the Baltic Sea. Helmut now had the only remaining one.

He'd already given up hope when the lifeboat had suddenly appeared beside him. He was now trying to work out what would be the wisest thing to do next.

The ship's doctor led him to the commander's cabin. Delacroix walked with shuffling steps and made a show of his trembling hands.

'Commander van Heerevelt,' the ramrod-straight man in uniform greeted him, pale blue eyes glittering with interest. 'How are you feeling?'

Delacroix let out a heavy sigh and slouched into the armchair that van Heerevelt pulled up for him.

'Did they throw you overboard? What about the other passengers?'

Delacroix heaved an even deeper sigh than before. Inwardly, he was frantically analysing the situation he was in. *They thought he was only a passenger.*

'I can't remember anything,' he whispered in a barely audible, rasping voice. 'Where am I? What's happened?'

***

'Tell your officers to continue at full speed towards Kaliningrad, then follow me.' Emilio was still dressed in his cleaner's uniform, speaking to Captain Bauer on the bridge of the *Ocean Emerald*.

The captain could hardly disguise his horror when he realized that one of the ship's own employees was among the hijackers. One – or maybe several?

In fact, this was a classic pirate ruse. A member of the gang infiltrated the ship's staff or crew, then sent information to his mates about the ship's location and cargo. Vessels could do little against this kind of plot, short of placing round-the-clock armed patrols on board, which wasn't considered a good idea, as it would lead to certain violence. Oil companies spent more on protecting a single petrol station than they spent on protecting a supertanker. Paradoxically, the best way of avoiding human casualties in hijacking situations was to minimize resistance.

Captain Bauer ordered his second mate to resume the course for Kaliningrad. He then reached for his embroidered cap and placed it on his head in a slow and deliberate gesture that was full of pride.

'Move, I said!' The insolent Emilio jabbed him in the ribs with his gun, and the captain could barely restrain himself from striking the man to the floor.

Back in Helsinki, Peter Baron was listening through his earphones to the excited, boyish voice of the commander of the Dutch frigate the *Zeeland*.

'*The man's in a state and can't remember a thing,*' van Heerevelt said. '*Could be the shock ... or he could be shamming.*'

'You mean he might be one of the hijackers?' Peter said into his microphone.

'We have no way of knowing – and I suppose there is no way of checking.'

'Maybe there is.' Peter shifted in his seat. 'Can you take his photo and send it to us?'

'We'll email you a digital photo.'

'OK.' Peter read out the email address and nodded at the officer operating the radio to indicate that the conversation was over.

Peter turned to his FNBI colleagues, to chair the analysis of the latest situation. He had also maintained close contact with his Europol colleagues in Brussels and The Hague, where international police co-operation was co-ordinated. The French police were sifting through all persons known to bear the name 'Juliette du Pont'. It was all but confirmed that she was indeed travelling under a false identity, as Luke had suspected. The passport that Juliette was using was in the name of a Parisian estate agent who had drowned in a sailing accident off the coast of Corsica the previous summer. Who she really was, was anyone's guess.

Oddly, however, the Philippe Delacroix mentioned in Luke's message appeared to have been operating under his own name. The one-time art dealer had long been suspected of contacts with criminals specializing in museum theft and the illegal art trade. But what would a professional criminal hijack a cruise ship for? Delacroix had dubious contacts, including with persons possibly involved with funding terrorism, but nothing in his own background suggested extremism.

The desktop gave a beep. An email had arrived from the *Zeeland*.

Peter opened the message and clicked on the attachment. The man in the photo was sitting in a cabin. Peter rushed to his feet and called for his colleagues. He had instantly recognized the face of the hijacker: it was the man that Luke had photographed on board the *Ocean Emerald*.

With a stony face, Thomson stared at the second spectacle, even sicker than the first, that was unfolding on the boat deck of the *Ocean Emerald*. Some of the hijackers and a knot of crew members had gathered under the bright lights, and a crowd of passengers was standing further back.

The gate in the railing, intended for launching the lifeboats, had been swung open once more. Captain Bauer stood five metres from the sheer drop into the roaring sea, eyes blindfolded with a black cloth, back straight and head held high.

Thomson forced himself to take long, calm breaths. He knew what the show was all about. Having lost their leader, the hijackers could feel their authority crumbling, and they were trying to regain the upper hand by the simple expedient of murdering the captain.

'Watch carefully,' Juliette shouted, her fanatical eyes glimmering in the floodlights. 'You defied our orders. Captain Bauer will now pay for it with his life. No lifeboats will be deployed after he has jumped.'

On board the *Zeeland*, van Heerevelt rushed to his cabin, where the man who had been rescued from the sea had made a surprisingly swift recovery.

'Mr Delacroix,' van Heerevelt said. 'We know who you are.' He was accompanied by two marines, in case the hijacker tried something desperate.

'Take me back to the *Ocean Emerald*,' the man said calmly, in a French accent. 'And keep your ship well away from mine.'

With a smirk, van Heerevelt met the eyes of the Frenchman, whose expression betrayed not a trace of uncertainty or hesitation.

'And why would we do that?'

'Because if my associates think I'm dead, innocent people will pay for it with their lives. This is a certainty.'

There was a long, heavy silence. Van Heerevelt looked at his armed marines. He thought of his service pistol, tightly wrapped in its holster in his desk drawer. What he really wanted to do now was to point that pistol at the arrogant man who was sitting on his bunk, resting his weight on his arms, like a tourist relaxing on a beach.

'If you don't take me back right now,' Delacroix said, 'and leave my ship alone, you'll be personally responsible for the lives of the passengers.'

'Your ship!' van Heerevelt spat out in helpless disgust. He looked at the scar on the Frenchman's neck. He couldn't believe he had no weapon with which to fight this blackmail – but so it was. The marines flanking him had taken a small step forward, but he waved them back.

'Well?' the Frenchman's eyes flashed.

'We'll radio the *Emerald* and tell them you are OK. And we'll take you back. But if you touch a hair on any of those passengers, I'll personally come and rip your head off. Looks like the previous guy didn't quite finish the job.'

32

'Jump, Captain Bauer,' Juliette shouted in the glare of the lights on the deck of the *Ocean Emerald*, and shoved the barrel of her gun into the blindfolded captain's back.

Beyond the open gate, far below, the dark sea churned.

He stumbled, but managed to right himself. 'This is a complex vessel, you need my help to sail it...'

'You underestimate your officers,' Juliette said. 'Move!'

The fierce wind made a keening sound and tore at the orange tarpaulin that covered the life raft.

As the captain took a small step forward, Thomson felt his skin crawl. The passengers had been told to watch, but in fact only a few of the tougher men actually had the stomach to do so. Others had averted their gazes. Some sobbed.

Thomson had no way of saving Bauer. If he tried force, the wrath of the hijackers would be unleashed on the passengers.

'Hurry up!' Juliette shouted over the wind.

Bauer took another blind step towards the edge of the deck, holding onto the end of the rail with one hand.

Suddenly Juliette's radiophone crackled. She raised it to her ear and the frozen expression on her face gave way to a blissful smile. Then the smile was replaced by a scowl.

'Captain,' she said. 'I have some good news and some bad news. My partner is alive and on his way here. That's the good news.'

'Delacroix... is *alive?*' Bauer took a step away from the precipice and felt for the railing.

'Now the bad news.' She blocked his way. 'Does a warship called the *Zeeland* mean anything to you?'

Bauer shook his head.

'Don't pretend. It's the Dutch frigate that you've been secretly communicating with.'

Juliette slammed her hands into Bauer's chest and he lost his balance, half-turning as he fell overboard. Somehow, by blind instinct, he managed to hook his arms over the edge of the deck. His cap went spinning into the storm, but he retained a strange dignity even as he hung there, suspended over the wildly surging waves of the dark sea.

'Wait!' Thomson sprinted over, throwing himself onto the deck to grab Bauer's wrists. 'Let Delacroix decide...'

Glancing up, Thomson met the wild stare of Juliette. It was a desperate gamble. Thomson's intuition told him that the woman's nervous intensity also implied total loyalty to her leader, Delacroix. She probably submitted to his power one hundred per cent.

A glimmer of hesitation passed over her face. Then her sharp eyes turned to the swarm of cowering passengers staring in stunned silence – she was no doubt calculating that she'd made her point already.

'OK then,' Juliette said. 'Haul him up. But don't expect pity from our leader.'

Curran hurried over to help Thomson pull the exhausted captain to safety.

***

Luke could feel the strength slowly returning to his limbs. He had spent an hour or so in Carol's cabin, buried under a heap of blankets, and the ship's doctor had examined him, finding no serious injuries.

Rosita had brought him some dry clothes from the changing room behind the kitchens: clean Y-fronts, checked trousers and a white T-shirt, as worn by the ship's catering staff. A small-sized crew member had contributed a pair of trainers and a yellow turtleneck sweater. Luke was glad that Toni and Emma couldn't see him in this get-up, but he really enjoyed being fussed over by Rosita.

He'd told Thomson about the radiophone conversation he had overheard in the hijackers' cabin earlier, when they'd referred to an accomplice called 'Helmut' who had 'the other one'. Was Helmut a member of the crew? He could also be masquerading as a passenger. It made sense for him to keep a lower profile than the others if he had the second radio control. But there was no ready way of finding him, as the computers containing the passenger and crew lists had been disabled and it was in any case unlikely he'd be travelling under his own name.

There was an impatient pounding at the door, then Rosita let herself in.

'I have bad news. Delacroix survived,' Rosita said breathlessly. 'I just saw him arrive in a military lifeboat. He was picked up by some warship nearby.'

It took Luke a few seconds to get his head round this. He knew he should have been upset, even terrified, to hear that the hijacker had returned to torment the passengers, but he wasn't. His first feeling was relief that Delacroix had escaped drowning. And the presence of a warship was a sign that someone, somewhere, was taking action.

But how would Delacroix, in turn, react to Luke's survival?

Luke's gladness evaporated and he could feel his mouth tightening with fear, although he tried to hide it from Rosita.

'I'll hide you,' she whispered, apparently reading his mind. 'I know places on this ship that they'll never find.'

Luke managed a smile. 'I hope you have space for a thousand passengers!'

A Gulfstream business jet landed at Helsinki-Vantaa airport at 7.50 a.m. Peter Baron watched as a tired-looking American with silver hair climbed down the steps accompanied by two slightly younger men.

Max Lownie Senior, CEO of the Emerald Cruise Corporation, was whisked through passport control as a VIP and within minutes he was sitting in an unmarked minibus, which drove him to the police headquarters, a short distance from Helsinki. The crisis group assembled by the Finnish authorities was ready to meet him. Close co-operation with the shipping company was needed to maximize the passengers' chances. But Peter knew that co-operation wouldn't be easy. The police had the media on their backs and they were under pressure to tell the truth sooner rather than later, whereas the ship's owners, fearing for the company's reputation, wanted to keep the hijacking secret as long as possible.

'Sorry to hear your wife and son are on the ship,' Peter Baron said from the front passenger seat, looking at the American in the rear-view mirror.

'I guess we're in the same darn pickle. Although from what I've heard, your son's doing a better job of helping us than mine is.'

Peter allowed himself a smile. 'Let's get straight to the point. About the media...'

'No media.' Lownie was shaking his head before Peter had even got started. 'It's in the passengers' interest that we keep this under wraps as long as we can. And I'm not just thinking about my own family.'

'This is an international crisis. Half a dozen Baltic countries are involved. The leaks are already starting.'

'Then plug them.' Lownie put his hand on Peter's shoulder. 'If you don't, my company will go belly up.'

They pulled up in front of the police headquarters and an officer rushed over to Peter as soon as he stepped off the minibus.

'Moscow wants to speak to you. They're offering us their special forces to help end the hijacking.'

At the sound of these words, Peter felt as though a hot knife had been stabbed into his abdomen.

'No,' he said. 'No special forces, especially not Russian ones.'

'They've already sent a taskforce to Kaliningrad.'

33

The wind over the Baltic had dropped during the course of the morning, and as noon approached, the sun flashed behind a milky layer of mist and cloud. Viewed from the outside, the *Ocean Emerald* looked handsome as it powered forward, a monument of glamour, wealth and optimism.

The mood on board was not so optimistic. The passengers were getting edgy and the hijackers were even more so, although they did their best to hide it.

Delacroix was watching on the bridge. He'd spared Captain Bauer's life. After the drama of the night, the man seemed at last to have recognized the advantage of keeping things on a businesslike footing. Neither spoke unless absolutely necessary. Neither had slept. The tension in the air grew thicker with every passing hour as the vessel relentlessly advanced towards Kaliningrad. Every so often, they caught a glimpse of another ship on the distant horizon.

Delacroix felt exposed without his scarf, and kept bringing his big hand to his throat. He couldn't get the arrogant van Heerevelt and his idle threat out of his mind. In other circumstances, Delacroix would have reacted differently. Very differently. It was hard, having to restrain oneself all the time, but that was what leaders had to learn to do.

Luke had read that rationing energy, fluids and rest was a golden rule for those who faced exceptional physical strain, be they special forces, explorers or athletes. The hardest thing, the experts said, was to force yourself to sleep under prolonged mental pressure. So after he'd been assured by Thomson that there was nothing useful to be done at present, Luke had decided to have a nap, and ended up sleeping most of the morning.

The hijackers had the upper hand, Thomson had stressed, and after the events of the night, it was best not to provoke them. Soon, however, something would happen, Luke felt sure of it. Perhaps it would take place in Kaliningrad, perhaps before, but something was in the offing. What was it?

As Luke had slept, he later gathered, Thomson and his emergency response team had been desperately and unsuccessfully trying to identify 'Helmut', who had the second radio control for detonating the explosives. The first one had presumably been lost when Delacroix fell overboard – at any rate, he was no longer seen holding it in his hand.

The German name 'Helmut' was the only clue they had, but there were more than a hundred Germans on board, and even Carol's excellent memory for names and faces hadn't brought up anything.

Rosita peeped in.

'Who's a sleepy boy, then?'

'That swim knocked the stuffing out of me.'

'Are you hungry?'

'Ravenous.'

'Well then.' Rosita took a note pad and tapped a pen against it. Luke noticed that she'd put on some lipstick that perfectly matched her pink nail varnish.

'What would you like? Dessert will be a surprise. We have a range of excellent main courses...'

Back in Finland, Peter Baron angrily slammed down the telephone, rushed to the window and saw what he feared he'd see: Gran swinging into the yard on her motorbike, dress fluttering in the morning breeze.

Hanna had just phoned to warn him, and he already regretted the tone in which he'd asked her why she hadn't stopped her mum from coming to see him on personal business – or any business – at the national police headquarters.

Hanna hadn't slept since Luke disappeared and Peter knew perfectly well that when Gran got an idea into her head, there was no talking her out of it – the vintage motorbike being a good example. Rummaging in the garden shed in the spring, she'd rediscovered it, a 1956 Norton Dominator 88, under a pile of old junk. It had belonged to her late husband, and Gran had immediately decided to start using it again. With the help of Luke's friend, Toni, it had been gorgeously restored.

The bike was a beauty, it had to be admitted, but Gran looked like a comedy act when she rode it in her helmet and baggy floral dress. Peter was fond of his mother-in-law, but right now, she was the last person he wanted to see.

It was almost noon and the night's fatigue had settled on him like a heavy cloak. He'd been jet-lagged before he even started and his mind felt sluggish. With a sinking heart, he watched Gran remove her helmet and take something from the pannier on the bike before setting off towards the main entrance. Peter rushed down the stairs, to ensure she didn't get the chance to speak to any of his colleagues.

As he crossed the small car park, Peter greeted a pair of officers who were heading out for an early lunch. He saw them exchange an amused look as he took Gran by the crook of her arm and drew her to one side.

'I have a message from Luke,' Gran said. 'I turned on my mobile and found this message from him. It was sent during the night.'

Peter grabbed the cheap mobile from Gran's fingers and cupped his hand around the display, to shield it from the bright sun.

Gran, Luke here. I'm OK. Look after Mum and Dad. Tell Dad about the credit card thing after this all is over. Miss you all.

'What credit card thing?' Peter said.

'That was just a small internet bet we placed together. It's not important.'

'If it's not important, then why did you come all this way?' Peter said sharply. 'I have a crisis on my hands and it's far from over.'

'I understand that, my dear. But I'm here for the first part of the message.' Gran squinted at the display. '*Look after Mum and Dad.*' She held up a small basket. 'Here. I brought you something to eat.'

Peter took the basket and gave Gran a kiss on the cheek. With a mischievous wink, she swung her leg over the Norton, slipped the helmet onto her head and placed her foot on the starter pedal.

'I'll travel less when we've got Luke out of this,' Peter said. 'I'll spend more time with him. I promise.'

'Good,' she said. 'And talk to him man to man. He's not a kid any more.'

'I know.' Peter was wondering how he could hide the basket for the walk back across the yard and through the building, to his desk. 'He's fourteen years old.'

'Then why do you treat him like a nine-year-old? He fixes computers, he reads grown-up books, he'll be shaving soon . . .'

Peter shook his head, nettled by Gran's meddling, but also stung by what she'd said.

'Age is a weird thing.' Gran dug a handkerchief from the pocket of her floral dress and blew her nose. 'When you're young, they take you for a baby. When you're old, they take you for a vegetable.'

'You're a star, Gran,' Peter said. 'Thanks for the food.'

'Some of us improve with age – like this baby right here.'

Gran kicked the old engine into life. The Norton, with its Featherbed frame, powerful brakes and 497 cc engine, was one of the great British motorcycles, and it sounded as good as it looked. It left quite a smell, too. Gran raised her arm and swung towards the exit, followed by a dancing plume of exhaust smoke.

Peter managed to get as far as his own corridor without being seen, but then the big-bellied figure of Deputy Director Kanerva came rolling into view.

'God, I'm tired.' Kanerva rubbed his sagging, red-rimmed eyes. 'Well, I never – it's Little Red Riding Hood. What's in the basket?'

'Food and a flask of coffee, by the look of it. Want some?'

'You know, I don't mind if I do.'

They sat on opposite sides of the desk in the office that Peter had been given and tucked into Gran's ham sandwiches and saffron buns. The coffee was strong and hot. Miraculously, the phone didn't ring for five whole minutes.

'What bread is this?' Kanerva buried his teeth into another ham sandwich. 'It's weird – it tastes like it just popped out of the oven.'

'It did. My mother-in-law stopped by.'

'Tell her to stop by more often.' Kanerva reached for a saffron bun. 'Mind if I try another one of these?'

Peter's thoughts were on his parenting skills. It was true he travelled a great deal, as did Hanna. It was true that Luke was a big lad now. When all this was over, he'd rethink it all and put everything on a better footing with his son. He'd talk to him, and listen, and maybe take him on a trip somewhere.

Then the phone did ring.

'*The* Ocean Emerald *is now in Russian waters,*' said Peter's colleague at the other end of the line. '*I'm afraid the Russians aren't listening any more. I think they want to storm it by force.*'

Peter jumped to his feet and tossed his unfinished sandwich back into the basket.

Three minutes later, they were sitting in a police car that was speeding towards Helsinki-Vantaa airport, where a Finnish Air Force jet stood idling on the runway, ready to fly them to Kaliningrad.

While Kanerva was briefing the Finnish Minister of the Interior via mobile phone, Peter took the opportunity to speak to his wife.

'I just talked to our liaison officer in Moscow,' Peter said.

'*Moscow?*' Hanna's voice faltered. '*Why on earth?*'

'Kaliningrad is part of Russia. Hanna... They want to send in special forces.'

Hanna let out a sob.

'They're called Alpha,' Peter went on. 'They're the Russian equivalent of the Finnish Karhu team and the British SAS.'

'Don't let this happen.'

'Trust me...' Peter cupped his hand around the mobile. 'We won't give them permission to storm the ship. But we can't stop Alpha from coming to the scene.'

'What makes you think they'd ask for your permission?'

'It will all be OK.' Peter looked up and saw the jet on the runway ahead. 'I have to go, or I'll miss my ride to Kaliningrad.'

'You didn't answer my question. Why would the Russians ask for your permission?'

'They won't ask for permission, but we can always forbid them from striking.'

'And will they listen?'

'Hanna, please...' Peter trotted across the tarmac after Kanerva. 'An armed assault would be the very last resort.'

34

A rusty and scratched old Renault Mégane hurtled south-
wards along the E411 motorway, heading from Antwerp
to Luxembourg. In the fields that stretched out on either
side of the motorway, ripening corn waved in the midday
sun. The floor in front of the empty child seat in the back
of the car was littered with sweet wrappers and baby
clothes. The state of the vehicle was bound to put off even
the most desperate car thief.

Eva kept a careful eye on the speedometer, as this was
no time to get stopped by the police, for several reasons,
one being the unlicensed firearm in the coat pocket of the
man sitting beside her.

The gun was needed for protecting the consignment.
Packed in the titanium briefcase in the boot of the car was
a grey Kevlar bag containing glass diamonds, a decoy, just
in case someone had got wind of the operation. The real
consignment was hidden inside the five cheap, floppy-
eared teddy bears innocently displayed on the back seat of
the car.

An hour later, Eva pulled off into a rest area behind a
petrol station, where a green Range Rover was waiting.
They abandoned the Renault and continued in the other

car. Soon after the Range Rover had crossed the border into Luxembourg, they stopped again. Eva reached into the boot, opened the titanium briefcase and poured the fake diamonds from the Kevlar bag into a large dark bottle, which she dropped into a glass-recycling bin. Then she unzipped the five teddy bears and took out the grey Kevlar bags, which she emptied carefully into a larger one. She binned the five empty teddy bears.

Then she transferred the single, bulging Kevlar bag containing the entire consignment of real diamonds into the briefcase and locked it.

After a lunch of fish-burger, chips and ketchup from a giant bottle, all wheeled up by Rosita on a serving trolley from the ship's kitchen, Luke began to feel like himself once more. He was lying on the bed in Carol's cabin, which was now reserved for his personal use. It felt weird, but not entirely unpleasant, eating in bed in the late afternoon.

'So what's the surprise dessert?' he said, rubbing the belly of his ridiculous yellow turtleneck jumper.

'The chef recommends fried bananas,' Rosita said, removing the tin foil from a shallow dish. With a flourish, she opened a small cold box. 'And pistachio ice cream. Do you want another lemonade?'

'Yes, please. And some of those chocolates over there. It's worth falling overboard, if this is how you're treated afterwards.'

'You saved my life, so the least I can do is try to put some flesh on those bones,' Rosita said. 'Your mum will thank me.'

Luke would have preferred to leave his mum out of it. 'Are my clothes dry yet?' he said.

'I'll go and see.'

Fifteen minutes later, Rosita was back from the laundry where the staff uniforms were washed and pressed.

'Washed and tumble-dried.' Rosita presented Luke with a pile of neatly folded, pleasant-smelling clothes: jeans, T-shirt, jacket, socks and underpants. His trainers and belt were in a separate bag. The belt was still wet.

'I'll leave you to it,' she said, sensing Luke's hesitation. 'Unless of course you need Mummy's help getting dressed.'

'You're such a comedian,' Luke said, scraping the last of the ice cream from his plate. 'I'm fourteen, you know. Not much younger than you.'

'Yeah, right. Luke C. Baron, fourteen.' Rosita winked. 'Oh, I also brought the snacks you asked for.' She tossed Luke a paper bag. 'In case you get peckish again. See you later.'

'I may never eat again,' Luke said. 'But thanks.'

Rosita flashed him a teasing grin. 'Seriously, what does the "C" stand for?'

Luke hesitated. 'Do you promise not to laugh?'

'Sure.'

'My name is Lucas Copernicus Baron. But everyone calls me Luke.'

'*Copernicus?*' Rosita fought in vain to keep a straight face, then started giggling. 'You poor thing... Copernicus, wow...'

'I knew it,' Luke said. Only his real friends – the inner circle – knew his middle name. But it felt good having told Rosita. It meant she was now in the inner circle, too.

Her laughter wasn't mean – the girl was cheeky, but also kind.

'My parents are into science and astronomy and all that.'

'Sorry...' Rosita was laughing silently, shoulders shaking, tears streaming down her cheeks. 'Copernicus...'

'Can you believe it?' Luke said, grinning. 'What were they thinking?'

'Lucas Copernicus... I can't breathe...'

Now Luke was laughing too. 'I don't normally tell people...'

'Sorry... I won't tell anyone...' Rosita disappeared into the corridor, still in stitches.

The door closed, leaving Luke alone. He wiped his eyes and heaved a deep sigh. He'd asked Rosita to bring him some dry foods that were easy to hide. She'd come up with beef jerky, individually wrapped biscuits, and small packets of raisins. Beef jerky was something Luke had never tasted before, but he'd heard it was delicious. The cruise ship was well stocked, and the ship's staff had received instructions to feed the hostages for free, but you never knew when the situation might change.

As he pulled on his black T-shirt, Luke decided that his recovery was complete. Feeling bloated after his meal, he had to force himself to stow the snacks into his clothes, mostly into his pockets. He also slid a packet of beef jerky into his sock and managed to squeeze another one into the secret compartment inside his belt. He took out the compass, but left the fructose tablets and the fishing line hidden inside.

Thus armed, Luke slipped out into the corridor and decided to take a stroll around the ship. He hastened up onto the deck, and using his compass, managed to establish that the ship was travelling southwestward. He knew that the authorities would be tracking the ship from a safe distance, but checking the course for himself somehow helped him to gain a sense of control. Keeping to the stairs as much as possible, he then went down to the Reception desk.

A tall, blond passenger stood waiting for the lift. He had a tidy beard and the air of a doctor. He looked very familiar. With a jolt, Luke remembered where he had seen him: at the fuse box on the ninth deck, when he was looking for the bridge. Then, just as the man stepped into the lift, Juliette stepped out of it, and Luke quickly turned away, not wishing to be seen. But he could have sworn he'd seen the pair exchange a glance that was slightly longer than natural.

Was the man Helmut? Had Luke caught him exchanging a glance with his accomplice? Or had the man just been staring at Juliette, the fearsome hijacker who also happened to be a beautiful woman?

Throughout the afternoon, he tried to keep a close eye on the tall blond passenger, who walked the decks tirelessly in his tweed jacket, always alone. Keeping a discreet distance, Luke followed him into the ship's library, where a clutch of anguished passengers sat whispering about the latest rumours. Apparently uninterested in joining this discussion, the man retreated to an armchair in the corner and opened a book. This made him the only person in the library to show the slightest interest in the contents of the shelves.

Luke was wondering whether he could address the man under some pretext or other, but the risk was too great. Almost everyone on board knew of Luke's ordeal in the sea and that he was close to the ship's crew, including the head of security, Thomson. Rosita, having been saved by Luke and having nursed him with Carol's help, was now also an object of suspicion in the hijackers' eyes.

'I guess you have to be a gangster or a hijacker to get served round here?' a familiar voice boomed in an American accent. 'All this walking is killing me.'

Luke saw Max Lownie Junior hitch up his shorts as he vented his wrath on some unfortunate waiter, who was collecting the glasses that passengers had brought into the library.

'This is the library, sir. We don't serve drinks here.'

At this point, the tall, bearded passenger rose to his feet and calmly left, humming as he went, one hand in the pocket of his tweed jacket. Luke waited before continuing the pursuit.

Suddenly Max Lownie Junior settled at the table next to Luke's, raising his fat forefinger at the offending waiter.

'When this is over, you'll regret what you did.' Max was taking off his trainers and socks. 'You'll regret refusing to serve a drink to a dehydrated passenger who also happens to own this ship.'

It was time to go, Luke reflected, or the American might start asking him awkward questions about his satellite phone.

Too late.

'Hey, kid, get back here. You took my phone!'

'I don't know what you're talking about.'

Max grabbed Luke by the front of his T-shirt. After a short struggle, Luke did the only thing he could think of: he stamped on Max's bare toes, crunching down with all his might.

Max screamed like a colicky baby with a future in heavy metal.

Luke slipped out of the library and broke into a run.

'You come back here!' Max yelled after him. 'Hey! I'll sue you for that!'

Luke looked left and right. There was no sign of 'Helmut'.

He hastened back to the bridal suite, where the response team was based. It was best to tell Thomson about his suspicions about the tall, bearded passenger in the tweed jacket.

'Good work, Luke,' Thomson said after Luke had finished his report. 'Again.'

'Thanks, Coyote,' Luke replied. 'What next?'

'I'll pass on the description to all the others. Let's find him and check. If he has the radio control, we take him out. OK?'

'OK.' Luke was gratified by Thomson's phrase, which clearly included him in the team.

'Don't get too close. You don't want another swim, do you?'

'Why not, Coyote?' Luke said. 'The sun's come out.'

He'd started to call Thomson 'Coyote' like everyone else, which seemed to go down well. In return, Thomson had stopped calling Luke a kid. The calm and centred security pro was like an American version of his father.

35

Peter was standing beside a Russian UAZ four-by-four at the airfield in Kaliningrad, in the company of the deputy director of the Finnish National Bureau of Investigation and two Russian officers. He couldn't fail to notice the olive-green bus parked to one side, which was full of Russian commando troops armed to the teeth.

'Alpha's on standby and we can strike at a moment's notice,' rumbled Mikhail Grimenko of the Russian Federal Security Service, the FSB. The man, who was a good half metre shorter than Peter, had the burly proportions of a bear and brown button eyes.

'Thank you,' said Deputy Director Kanerva. 'But let's hope we won't need it.'

'Tell him upfront we won't use Alpha under any circumstances,' Peter said in an undertone, but Kanerva ignored him, loosening the collar of his tight shirt to make room for the folds of his neck.

'Time is of the essence,' Grimenko growled, staring with his button eyes. 'We've developed an aerosol anaesthetic, much more powerful than the gas used in the Moscow theatre siege.'

'Tell them *no way*,' Peter hissed at Kanerva.

'We'll listen to what they have to say,' Kanerva replied, turning to Grimenko. 'Go on,' he said, patting the Russian on the arm.

'We'd like to outline our plan for retaking the ship—'

As the afternoon wore on, the weather behind the tinted windows of the *Ocean Emerald*'s bridge became overcast once more. A mist rose as dusk thickened, causing evening to fall with unnatural suddenness.

'Captain Bauer,' Delacroix said at the chart table. 'Show me our precise location.'

Avoiding the hijacker's eyes, and doing his best not to stare at the ugly scar on his neck, Bauer bent over the chart and used a telescopic pointer to indicate a location on the Baltic coast, between Lithuania and Kaliningrad.

'Six miles offshore,' Bauer said. The shock of what had almost happened to him during the night burned like an open sore deep inside his sleep-deprived mind. Something about the hijacker's behaviour told him that a new surprise was imminent.

Delacroix tapped at the chart with a ballpoint pen, showing a spot just south of the vessel's current location, near the Russian town of Pionerskij, north of the Bay of Gdansk.

'Stop the vessel at the tip of this headland,' Delacroix said. 'Get us as close to the shore as you can.'

'That's in Lithuania...' Bauer glanced up from the chart. 'It's at least five hours to Kaliningrad. We'll need a pilot from Baltijskij—'

'Do as I say. Anchor the ship and evacuate all the passengers and crew.'

Bauer's mouth felt dry. He swallowed. 'I don't under-stand... There are sixteen hundred people on board.'

'And you'll use the lifeboats to take them ashore. Or they can swim, if you prefer.' Delacroix's voice was icy. 'Do it. You have half an hour.'

'*Half an hour?*' Bauer could hear his voice rise to a falsetto.

Delacroix spun away.

Bauer scuttled to the back of the bridge and fumbled for the microphone.

'Ladies and gentlemen, this is Captain Bauer speak-ing...' He tried for an encouraging tone, but could hear the weariness in his own voice. 'We have been told to evacuate the ship. I must invite you all to assemble at the muster stations on the Promenade Deck. Please equip yourselves with life vests, warm clothes and any medica-tion you might need. Don't panic. We're close to land and the lifeboats will take everyone ashore...'

'*I must ask you all to assemble as swiftly as possible. I apolo-gize – as you know, this situation is not of my making...*'

A thin, stooped man was sitting at the small writing desk in his cabin listening to the captain's announcement over the speaker system. He noticed that the captain was speaking in a taut voice and the observation sent him back to his task in an even greater hurry. He was writing instructions to his accountants and lawyers – just in case. If the hijacking came to a bloody end, they'd need to know what to do.

The luxury cabin on the seventh deck was pleasant enough, but it was far from the most expensive on the

Ocean Emerald. The American property tycoon David C. McMorgan had chosen a moderate price category, even though he was rich enough to buy the entire vessel. He swigged brandy from the glass on his desk and paused to knead his arthritic fingers, which were covered in freckles and blotches. It was getting dark again outside and he could see his own reflection in the window.

There was a rustling sound behind the door, then someone turned the handle. McMorgan jumped as the stranger unleashed an aggressive knock. McMorgan glanced around desperately. He thought of taking refuge in the small bathroom, but what would have been the point of that?

The knock was repeated.

'Mr McMorgan?' a woman's voice demanded. 'Open up or we'll break down the door.'

McMorgan rose to his feet and straightened his back. He had to gather all his strength in order to remind himself who he was and what he stood for: power and wealth. He went back for another mouthful of brandy, then strode across the carpet and opened the door.

'What do you want?' he demanded, but his voice broke into a sob.

'Follow me, Mr McMorgan.'

'Wouldn't you like a drink first?' He cleared his throat. 'I know I would. If you let me go, I can make it pay for you ...'

'You're our best hostage. You'll stay with us as long as it's necessary. Let's go.'

McMorgan could feel the blood draining from his face. 'But I need my medication. As the captain just said—'

Juliette pounced into the bathroom and swept all the medicine bottles into McMorgan's leather sponge bag.

'Now move!' Juliette had him by the arm and yanked him out into the corridor.

On the boat deck, Luke had to fight his way through the hordes of panic-stricken passengers. Outside, the powerful lights cast a yellow gleam that failed to penetrate very far into the dark mist that had enveloped the vessel like a shroud. The storm had died down. Working as fast as they could, the crew were ushering the passengers into the covered lifeboats. The barrel of a sub-machine-gun flashed rhythmically as warning shots were fired into the sky.

'Keep calm and do as the crew tells you!' roared one of the hijackers, but his own tone was anything but calm.

Luke understood that things had come to the crunch. What were the hijackers doing? He couldn't keep his thoughts away from the remaining hidden explosives, which could go off at any moment, sinking the vessel.

A woman clutching a handbag began to scream uncontrollably as she became caught in a rushing stream of passengers. Luke saw her go sprawling across the deck, her golden handbag trodden underfoot by the crowd. Most people were clearly thinking of only one thing: their own survival.

The deck hands swung open the gate in the railing and set to work on the davits that lowered the two-engine lifeboats into the sea. Each lifeboat was a vessel in itself: ten metres long, with a covered cabin. First, they were lowered flush with the deck, so as to allow the crew to test and warm up the engines. Diesel fumes drifted across the misty deck and the roar of the engines added a note of insane menace to the already nightmarish mood. Then the crew of each lifeboat began to usher passengers on board and as soon as the rescue station was emptied, the lifeboat was lowered onto its steel cables operated by the davit's electric motor.

Juliette dragged the stooped, pale-faced American property tycoon into one of the boats – the one where the sacks full of the passengers' jewellery and watches were also being loaded by Emilio Fernández.

'I have priority!' insisted a familiar voice. 'I represent the Emerald Cruise Corporation, let me through!' Max Lownie Junior was shouldering a path through the throng, indifferent to the imploring shrieks of his step-mother, who had fallen far behind.

Some passengers rushed eagerly for the safety of the lifeboat, while others held back, muttering among themselves. Suddenly there was a commotion when an old lady refused to get into the lifeboat and turned to rejoin the crowd, scared off by some rumour or other that had reached her.

Luke froze. There he was again: the tall blond man he suspected of being 'Helmut'. As before, the man seemed the only calm figure among many distraught faces. Leading the way when others hesitated, he boarded a lifeboat and offered his hand to the old lady. The old lady, totally hysterical now, was pushed forward by the crowd and the man pulled her up, but the woman's leg got caught in the narrow gap between the lifeboat and the side of the ship. When at last she was safely in the lifeboat, she still wouldn't calm down, bending over to scoop up the asthma inhaler that she'd dropped. No one paid her any attention. The inhaler was kicked out of reach by the tramping feet of others. The woman broke into a wail. Suddenly Luke saw a second, smaller pair of hands trying to reach the inhaler, flicking among the shoes and somehow managing to catch hold of the lost object.

It was Rosita! Luke saw her hand the asthma inhaler to its owner, but the lady, weeping hysterically, grabbed Rosita by the hair and began clawing at her face. Rosita screamed. Luke rushed forward to help. Just as he got into the lifeboat, he saw Rosita trying to reason with her adversary, but the old lady wasn't taking anything in.

Suddenly a strong arm sliced through the air and Rosita was thrown backwards by the force of the blow. Juliette had put an end to the skirmish.

Luke saw Rosita bring her hands up to her face, then the blood coursing between her fingers and down the backs of her hands.

'I was trying to help,' Rosita said.

'Get out of the lifeboat,' Juliette said. 'Stop interfering.'

Rosita climbed back onto the deck of the cruise ship. Luke tried to follow, but his path was blocked by a chain of men, members of the ship's crew, who were enforcing the hijackers' instructions.

'This is mine,' Juliette snarled at the old lady, grabbing hold of a pearl necklace half-hidden under the woman's shirt.

She ripped at the necklace and it snapped, sending pearls bouncing along the deck of the lifeboat. Juliette tossed the remains of the necklace to Emilio, who was standing in the next lifeboat along, surrounded by sacks of loot.

Within minutes, the rest of the passengers herded into the rescue station had been crammed into the lifeboat. Luke followed the weeping women and grimly staring men into the quarters below deck, which seemed ludicrously cramped compared with the vast spaces of the cruise ship. He glanced back and saw the deck hand give a signal to his colleague operating the davit. The lifeboat lurched, then began its slow descent towards the water.

All seats were taken, but Luke squeezed himself beside the window. By twisting his neck, he could still see the edge of the cruise ship's deck a few metres above him, but receding fast. Suddenly, a dark figure loomed against the misty sky, struggling with a smaller figure, who was being dragged to the gap in the railing from which the lifeboat was being launched.

Rosita. Luke felt a cold sensation around his heart as Emilio hurled the girl overboard, drawing screams from some of the passengers who were still on deck. Then there was a sickening thud overhead as Rosita landed on the roof of the descending lifeboat.

Luke scrambled towards the exit, which was easier said than done with so many passengers squeezed into the boat. He came to the steps leading out of the boat just as a member of the crew appeared, supporting Rosita, who could barely walk. The man led her to the space behind the wheelhouse, which was higher than the main cabin.

Rosita lay down on the floor. There was a gash on the back of her head and she was white, but when Luke took her hand, her dimples soon reappeared.

'They'll take you to hospital as soon as we get to dry land,' Luke said in a choked-up voice. 'You'll be OK.'

From close up, Rosita looked frighteningly pale. She had a lifeless air and it wasn't clear whether she was able to take in Luke's words. His heart lifted when she suddenly moved her lips and put her fingers to her chest.

'Take this... for good luck.' She held up an amulet hanging from a leather cord. 'I found it near an Aztec temple in Mexico.'

'No...'

'You need it more than I do... Lucas... Copernicus...'

'No... You do...'

Rosita sat up a little and Luke gently slipped the leather cord over her head. Her brow felt cold and clammy. He squeezed the amulet in his hand. He cleared his throat, but was unable to say anything. This was no time to start blubbering.

The moment the lifeboat splashed onto the waves, its engines burst into life and it surged forward, away from the cruise ship. Luke looked back through the open doorway. Within seconds, the *Ocean Emerald* was swallowed by the mist.

36

'People are being thrown overboard!' Captain Bauer roared at Delacroix on the bridge. 'You murderer!'

'One or two hysterical passengers have slipped off the deck, but your crew will fish them out.' The hijacker was calmly watching the chaotic scenes that were unfolding outside on the deck. He didn't even turn to look at the captain. 'A cold bath won't kill them. I should know.'

'I don't like your joke. I am responsible for the lives of my passengers. You're treating them like cattle.'

'They've given in to panic. The only thing that will help is a firm hand. You must lead by example.'

Bauer couldn't believe his ears. 'Don't think I'll get into a lifeboat before my ship is safely evacuated.'

'You're no longer the captain.'

'And you're no longer in your right mind.' Bauer stopped even trying to control himself. 'The captain never abandons his ship. You ignorant freak!'

At this, Delacroix finally turned from the window and fixed Bauer with a cold stare. 'You've done your heroic bit, so your reputation is safe. Now swallow your pride and do as you're told. It's best for your passengers as well.'

'What guarantee do I have of that?'

'None whatsoever. But you're getting on my nerves. Don't make the mistake of assuming I'll spare your life a second time.'

'I'll stay here on the bridge until the last passenger has been evacuated.'

As the conflict came to a head, Bauer noticed something that surprised and pleased him. *He was no longer afraid.*

Delacroix glanced at his watch.

'Suit yourself, Captain Bauer,' he said, and calmly left the bridge. Moments later, Bauer saw the Frenchman get into one of the last lifeboats.

Luke narrowed his eyes inside the dim, battery-lit cabin of the lifeboat, watching his suspect as closely as he could without being seen. The blond man looked like a tourist in his tweed jacket. Was he carrying one of the radio controls that could blow up the *Ocean Emerald*? If so, what was the range of the device?

Luke tried to peer out into the half-darkness, but the dark porthole only showed him his own reflection against the tongues of drifting mist. Suddenly, the engine tone changed. The sailor at the helm of the lifeboat called out: 'Prepare to disembark! There's no jetty, so we'll all get our feet wet. I'll pull up as close as I can.'

He stopped the lifeboat and began to help the passengers wade through the shallow water to the sandy beach. A dark forest loomed over the beach. Luke saw a group of passengers carrying Rosita to dry land. He hesitated, then joined another group, which was walking in the same direction as Helmut. Doing his best to stay out of sight, Luke kept his eye on his prey. He wasn't going to lose him a second time. The foggy air gave the scene an unreal, dreamlike quality. The passengers were gradually adjusting to the good news: they were no longer under armed guard, and the hidden explosives on board the *Emerald* could no longer hurt them. So were they saved? It seemed so, yet they felt disorientated by their surroundings. Many of the old-timers squelching through the mud towards the shore hadn't set foot in sea water for years.

As the passengers reached dry land, they pulled off their yellow life vests and tried to peer into the misty dusk. People spoke in whispers. The engines of a second lifeboat drew close, then went silent. More ghostly figures could already be seen landing a little further down the coast.

Luke was still watching when his man quietly slipped away from the other passengers and began to walk across the sand towards a small group of pine trees near the rocky shoreline. His stride was purposeful. Luke looked around for a member of the security team, but he was alone. He followed the man, keeping under cover of the pine trees bent by the sea wind.

Suddenly a twig snapped under Luke's foot. He froze, holding his breath. Just ahead of him, the back of a tweed jacket was half visible behind a fir tree. The man seemed to have stopped to listen. The sea wind whispering in the branches was almost the only sound.

The man continued on his way, apparently reassured, advancing into the forest along a narrow gravel track. Luke waited a good while before setting off after him.

The track curved behind the trees, but the crunching footsteps were clearly audible in the evening air. 'Helmut' – if it was him – was striding more rapidly now. Luke saw red lights glinting in the dusk – a car? Thinking he could hear voices ahead, he dashed behind a large, moss-coated boulder, and peered carefully round its edge. A grizzly old fir tree provided cover, but its swaying lower branches also made it difficult to see.

Luke could make out a Land Cruiser surrounded by a dozen or so people.

He recognized some of the faces, including Emilio and Juliette. And the skinny, stooped form of the property billionaire McMorgan – Thomson had pointed him out to Luke. Why had they taken the old man with them?

Luke's chest tightened when he suddenly saw the man he'd been following walk up to Delacroix and hand him a small black object.

'*Merci, Helmut!*' Delacroix gave his accomplice a slap on the shoulder. '*Du bon travail...*'

Suddenly, Helmut pulled off a false beard and stuffed it into the pocket of his tweed jacket. Luke understood at once: Helmut was a crew member, who'd mingled among the passengers in disguise.

Delacroix took out his radiophone and moved to one side.

'Captain Bauer, can you hear me?' Delacroix was speaking into the radiophone. His voice carried well in the silence of the dark forest. 'Please listen very, very carefully.'

Luke strained to see. In the hijacker's other hand was the black device that Helmut had given him. It had a flashing red light on it.

It was the second radio control for blowing up the ship.

Luke swallowed. Leaning his back against the boulder, he slid down, sitting on the soft carpet of pine needles on the forest floor.

* * *

From his station on the bridge, Captain Bauer could see nothing of the coast, just mist. Knowing he was the only person left on board filled him with immense pride. After a wobbly start, he'd stood up to the hijackers, twice, and won.

Or had he? Was the situation over? And if so, what had it all been about? Just the loot? The hijackers knew he was now at liberty to communicate with the outside world, but they didn't seem to care. Why?

He'd radioed the *Ocean Emerald*'s precise location to the authorities and explained the latest developments. He'd been told very little about the response to the hijacking in return – the authorities no doubt feared that any information they gave him would trickle through to the hijackers as well. However, he did discover that Max Lownie Senior, the company CEO, was in Helsinki, and had insisted on speaking to him personally as soon as possible.

Suddenly the radio crackled into life. Delacroix's steady voice filled the bridge. '*This is the last warning, Captain Bauer. Your passengers are safely on shore, as are we. Leave the ship. It's about to explode.*'

Bauer leaped for his microphone, intending to reply, but the line was dead. Why would the hijackers first evacuate, then sink and destroy the *Ocean Emerald*? It made no sense.

Bauer radioed Helsinki and was put through to Lownie. 'This is Captain Bauer on board the *Ocean Emerald*. All the passengers are safe. However, I'm afraid the hijackers have threatened to blow up the ship.'

'*That's insane... They already robbed it clean!*' The CEO's voice betrayed his turmoil. '*Are you sure all the passengers are safe?*'

'Yes, sir. The vessel is empty. I am here alone.'

'*Then get the heck out of there! You've done your duty, Captain.*'

'I'd rather wait here for the rescue team. I doubt the hijackers will set off those explosives. It's all smoke and mirrors – they're sowing confusion as they escape. Besides, Thomson's men managed to dispose of some of the bombs.'

'*They only found two. There are more bombs. Don't risk it. Leave the ship.*'

'With all due respect, I'll follow developments from here, then do as the situation demands.'

Bauer stared out into the mist that glowed in the lights of the immense ship. He felt almost dizzy with his new-found courage and pride.

37

'*Captain, you were warned and now it is done. The ship will explode in thirty seconds.*'

Captain Bauer was still standing at the front of the bridge, gazing over the brightly lit bow deck.

'*Twenty seconds... Captain? Can you hear me?*'

Bauer's eyes wandered to the Swiss wall clock, whose thin hand twitched forward in perfect silence. The framed picture on the shelf under the clock showed Bauer's wife and daughter, laughing at the camera...

'*Fifteen seconds.*'

Bauer stared at the photo, then suddenly came to himself and rushed for the door, wrenching down the handle. *Locked.*

Bauer turned his attention to the window that doubled as an escape hatch – a facility that the captain of a vessel this size never expected to use.

'*Ten...*'

Bauer worked the handle. The mechanism was poorly oiled and would barely move. It had probably never been touched since it had been made. Bauer grabbed it with both his hands, cursing aloud.

'*Five seconds, Captain. If you're still there, too bad for you. So long.*'

At last the window was unlocked and could be pushed open. Bauer hoisted himself up and thrust out a leg, reaching for the railing, which he used as a springboard for his leap into the darkness. The fall seemed to go on for ever. At the precise moment when he made impact with the sea, Bauer also felt a wave of pressure blast over him. Immense sheets of fire burst from the cabin windows, blazing high against the night.

A succession of deafening explosions shook the *Ocean Emerald*, and within moments, billowing smoke had covered the whole length of the vessel in a foul black cloud. Then the fire began to rage, licking at the misty air. Gagging and spluttering, Bauer spat sea water, raking at the freezing waves with his arms.

The hijackers had done it. Why, in God's name, had they finally done it?

Luke could see a monumental pillar of black smoke and an orange fireball blurred by the mist. There was a succession of booming sounds. For a fleeting moment he thought it was an earthquake, then he realized what had happened. He stared. A towering wall of flame rose up from the sea, as though the horizon itself was burning. He could see people on the beach taking photos – the photos that would be on tomorrow's front page.

He forced himself to return his attention to the group of hijackers behind the trees. The explosion had raised the stakes massively. The hijackers had wilfully committed a major-league crime – and were much, much more ruthless than Luke had realized. They were clearly working on the assumption that they wouldn't be caught. What if they found him spying on them now? By lowering himself onto the ground, under the trees, he got a better view. His elbows sank into the moss. He saw Delacroix fling the radio control casually onto the back seat of the seven-seat Land Cruiser.

There was a white 'D' surrounded by yellow stars on the left of the number plate. 'D' for 'Deutschland' – the car was registered in Germany.

Luke felt with his finger into his breast pocket and found the notepad and pencil stub he'd taken from his belt. It was difficult to write against the soft ground. Slowly, he recorded the registration number, the make and colour of the vehicle.

'You don't give up, do you?'

Luke's heart seemed to contract inside his chest. The voice told him who it was, but he received a second, more powerful shock when he turned and saw the rage blazing on the Frenchwoman's face. Juliette du Pont was standing right behind him, pointing a gun between his shoulders. The burning cruise ship made a flaming orange backdrop and gave her the air of a bat out of hell.

She took Luke's notepad and slapped him across the face. Surprised by his own nerve, Luke managed to hide the pencil in his fist, from where he transferred it to his jacket pocket.

Suddenly, Luke felt a big hand on his shoulder. He turned to face Delacroix, whose face was stained deep red by the glow of the fireballing ship.

'We meet again,' Delacroix said. 'Give me one reason to spare your life.'

Luke tried to think quickly. This was the first time he'd

set eyes on Delacroix since the moment they'd fallen over-board together. The man's eyes looked somehow naked without the glasses. Juliette gazed up at her master, wait-ing for his decision.

'Please,' Luke said. He couldn't think of anything else.

Delacroix ran his finger across his throat. Then Juli-ette and Delacroix began dragging Luke towards the Land Cruiser.

'Let me go . . .'

The hijackers didn't reply. They were close to the vehicle now. Someone held the back door open. The engine was running.

'Wait . . . There's something you should know.' Luke squirmed with all his strength. 'My dad works for a secret unit in Europol.'

Delacroix stopped. A look of shock passed over his face. He glanced at Juliette then shook Luke by his collar.

'Is that true?'

'Call him, if you like . . .' Luke was hyperventilating. He had to struggle to get the words out. 'If something happens to me, he'll never rest until you're all behind bars.'

'This is getting interesting.' Delacroix gave a dry laugh. 'Let's call him right away.'

PART
THREE

38

'*The* Ocean Emerald *has caught fire and is sinking just west of Pionerskij,*' screamed a voice through the radio speaker.

Peter Baron could feel his legs giving way beneath him, but by mustering all his willpower, he regained his self-possession.

'*There are lifeboats on shore . . . and crowds of people . . .*' continued the voice transmitted from a helicopter belonging to the Lithuanian Coastguard.

For Peter, these words were a ray of light in the darkness that had overwhelmed him – it was still possible that Luke was safe. He had to be.

Peter was standing among a huddle of officials in an office within the air-traffic control centre at Kaliningrad airport. The room was tall and dreary. On the huge wall map, the location of the *Ocean Emerald* was marked with a red pin. The text of the map was printed in Cyrillic letters.

'We have contact with the hijackers,' exclaimed Deputy Director Kanerva. His deep flush extended from his face to his swollen neck. 'And it looks like the media are all over this now. Several passengers had kept their mobile phones and have been calling home and TV stations from Lithuania.'

Peter bounded across to Kanerva and seized the extra headset that lay on the aluminium case containing the field communication centre. From the corner of his eye, he could see the bearlike figure of Mikhail Grimenko observing him with close interest.

'*This is Philippe Delacroix,*' said a calm, heavily accented French voice at the other end. '*Are you Peter Baron?*'

'That's me. Are the passengers all safe?'

'*Oh yes. Two of them are extra safe. An American billion-aire and your son.*'

'What do you mean?' Peter said. 'Why have you taken my son?'

Luke sat squeezed into a narrow gap between Delacroix and McMorgan in the back of the Land Cruiser. The hijackers hadn't counted on picking up an extra passenger at the last minute.

Luke was furious with himself. The previous day in Helsinki, he'd said nothing to Juliette about Dad's work, but now he'd cracked and Delacroix had a hotline to Dad.

Meanwhile, Juliette checked Luke's pockets, confiscating his biscuits, raisins, compass and pencil. She glanced at Luke's notepad, then laughingly tossed it onto the floor with some mocking remark in French about 'Young Sherlock Holmes'. Let them laugh, Luke thought to himself. He still had the beef jerky, the fructose tablets and the fishing line and hooks hidden inside his belt, and another stick of beef jerky in his sock. He was better rested than his captors. He was younger, too, and had sharper senses.

Delacroix was still on the phone.

'Mr Baron, your son is under my personal protection.' Delacroix put his hand on his prisoner's neck and clutched it lightly. 'He will remain safe as long as you follow our instructions to the letter.'

Luke shuddered at the touch of Delacroix's leathery fingers. He bit his lip. He couldn't hear Dad's reply. Delacroix hadn't said how he'd discovered that Luke was Peter Baron's son, but Dad would work it out. Luke wondered whether he'd done the right thing. Would they have killed him if he'd kept quiet?

'The passengers were all safely evacuated onto the Lithuanian coast before the *Ocean Emerald* exploded. I know you have a ship and a helicopter in the immediate vicinity. As soon as we give you the green light, they can move in to rescue the passengers. Good bye.'

'Where the hell are you taking me?' McMorgan shrieked. The freckled old American sitting next to Luke stank of spirits, and his voice carried none of the defiance he tried to put into his words. He clutched an overflowing sponge bag in his hands.

'I'm a sick man,' he continued. His face was a curious sickly shade of grey. 'I'll transfer you as much money as you like… Please let me go… Please…'

'Stop grovelling, Mr McMorgan!' Delacroix barked with sudden violence. 'The kid's got more guts than you have.'

Luke didn't like Delacroix's tone, but he felt a little flattered nevertheless.

'My medication…' McMorgan's voice was almost tearful. 'I can't read the labels…'

'Shut up!' Delacroix's eyes flashed with anger. 'Do you understand?'

Apparently the American did understand. Suddenly, there was silence in the Land Cruiser. The potholed, winding road was making Luke's stomach churn. The hijackers must have been bursting with relief at their successful escape, but they didn't speak, which was somehow inhuman. The headlights licked at the undergrowth and the trees that came dancing out of the mist.

Luke wondered what had become of Rosita – he hoped she was already safely in hospital.

He registered the signs of human activity on the roadside: here, a heap of rubbish; there, an abandoned car wreck. Yet the area seemed uninhabited. Luke hadn't seen a single house or light among the trees.

As they drove deeper inland, the mist thinned, then disappeared. The forest grew thicker and taller. Black clouds drifted in front of the full moon. The road that flickered under the headlights seemed to be getting narrower and even more winding. Soon, it would be impassable terrain, even for the Land Cruiser.

'They chose me because I am rich,' McMorgan said, blinking at Luke. 'Are you rich too?'

'I wish,' Luke said.

'Do you mind if I hold your arm?'

'Go ahead.'

Clutching Luke's arm with his claw-like hands, and resting his head against Luke's shoulder, the old man fell asleep – impressive, given the state of the road. Suddenly Luke saw wire netting in the headlights. A row of rusted and bent fence posts stood askew, half-supporting coils of barbed wire. The car swung through a rickety gate. Could this be the hijackers' base? Didn't they understand that the whole region would be searched?

The door of a small warehouse swung in the wind, its shattered windowpanes staring blindly. The headlights flashed in the broken glass that littered the ground. Suddenly, McMorgan slumped on top of Luke. After a struggle, he managed to heave the skinny, snoring billionaire into an upright position.

The Land Cruiser crawled past the shell of an abandoned car, its tyres long gone. Bricks and bits of black rubber lay scattered on the ground. A bump almost sent McMorgan keeling over again. Rusted through, the abandoned barrels looked like oversized drink cans. Nature had got the better of a concrete slab, pushing grass out of its cracks. Suddenly Luke realized they were on an abandoned airstrip.

The realization set his heart racing madly. Unable to take notes or to check his bearings, he tried instead to memorize everything he saw: the charred carcass of a large military helicopter, wheels from an aircraft's undercarriage, the remains of an armoured personnel carrier... The Land Cruiser hurtled through the fog onto the pitted surface of the landing strip. The vehicle bounced and Luke almost hit his head against the ceiling. Incredibly, McMorgan slept on, mottled head rolling from side to side like a ball.

Then the driver applied the brakes. Luke gasped. They'd pulled up beside a small business jet and he'd immediately recognized the sleek contours of a Learjet, which looked like a miniature passenger jet. The purple fuselage sparkled in the headlights. Apparently brand new, the beautiful little plane looked utterly out of place in this Godforsaken place.

The hijackers dismounted and hurried towards the folding steps leading up to the aircraft door.

'You too,' Juliette shouted over the roar of the idling jet, addressing her words to McMorgan and Luke.

Luke got up as told, glancing at the sleeping figure of McMorgan, who seemed oblivious to the noise around him. The sponge bag had spilled its contents all over the floor.

'He needs a hospital,' Luke said. 'You should let him go.'

Delacroix shook the old man by the shoulder, to no avail, then grabbed his wrist, feeling for a pulse.

'Get me some light,' he called to Juliette.

Juliette handed him a torch, which Delacroix shone into McMorgan's face, using his free hand to pull up the man's right eyelid.

'The old man's had an attack of some sort.' Delacroix's voice was thoughtful, and completely calm. 'We should let him go, as the boy says.'

'But the strategy was to keep one high-value hostage!' Juliette screamed. 'McMorgan is a billionaire! This boy is worth nothing!'

Delacroix stared at her. 'Are you done?'

'Sorry,' Juliette seemed to shrink a little. 'Of course, you decide…'

'I say this boy is now the most valuable hostage we have.' Delacroix clutched Luke by the neck. 'Does your dad care about you, boy?'

'Of course,' Luke said, without a moment's hesitation.

'We'll see. I know mine didn't. He left us.' Delacroix pushed Luke away and gave his cheek a hard pinch with his calloused fingers. 'Then the old bastard went and died. But at least he didn't become a cop.'

Leaving McMorgan asleep on the back seat of the

Land Cruiser, the hijackers marched Luke up the steps and into the narrow cabin of the aircraft. Luke found himself in a cream-coloured seat. The interior was decorated with wood panelling and dark felt. In more auspicious circumstances, he would have loved the chance to fly in a Learjet. As things stood, the fear was almost more than he could handle.

What would happen when they didn't need their last hostage any more – the hostage who knew their escape route?

He fastened the seat belt and summoned all his will-power to quash his fear. He had to focus on something practical he could do. There was no point fretting over things he could neither predict nor control. He'd made it this far, so why shouldn't things turn out for the best?

He suddenly realized that he was weak with hunger. He bitterly regretted not having eaten his biscuits and raisins while he had the chance. He'd neglected his intake of calories and fluid – an elementary mistake. There was a bottle of water in the small woven pocket at the side of his seat. Without asking for permission, he opened it and gulped down the contents.

Juliette took the seat facing his and Delacroix soon buckled himself into the seat across the aisle from Luke. The cabin was surprisingly cramped, with a total of eight seats, four on either side of the narrow aisle. So this little tin of sardines was what the likes of Bill Gates and Lewis Hamilton used to shuttle across the world?

The engines revved up and the Learjet nudged forward. The state of the runway made itself felt as the taxiing plane bounced and clattered along. Luke saw Juliette peering out of the oval porthole, but she wasn't likely to see much in the darkness, unless it was her own unpleasant reflection.

The Learjet turned and the engine noise became yet louder. Luke tried to glance out of his own porthole, and as he feared, there was no sign of any runway lights. Could the plane take off without them?

It was to be hoped so, because suddenly the pilot brought the turbines to full power and the Learjet went rocketing forward, juddering along the pitted tarmac. Luke clutched at his armrests. In front of him, Juliette looked as composed as she had when she'd met him at the Reception desk the day before.

At a stroke, the plane stopped vibrating as it swept into the air and went howling into the night.

39

Peter Baron stared down at the oil slick on the sea from the window of a Russian Mi-8 military helicopter. It was hard to accept. The oil that glistened in the chopper's searchlight was all that was left of the two-hundred-and-forty-metre luxury cruise ship.

Peter clenched his fists. It had now become obvious that the hijackers were ready to do anything. And Luke was their hostage.

Peter could only pray that his son wouldn't go and try anything clever again – clever though the boy certainly was, on occasion. He was good at sizing up difficult situations and a past master at manipulating adults. He could lead his mother and grandparents by the nose, and Peter, too. Luke sometimes even amused himself at the expense of complete strangers. Riding the Paris metro on a school trip from Brussels, he had once persuaded a group of Asian tourists to visit the palace of the King of France – although France had abolished the monarchy after the Revolution of 1789.

The helicopter cabin was austere in the extreme, with not a shred of unnecessary padding or decoration. Down below, the orange lifeboats rocked in the shallow water.

Then the searchlight swept onto a group of people, a huge mass of them, waving up at the helicopter from the shore. The chopper swooped towards them.

Unable to help himself, Peter scanned the crowd for his son, but he knew he was kidding himself. The passengers looked cold and shaken, and some were lying or sitting on the shore, but they seemed to have got off lightly.

The pilot guided the helicopter a little way inland and touched down on a patch of field in the forest. The beach wasn't a good option, as the sand whipped up by the blades of the chopper could have damaged the engine. Peter flicked off his seat belt and was on his way to the hatch when Mikhail Grimenko gave a grunt and pulled him back into his seat.

'*An unidentified plane has taken off from an abandoned airfield in Romanovo, refusing to contact air-traffic control in Kaliningrad.*' The heavily accented voice in Peter's earphones was harsh and metallic. '*Hold it... We now have a visual on a Learjet, which took off without authorization... It's them.*'

'They must be dreaming if they think they can just fly away.'

'We have an ID from the unidentified plane,' a voice from the cockpit cut in. 'They'll patch it through to us.'

'Put that through to everyone's earphones,' Grimenko said, squaring his shoulders.

'*Kaliningrad, do you hear me?*'

'We hear you,' Grimenko replied.

'*I won't remind you what will happen to our hostages if we're followed or interfered with. We'll tell you our final demands after we've reached our destination. Until then, we'll observe radio silence.*'

The voice was cut off briefly, then continued again.

'*We left an American passenger in a car at Romanovo military airfield. His medication is on the floor of the vehicle.*'

Then the voice went off the air for good.

'We'll scramble some MiG fighters to intercept them and force them to land.' Grimenko's voice boomed with relish. 'We'll squash these bastards like a rotten fruit.'

'Not so fast.' Peter Baron tried to keep his voice as mild as he could. 'We need to reach a joint decision.'

Peter glanced at Deputy Director Kanerva, but the man kept his eyes on the floor.

'That just sums you up!' Grimenko barked with surprising violence, turning deep red. 'Europol! You Westerners consult and dither. Action! We need action! Time is on the hijackers' side.'

'There's precisely nothing we can do while the plane is airborne.' Peter removed the Russian's big hand from his shoulder, took off his helmet and hurried to the hatch.

'Are you new to this game? We've got decades of experience fighting the Chechens and other terrorists.' Grimenko followed Peter out of the chopper. 'Those bastards won't know what hit them!'

'Let's debrief the passengers first, and see if we can get a sense of what the hijackers are after.'

Peter went down the steps and hopped onto the grass, followed by Grimenko, the four other Russians and the waddling figure of Kanerva. Dust and dry leaves spun in the air agitated by the idling rotors. The searchlights threw elongated shadows of the men and lit up the surrounding trees.

A big-jawed American came running from the direction of the shore to meet them. His trousers were wet up to the thighs. His hair had been shorn off, but someone had made a patchy job of it.

'I'm Craig Thomson, head of security on the *Ocean Emerald*,' the American shouted over the clamour of the helicopter. 'Who's in charge of the operation?'

'I am.' Peter extended his hand. Strictly speaking, Kanerva was in charge, but this wasn't a time to be pedantic. 'Peter Baron. Does the name Luke Baron mean anything to you?'

The American's eyebrows shot up. 'Sure. The kid on board. Quite a trooper. Why, is he your…?'

'Yes, he's my son. They still have him.'

Grimenko shouldered in between them. 'With all due respect to Europol, may I suggest a firm approach?'

'The hijacking took place in international waters. As the representative of Europol, I'm responsible for coordinating the international police operation.' Turning his back to Grimenko, Peter tried to pull Thomson to one side. 'Are all the passengers safe?'

'We know the hijackers took a wealthy American with them,' Thomson said. 'And you've just told me your son is also being held hostage. I can't confirm it, but I didn't see him after the freed passengers came ashore.'

'And how are they doing?' Peter forced himself to take a professional view.

'They're in good shape. A few minor scratches and sprains and some of the old folk are pretty shaken up. One young woman is more seriously injured and must be flown to hospital as soon as possible.'

'What about the captain?'

'Captain Bauer was the last to leave the ship. He only just made it out on time and is currently resting. It was a cold swim.'

Two more helicopters appeared through the darkness and prepared to land.

'Fantastic, more choppers at last!' A seriously over-weight young American came limping up behind Thomson. 'My name is Max Lownie Junior. I'm the son of the CEO. I'm injured, and it's really important that I see him as soon as—'

'Wait your turn.' Thomson cut him short and set off at a brisk pace. Peter kept close to his side.

'Any idea where the hijackers are going?'

'None. They haven't played to a predictable pattern.'

'Who, apart from my son, had the most contact with them on board?'

'I, my team and the captain had that pleasure. The injured girl, who worked in one of the ship's kitchens, was also in contact with them.'

'If you'd be so kind, I want a quick word with all three of you right now.'

No matter how many times he swallowed, Luke couldn't unblock his ears. The Learjet jolted and bucked in the turbulence, and the steady roar of the engines made it hard to think straight. His hand strayed to the leather cord and the amulet that Rosita had given him. He hoped she was OK. Surely she was safely in hospital already?

Luke had no watch, but he estimated that they'd been flying for about an hour. He glanced around. Delacroix had reclined his seat, as though to rest, but his eyes were wide open. In the seat facing Luke, Juliette sat simmering with nervous tension. It scared him even to think how that tension might be released. On the folding table in front of Delacroix lay the familiar black-leather diary. He'd left it there when he got up to use the bathroom, but Luke couldn't risk a closer look in full view of Juliette.

'May I also use the facilities?' Luke asked when Delacroix returned to his seat.

'*Plus tard*,' Delacroix said and a small, sadistic smile played at the corner of his mouth. 'Later.'

'Later,' Juliette parroted.

They made him wait for half an hour, or more, before Delacroix nodded at him, like a tyrant dispensing an enormous favour.

'Where are we going?' Luke asked when he returned to his seat.

'No questions,' Juliette snapped.

Luke could hardly believe he'd found this woman attractive when he first saw her. The sharp, paranoid stare was chilling. He felt it on his skin right now, as he closed his eyes and pretended to sleep.

His mind was working furiously. The Learjet would be tracked by radar; that was certain. And as soon as it landed, special forces would be sent swarming all over it. But if the airport happened to be a remote one, Delacroix and his team would have a head start... So were they heading somewhere inaccessible?

But what if no one had even noticed when the jet took off? That would mean it might never be found – and that Luke was completely on his own.

Perhaps escaping by business jet wasn't such a stupid idea. The hijackers seemed to have planned every detail of their operation with absolute care, and the getaway was probably designed most carefully of all.

40

With a sinking heart, Peter watched the small green dot as it crawled slowly across the radar screen in Polish airspace. That was the Learjet carrying the hijackers and, possibly, his son.

He'd just returned to the air-traffic control room at Kaliningrad airport, having debriefed those members of the *Ocean Emerald*'s crew who had personally communicated with the hijackers: Captain Bauer; Head of Security, Craig Thomson and his team; and Rosita Jimenez, a kitchen maid. None of them had discovered anything that might shed light on the hijackers' deeper motives or destination.

That they lacked any scruple or restraint had become abundantly clear when they'd calmly sunk the *Ocean Emerald*. Rosita's account of Luke's bravery filled Peter with pride.

The valuables and credit-card payments extorted from the passengers suggested a financial motive. But it could have been subterfuge. And if the hijacking was just a heist, why sink the vessel without any reason?

Judging by its current course, the hijackers' little plane would soon slip outside the range of the surveillance radar and into German airspace. The elite German *Grenzschutz-gruppe 9*, or Border Guard Group 9 – known as GSG-9 – had been put on standby in St Augustine, east of Bonn, in case the plane tried to land in Germany. Peter's unit in Europol had no operational resources or even powers of arrest of its own, but relied entirely on the national police forces: they were its only teeth.

An unmarked Russian Air Force Yak miniature jet was ready for take off at Kaliningrad airport, but no one had issued the command to give chase just yet.

Another plane also waited at the airport – this one chartered by Max Lownie Junior at his personal expense from a business jet service provider in Kaliningrad. The son of the ship's owner was impatient to go home, it seemed.

Grimenko cleared his throat and spoke in his booming bear's voice. 'I suggest we intercept now and force the suckers down at Gdansk airport. Alpha is ready to go.'

'Let's not panic. They still have a hostage,' Peter said calmly. He knew he couldn't restrain Grimenko for ever.

Luckily, the Germans would soon have a stake in the crisis. A representative from the Federal Criminal Police Office of Germany (BKA) was already liaising with Baron's team. Kanerva had flown back to Helsinki, and good riddance. The operation was no longer a national problem. It was a European problem, and that made it Peter's and Europol's job to sort it out.

'Don't you understand?' Grimenko bellowed. 'They're using diversionary tactics. I say they'll head straight back to Mother Russia, and when they do, we'll be ready.'

'This is an international incident,' Peter said. 'You don't have a monopoly on decision-making.'

'*I agree with the previous speaker,*' said the voice of a German official over the speakerphone, to Peter's relief. '*We're ready to provoke a forced landing if we have to. GSG-9 has ample experience of hostage-taking situations.*'

Peter's relief gave way to another surge of anguish. If the Germans chose to get physical in German airspace, that was their decision. At least GSG-9 was a quality outfit… Peter flicked his gaze back to the radar. The course of the green spot had changed fractionally, bending towards Czech airspace.

'What are they playing at?' he said as much to himself as to his colleagues around the radar screen.

The plane described a turn that seemed to go on and on. Finally, the course straightened out, heading for Austria. It was now miles away from Kaliningrad and Russian jurisdiction.

'Unpredictable, these bastards. Oh well.' Grimenko crossed his short, thick arms and went into a sulk. 'We remain at your disposal if you want help.'

The plane slipped off the radar and Peter turned his attention to the huge map of Europe on the table. Air-traffic controllers would update them on the plane's movements.

What on earth were the hijackers planning? Only one thing could be predicted for sure: the Learjet would need to refuel within a few hours at most.

'*Radar cover is patchy over the Alps and we might lose them,*' the German voice on the speakerphone broke the silence. '*Maybe that's their plan.*'

'We need a list of Alpine airfields or other landing strips,' Peter said. 'Everything that's off the radar.'

'*It's just a handful of valleys. We'll send patrols to each one just in case.*'

Peter rested his gaze on the patchwork that was Europe. 'I suggest we also move closer to the area where they seem to be heading.'

Luke felt his seat drop away under him before leaping up once more, as the Learjet rode the turbulence. He needed every cell of his body to fight the need to vomit. Looking on the bright side, the nausea was a welcome distraction from the burning fear.

It brought back the memory of a car trip to the South Downs when his grandfather was still alive. That time, he'd lost the battle and vomited into a crisp packet – to the appalled amusement of his cousins, who still reminded him of it to this day.

He tried to peer out of the porthole, but night had fallen. He had no idea what direction they'd flown in. Surely the fuel would run out at some stage?

Across the aisle, Delacroix rose to his feet and opened a locker above his seat. Luke sensed the tension mounting in the cabin. The Frenchman lowered a backpack onto the floor. Emilio and Juliette did the same, and Helmut followed suit.

Luke wondered what the hijackers were doing with their backpacks before the plane even landed... Then, with a jolt of alarm, he realized what the taut packs in fact were: parachutes.

The drowsy calm on board gave way to swift but orderly activity. The hijackers strapped their chutes on and helped each other check the equipment. The door of the cockpit opened and the pilot shouted out a set of co-ordinates – probably the plane's location.

Luke turned to his porthole and was amazed to see a majestic white mountain range glowing in the moonlight. The Alps? The Caucasus? The Urals? Or somewhere even more exotic?

Once the others were ready, Delacroix pulled on a pair of grey overalls and harnessed himself into his parachute, leaning on the armrest of his seat to fasten the thigh straps.

Luke saw the simple brilliance of the plan. The hijackers would disappear into the sky and the plane would land somewhere far away with just the pilot and the hostage on board. By then, the hijackers would have got away. But the pilot was also an accomplice... how would he evade capture?

Then he saw exactly what he had feared: the pilot appeared in the cabin and he, too, began strapping on a parachute. He'd apparently put the Learjet onto autopilot.

Luke felt panic wrenching at his insides. *How many parachutes were there? Was there one for him? Or were they going to abandon him on board the doomed plane?*

41

Eight hundred kilometres away, the unmarked Russian Yak mini jet that had been standing at Kaliningrad airport had finally taken to the air.

Peter was sitting in the rear of the plane, facing Grimenko. He was in constant communication with his Europol unit in Brussels, where the international police operation to apprehend the hijackers was being co-ordinated. Also on board the Yak were several Russian officials, although the Russian Federation had no powers outside its own territory – thankfully, Peter thought. Whatever country the fugitive plane decided to land in would become responsible for the immediate response and local manhunt.

The credit card payments extorted by way of a ransom had been traced as far as the Cayman Islands, but then the trail went cold, for now. The local banking secrecy rules meant that a court decision was needed before the transactions could be investigated any further, which meant waiting until the next day.

Peter had been using a red pen to trace out the path of the fugitive plane onto the map on the folding table in front of him, his heart sinking further with each cross he drew. According to Swiss control, at present, the Learjet was somewhere over Lucerne, heading west.

'*They're reducing their altitude,*' Zurich local air-traffic control reported over the radio.

'Is there an airport in the vicinity?' Peter demanded.

'*Bern is closest, Geneva is second closest.*'

'Any other place to land?'

'*None whatsoever. The valleys in the area are just narrow ravines. They're accessible by four-wheel-drive, at best.*'

Peter let out a sigh. The hijackers still had the whip hand. So far, every move by the authorities had been like a reflex determined by what the hijackers did first. The perpetrators would call the shots until they lost control of their hostages... Until Luke was safe... Yet again, Peter the dad came onto a collision course with Peter the professional. One said softly, softly, avoid all risks, while the other analysed the situation with cold precision and sifted alternative courses of action – including force. How could he ever decide between the two?

He looked at his personal mobile and found yet another text message from Hanna, demanding news, begging him to keep Luke safe.

'We'll have to refuel in about one hour at the latest,' Grimenko grunted, rolling his chunky shoulders. 'This piece of '70s Soviet junk is as thirsty as they come.'

'They'll be refuelling, too.'

'Not as soon as us. A Learjet has a good range.'

'OK then.' Peter tapped the map with his finger. 'Let's land in Zurich and see what they do next.'

***

Luke watched helplessly as the hijackers and the pilot prepared to bail out.

'What are you doing?' He had to shout over the screaming engine. 'Don't leave me—'

'Shut up and wait for instructions.' Juliette nodded in the direction of Delacroix, who was standing further down the narrow aisle.

Luke sat frozen. The pilot tramped back into his cockpit with the parachute on his back. The plane seemed to turn a fraction and it was steadily losing height.

Luke tried to make out the shapes in the cloudy darkness below. Here and there he saw a toothy ridge or a snow-covered peak bathed in moonlight, but the valleys between were plunged in darkness. He was caught in a nightmare. Something like this could only be a dream, yet he knew for sure he wouldn't wake up in his own bed.

Delacroix got down onto his knees beside Luke's seat and spoke with a new urgency.

'Listen carefully to what I say. You and I will do a tandem jump.'

'I take it you're being funny?'

'It's a routine procedure.' Delacroix clutched at Luke's cheek with his leathery hand. 'Don't worry, son, you won't have to do anything.'

Luke had to fight for breath. Although it was better than being abandoned on a pilotless plane, the prospect of hurling himself off the plane in mid-flight with this character filled him with terror.

He struggled to his feet and took the overalls that Delacroix handed him. They slipped on easily and he had to roll up the sleeves and legs. Delacroix clipped on the harness and showed Luke how to fasten the thigh straps.

'Good work,' Delacroix said. 'Lucky it's you, not McMorgan.'

'Lucky for him,' Luke said.

The metal links snapped into place, binding Luke's fate to that of his captor. If something went wrong, they'd plummet to their deaths together. Strapped to the hijacker, Luke felt like a ventriloquist's dummy. His heart raced inside him, like some deranged clockwork toy.

Only now did Luke notice the four grey sacks that had been tethered together and equipped with their own parachute and automatic activation device.

Emilio was already crouched beside the door. Juliette was saying something into her radiophone, her face burning with nervous excitement. She was probably talking to someone on the ground. The hijackers all seemed to know exactly what they needed to do at a given moment – they had no doubt rehearsed the jump over and over again. But this was the real thing and it showed on their faces. Even ever-relaxed Helmut was looking distinctly green around the gills.

'Did you know,' Luke said aloud, wondering whether Delacroix could hear, 'that the world record for a freefall without a parachute is—'

'Hold onto that seat,' Delacroix said into his ear.

Luke grabbed the armrest just as Emilio opened the plane's door and the cabin pressure was sucked out into the cold night.

Juliette clutched the radiophone closer to her ear, struggling to hear. Finally, she signalled to Emilio with her hand.

Emilio shoved the sacks out of the door and into the void, then grabbed Juliette's hand and helped her dive after them.

'Go!' Delacroix shouted into Luke's ear.

For the first time in his life, Luke knew what it felt like to have his legs paralysed by fear. He just managed to shuffle forward to the rhythm of Delacroix's steps as the Frenchman frogmarched him to the oval door. The air rushed past at such violent speed that it was difficult to snatch a single breath. Without so much as pausing at the door, Delacroix tensed his legs and sprang into the void with Luke in front of him.

The lurch that Luke felt in his stomach was a hundred times wilder than anything he'd ever experienced on a funfair ride. White crags floated like islands in the inky darkness far below. The roar of the plane died away, and Luke experienced a moment of thrilling excitement that almost made him forget the situation he was in. It didn't even feel like falling, because they were travelling so fast that the atmosphere pushed back at them like a huge airbag.

They'd been falling for many seconds now. What if the parachute failed to open? Hot fear squirted into Luke's limbs.

'Is everything OK?' he shouted but his voice was swept into the darkness that was speeding past.

'I can't hear you,' Delacroix said into his ear. 'Relax, son, everything will be fine.'

'I'm not your son, mate,' Luke mouthed into the cold air.

Moments later, Luke felt the hijacker make a sudden jerking movement, and with a flutter and a snap, the parachute blossomed out behind them. Luke glanced up and saw the taut fabric above him. The hurtling freefall came to a stop and they were floating softly through the air.

It felt like being on a swing suspended from an immense height. Luke's eyes were stinging from the cold breeze, but he couldn't help staring in awe at the sublime mountains around him. Some distance ahead and below, another parachute was floating towards the ground. Delight at the experience got the better of Luke's fear.

He could now see jagged rocks on the black mountain slopes below, rocks that looked like they could cut you to pieces. But Delacroix was steering the chute with visible skill, and they skimmed deeper and deeper into a valley surrounded by massive mountains on all sides.

As they approached the ground, their speed seemed to increase.

'*Attention!*' Delacroix shouted. 'Pull up your legs.'

Luke had, in fact, already instinctively done just this. Let the Frenchman by all means take the impact of the landing, cushioning his unwilling passenger. The wind buffeted the chute during the final approach. At last, they made contact with the ground, tumbling into the dark vegetation.

As they recovered for a few seconds, Luke realized that they were on a sloping meadow, probably in the Alps. Then he heard the snap of metal and he was free of his harness.

Delacroix began to fold away the parachute. Luke was euphoric: he'd survived! Then, at a stroke, the feeling disappeared. He was still a hostage whose life only had value as a bargaining chip. The moment he lost that value, he would become a liability.

That moment was close now.

'Take off the overalls.' Delacroix began stuffing the parachute back into its backpack. 'We're continuing right away.'

Someone – Emilio, perhaps – thudded to the ground a few hundred metres away. Another figure stowing his parachute could be made out up in the distance. The moonlit silence had a dreamlike quality. A third parachute was still making its way down. The sacks of booty had presumably been the first to land. But what would happen to the Learjet, which Luke could no longer see or hear?

Delacroix had finished packing up his chute. He said a couple of words into his radiophone. The figure higher up the slope began signalling with a bright lamp, playing its beam down into the valley.

Luke scanned his surroundings, desperately scouting for a means of escape. The moonlit mountain range laid siege to the forested valley below. He'd skied in the Swiss Alps when he lived in Geneva, and he knew that the more secluded Alpine valleys could be dozens of kilometres from human habitation – assuming these were the Alps. The hijackers had probably chosen the remotest spot they could find. Luke had the wrong clothes and footwear for a mountain hike… One thing was clear: running away in this location would be suicide.

He was a valuable hostage, but Luke knew he was also a dangerous witness. What reason would the hijackers have to keep him alive?

Suddenly Luke heard the growl of a car engine and saw a pair of silvery Xenon headlights cutting through the gloom. The powerful four-by-four handled the gradient without any trouble at all. He recognized the hulking, streamlined features of the approaching vehicle: a Porsche Cayenne. It groaned up the last stretch of meadow and stopped right beside them. The driver hopped out, leaving the engine idling, and greeted Delacroix in French before going round the back to open the boot. Delacroix swung his backpack inside.

Luke kept his eyes on the open driver's door and the rest of the hijackers standing behind the boot. Suddenly, acting by instinct more than reason, he flung himself behind the wheel of the Cayenne and jerked the door shut. His driving experience was limited to Toni's clapped-out old Nissan, but he'd raced countless times in Paris-Dakar, Daytona and Hockenheim, even if it was only on games like *Driver* and *Midtown Madness*.

The Cayenne was an automatic. Luke shifted from Park to Drive. As he slammed the accelerator to the floor, he glanced at the side mirror and saw Delacroix lunging for the driver's door. The mighty engine roared and the Cayenne reared forward. Beeps and flashes from the on board computer warned him that the boot was open. He'd overdone his initial acceleration, almost losing control, but the beast settled under him. It was solid as a tank, but it wasn't designed for a desperate fourteen-year-old without a licence on a dark mountain slope. Yet it did more or less what he wanted.

Resisting the urge to stare into his mirrors, Luke focused every brain cell on the search for a route away from the meadow. He'd hoped to find a road, but the dreadful thought dawned on him that maybe there wasn't one: the Cayenne might have driven off-road for miles.

Squeezing the wheel, Luke tried to read the alien landscape stroked by the bluish headlights. To his right, the meadow sloped steeply upwards. To his left there was pitch-black forest. The meadow seemed to be narrowing, but Luke had been watching carefully and he was one hundred per cent sure that he was driving in the direction from which the car had come.

The colourful screen of the GPS system on the dashboard caught his eye. He studied the map, then felt a hard thud under the front of the car. The meadow was getting bumpier and the space between the trees had dwindled to almost nothing. Immediately ahead, sparse forest could be seen and leading through it, a narrow passage.

Luke felt like shouting for joy. The track would bring him down to a real road, civilization. Toni would be very impressed when he heard about this. Luke could hear the tyres spewing dirt and stones against the wheel housings. Fear and triumph battled inside him. He was awash with adrenaline. The stench of damp earth he'd noticed up on the meadow had been replaced with a refreshing scent of pine, which made its way into the car despite the windows being closed.

The track widened at last, the forest ended and Luke saw a stony ridge, with sky behind it. He allowed himself a sigh of relief and felt his face relax into a smile.

He paid the price at once, when a massive boulder loomed up out of the darkness and he had to swing the wheel to the left, to avoid a crash. But this put the Cayenne into a slide. With a lurch, the car came out of the slide, and then went fishtailing the other way. He was going too fast, but fearing another skid, Luke didn't dare apply the brakes, letting the car run out of momentum instead. Somehow, he managed to tame the vehicle once more. The smile was well and truly wiped off his face and he could feel cold sweat dribbling down his temples.

As he slowly took the next corner, his heart almost stopped. He was on a narrow ledge that skirted the edge of a ravine on his right. With a shudder, he realized what a close call it had been. If he hadn't brought the vehicle back under control, he'd have driven off the mountain to his death. It was right there in the rear-view mirror: the moon, the stars and the void beneath. He knew he was holding the wheel too tightly, but it was better that way. Gently, gently, he eased his foot off the accelerator, slowing down to a crawl.

At least he was now on a road, of sorts, even if it had a wall on one side and nothingness on the other. Rocks and potholes streamed towards him in the bright headlights. Behind the ravine on the right, the dark mountains towered majestically against the starlit night. It was like the Corsican leg of the *Colin McRae* game – although Luke had never experienced heart palpitations at his computer screen.

He couldn't fight away the image of the tyres losing their purchase, of the plunge into emptiness... Would he have time to think? Would he see his life flashing past? Or would those seconds pass in agonizing slow motion?

Luke redoubled his concentration. The lip of rock on which he was driving seemed to be getting smaller and smaller. On his left, the mountain soared up almost vertically, and on his right, it dropped away right behind the passenger door... Suddenly, the right wheel hammered into a pothole and Luke instinctively swung the wheel in the opposite direction. The left side of the Cayenne grazed the rock face. The screech of grating metal was painful to hear. Sparks showered off the bodywork behind the window. Had the pothole been on the other side, Luke's reflex would have put him into the ravine...

Then, suddenly, the ledge ended and Luke found himself in a short tunnel, which led into another valley. He was now on a serpentine road, with shelving rock on either side. Small bits of stone pattered onto the bonnet and went skimming up the windscreen. What if a bigger stone came rolling off the mountain?

He quickly had his answer when, seconds later, it happened. He knew at once there was nothing he could do.

Flashing past, the boulder crashed into the bonnet and leaped into the ditch.

Luke stamped on the brakes and prayed for good luck. He thought he saw lights ahead, but he didn't have time to think. The car limped on, then suddenly came to a stop with a loud bang. The headlamps shattered. There was a sound of crunching metal and the whole world went suddenly white as Luke's head jerked forward into the airbag ballooning out of the steering wheel. He'd always assumed airbags were soft, but it took him a few moments to get over the blow.

With a slow hiss, the airbag emptied under him. When he raised his head, Luke was puzzled to see bright lights immediately ahead. Then he understood: he'd crashed into an oncoming vehicle. He sheltered his eyes with his hand. Through the high-pitched whistling in his ears, he could hear an angry voice speaking in French.

Sweet relief welled up inside him. The other driver would surely have a mobile and they could use it to call the police.

'Get out,' an entirely unsympathetic female voice ordered in French, then continued into a phone. 'We've got the little bastard. The Cayenne's wrecked, but the Range Rover is still driveable.'

With a crushing sense of defeat, Luke understood. The hijackers had two pick-up cars and he'd just crashed one into the other. He looked at the driver of the other car and felt a queasy jolt of recognition. Fear stirred deep inside him. He hadn't seen her before, but she had the same, nervous energy as Juliette and the same wild eyes. *It had to be her sister.*

'I'm Eva,' she said. 'Don't mess with me.'

42

In the air-traffic control room at Kloten Airport near Zurich, Peter tugged out the pin that showed the location of the hijackers' Learjet on the map. They were heading west across the Alps, towards France.

'*The French special forces are on standby at Le Bourget,*' said the voice of the officer leading the operation in Paris. The speakerphone was set up for a conference call.

It was looking more and more obvious that the hijackers were escaping to France. In any case, they only had fuel left for another hour or two at the very most.

'*We've tried to make contact with the plane, but with no success,*' the French voice continued.

'That's no surprise,' Peter said, hearing the exhaustion in his own voice. 'They said they'd observe total radio silence from now on.'

Peter had concluded some time ago that consistency and an unusual degree of tough-mindedness were the hallmarks of these hijackers. These traits combined to create a certain candour: these people meant what they said. But what were they after? Professional thieves wouldn't engage in wanton destruction by sinking a brand-new forty-five-thousand-tonne luxury cruise ship. In terms of the material damage caused, the act was tantamount to levelling a small city.

'*The Learjet is now passing just north of Lyon and continuing towards the Dordogne,*' said the French official over the speakerphone.

Frowning at the map, Peter jabbed the red pin into the new position.

Passing through the tunnel and back onto the mountain ledge, where the ravine now yawned on his left side, Luke knew his popularity hadn't been improved by his escape attempt. Eva drove with calm concentration.

They'd left the Porsche Cayenne by the roadside and were travelling in the green Range Rover that Luke had rammed into. Luke felt dizzy with shock and exhaustion, but it was impossible to sleep – his mental state, the steep road and the strange beauty of the starlit night took care of that. He tried to count the ascents and descents, but there were too many and he now gave up even trying to keep track of his bearings. He still wasn't even sure he was in the Alps, although the French registration plates on the two getaway cars and the look of the terrain strongly suggested it.

They soon returned to the spot where Luke had stolen the Cayenne. His pockets were searched again, and he was frisked by Juliette, who found the beef jerky in his sock, but didn't discover the contents of his belt. She tossed the beef jerky into the undergrowth, casting her trademark stare at Luke.

Now, for the first time during his ordeal, Luke had nothing with which to fight the despair. Sitting between his captors in the back of the Range Rover, his face sore and battered from the crash, he drifted between unpleasant half-dreams and the waking nightmare that his life had become. His sense of time was dissolving... Then, to his surprise, he dozed off into a profound sleep.

When he awoke, they'd come to a crossroads. The road sign to the right said Les Rochers. So they *were* in France, or in Switzerland... He was immediately one hundred per cent alert... The nap had helped.

Eva turned the Range Rover right, swinging onto the broad, well-maintained tarmac road, then accelerated purposefully. An oncoming car brought Luke a tiny ray of hope – at least he wasn't in some wilderness, miles from help. He tried to read the registration number, but it was too dark. However, he did glimpse something significant. There was a shield on the left side of the plate, with a white cross against a red background: the Swiss flag. Then another car swept past – also with Swiss plates. Luke couldn't be sure, but it seemed likely that they were in Switzerland.

The straight, flat ride felt almost comically smooth after the hammering terrain of the mountain. Once again, Luke forced himself to concentrate, watching the road, listening, certain he couldn't afford to miss the next opportunity – if it ever came.

Peter battled to steady his hand, but it trembled as he plucked the red pin from the map and transferred it to the latest coordinates received from the French. Bordeaux air-traffic control had just clocked the hijackers' plane.

To everyone's horror, the pin now moved to Cap Ferret, a tiny town on the Atlantic coast. The Learjet had cut France in two and was headed out to the open sea, over the Bay of Biscay.

'There's nowhere to land out there,' Peter said. His mouth was almost too dry to speak. 'Is there?'

'*Non,*' the French official said over the speakerphone. '*Unless you continue to the Azores, in the middle of the Atlantic.*'

Peter thought he was suffocating. If they headed out over the Atlantic, the hijackers couldn't land and they couldn't refuel – yet refuel they must, because the plane's tanks were almost empty already.

The hijackers had planned and executed an operation of almost unprecedented ambition and perfection. Why end it by committing suicide out on the ocean?

The Learjet was about to drop out of the sky. It made no sense. It was surreal. There was only one rational explanation. The hijackers were no longer on the plane. They must have parachuted out.

What of the hostage, then? Was he still on the plane? Peter asked himself. The thought of Luke sitting on the plane, roaring out over the waves, towards its imminent extinction, was too much to bear.

Meanwhile, Grimenko had reached the same conclusion as Peter.

'They've bailed out, haven't they? But where?'

Peter groped for a felt-tip pen and said in a strangled voice, 'Let's mark all the blind sectors on the radar network on the plane's route.'

* * *

Luke knew instinctively that they were getting close to their final destination. It froze his blood. They'd left the main road, taking a dark, forested track that forked and split in a bewildering succession of turnings, rising steadily up the mountain. As they climbed, there were fewer trees and the sleeping villages grew ever smaller. Finally they came to a steep, zigzagging track.

The Range Rover slowly negotiated the hairpin bends, huge engine groaning. Luke was worried that the tyres would lose their grip and the car would skid backwards, or into the vertical ravine on their right.

The vehicle was moving slower and slower, until it finally inched through a narrow stone gate, turned sharply and stopped. The driver killed the engine and everyone clambered out. Luke was surprised to feel cobbles underfoot. Then he let out a gasp. On the summit that rose immediately above them, there soared the ruins of an ancient castle, its single tower jutting like a finger against the night sky. The Range Rover was parked on a tiny round terrace at the foot of the peak on which the castle stood. Luke leaned back his head to take in the profile of the tall, narrow structure, presumably built long ago to guard the mountain pass. The top of the tower overhung the terrace and Luke could just make out the jagged profile of the battlements, designed to allow defenders to shoot arrows between the blocks of stone – crenellations. Even through his weariness, he remembered the technical term.

What had driven someone to build something so imposing somewhere so remote? A ghostly light filtered down from the moon and the stars. Leading off from the cobbled terrace, Luke saw a set of stairs carved into the rock, covered in moss.

Luke inhaled the Alpine air, fresh, humid and thin. The tinkle of the cooling engine of the Range Rover behind him was the only sound. Then something caught his attention. A cross and an inscription carved into the stone wall. It looked like Latin. Was it a monastery? If a monk wanted to retreat from the world, this wouldn't be a bad spot to choose. The place definitely looked like a castle, but he knew that religious buildings sometimes doubled as defensive ones in the Middle Ages.

Delacroix took what looked like a small credit card from his pocket and slid it into a narrow slit in the stone. Luke felt like rubbing his eyes, it seemed so unreal. A small red LED lamp flashed three times. Then something magical happened: the contours of the stairs ahead were illuminated, each step drawn with a line of light. Luke knew what this was: fibre lighting. It allowed you to see where you were going, but would not have been visible from a distance – from a satellite or a plane, for example.

'Welcome to Sorde de l'Abbaye,' Delacroix said and trotted up the stairs, which seemed to have been cut directly into the rock. 'The Benedictine monks built this castle as a monastery in the fourteenth century. Two hundred years later they were kicked out by the Duke of Savoy, who needed a place to hide from the Bernese.'

With a flick of her head, Juliette ordered Luke to go next. Emilio and the drivers came after her, followed by Eva and Helmut. Eva was carrying a small metal briefcase. Luke's eyes had now grown used to the darkness. Rough repairs had been made to the walls using concrete and steel. Without these interventions, the ruins might well have slid down into the valley long ago.

Luke had been silently praying that the hijackers would blindfold him, but they didn't. This was the worst possible sign. It meant they didn't care if he saw the hideaway. Which in turn meant they didn't intend to let him talk.

The stairs curved and Luke saw the black plastic casing of a security camera embedded in the stone wall. Like the magnetic card reader, it looked completely out of place in an ancient monastery. The only security features that Luke associated with medieval castles were catapults, arrows and cauldrons of boiling oil ready to be tipped over unwelcome intruders.

The stairs seemed to go on for ever. Luke's thighs were hurting and he had to fight for breath. Behind him, Juliette was doing some kind of a rhythmic skipping exercise as she climbed. At last they came to a massive oak door under a pointy Gothic arch. The iron knocker was blackened with age. Delacroix didn't touch it but reached for his card again, inserting it into another hidden reader. There was a quiet beep and the sound of an electric lock. The door opened and Luke noticed a damp smell wafting up. Behind the door another, narrower set of stairs corkscrewed upwards in a narrow shaft. Rusty spikes for holding candles or torches jutted from the brackets set at regular intervals in the round walls.

Luke was gasping from the climb and he noticed that even Delacroix was clutching his thighs. The stone wall didn't have a single window, but every so often they passed a small niche that narrowed to a vertical slit. These, Luke knew, were loopholes, built in medieval times to allow the defenders of the building to shoot arrows without danger to themselves.

At last they reached the main body of the castle. Delacroix led the way into a small passage with lancet windows and a timber floor. Luke followed. He could have sworn that the timbers bent slightly under his weight, and tried not to think of hidden trapdoors and dungeons below.

Delacroix opened yet another door and Luke slipped through. Juliette and the others followed close behind him. They now came into a long hall, with rows of pillars supporting the timber ceiling. It was dry here, and warm. The dank, churchy smell was replaced by the scent of cigars. The hijackers gathered around the long trestle table. Delacroix lifted several bottles of mineral water onto the table and Juliette distributed bags of dried fruit and what looked like energy bars to the group. Luke wasn't offered anything. Eva drew the curtains across the amber-coloured stained glass windows and lit some candles. The hijackers ate and drank in silence.

Luke studied his surroundings. The floor had been stripped of its Oriental carpets, which lay in rolls at the back of the hall, next to a row of wooden crates and neatly stacked cardboard boxes. A dozen or so framed paintings still hung on the whitewashed walls. Luke froze when he recognized a crucifixion stolen from the Hermitage museum in St Petersburg the previous spring. He quickly looked down at his trainers. He was sure of what he had seen – the stolen masterpiece had been shown on TV and reproduced in all the newspapers. Presumably, the other canvases were stolen as well. Why were they here? Had some crazed collector hoarded them up here for his own enjoyment? Why not sell them for money?

Luke returned his gaze to the tormented, sallow figure of Christ on the cross, the thin arms stretched by the weight of his body.

'Lovely picture, isn't it?' Delacroix said. He was still short of breath from the climb, but there was pride in his voice and a new energy, as though arriving here had given him a boost. Was this his home? Luke glanced around. Some of the white walls were bare, but you could see the outlines of the works that had hung there and the mounting hooks were still in place. A large blue-and-white vase stood in the middle of the trestle table. He noted an orderly row of sturdy transport crates. Someone was getting ready to move...

Juliette opened another door and flicked a light switch, and Luke was amazed to see a row of modern exercise machines. She picked up a pair of hand weights and began shadowboxing in front of a full-length mirror, skipping and bobbing silently, eyes blazing back from the mirror – even after the night's ordeal and the arduous climb, she had energy to burn.

'Let's take the boy up to the garderobe,' Delacroix said.

Juliette instantly set down the weights and led Luke up a set of stairs to the floor above. He found himself being trundled along a narrow, brightly lit passage with a succession of doors leading off it. Delacroix brought up the rear. Luke glimpsed a room like a hotel bedroom. The very last door was smaller than the others and had a threshold that came up to Luke's shins.

Juliette opened the door and gave Luke a firm shove. He stumbled into a dark cubicle. The door was pushed shut behind him. The key turned in the lock.

He'd assumed the word garderobe referred to a wardrobe, but standing in the cramped little space, he suddenly remembered that the word was also used for medieval toilets, built to project from castle walls, so that the waste fell straight into the moat below… He'd seen several garderobes in a castle somewhere in England. He'd visited many historic sites in Sussex and Kent when his dad still had time for that kind of thing.

Hearing the voices of his captors retreating down the passage outside, he pressed his ear against the gap between the door and the jamb.

'When do we leave?' Juliette said. 'And where will we go?'

'Impatient girl! I thought we agreed it would be a surprise.'

'Tell me now.'

'Argentina.'

'And what will be my name?'

'I will be Vincent Leonard, a real estate developer, and you will be my obedient wife, Martha.'

There was the sound of a kiss. Luke strained to hear more.

'I can't wait,' Juliette said. 'How long do we keep the boy?'

'Only until tomorrow evening,' Delacroix said. 'If they haven't found us by then, they never will.'

The words made Luke turn cold all over. The conversation confirmed what he already knew, but the cruelty of his captors still shocked him. This was obviously their sanctuary. He'd been allowed to see it. It meant he couldn't be let go, ever.

He heard the hijackers return to the floor below. A cork was pulled from a bottle. Luke sat down and buried his face in his hands. He would be dead by the following evening – at the latest.

43

Peter stared at the map, biting his lip. Judging by the manner in which it had simply disappeared off the radar, the Learjet had indeed now crashed into the sea. The cross marked the site in the Atlantic Ocean, in the Bay of Biscay, just under a hundred kilometres west of Cap Ferret.

'*The rescue helicopters are at the scene, but there is no sign of any survivors,*' the French voice said calmly over the speakerphone.

Peter retraced the route of the plane on the map. Certain stretches over the Alps were marked with a broken line, where the plane had traversed areas that had only intermittent radar coverage.

In one of those areas, the hijackers had bailed out. And Luke? Where was he?

Peter kept clenching and unclenching his fists. It was a torment, having to rely on pure conjecture. But he felt sure of one thing. No one would execute such an elaborate, clockwork plan, only to deliberately crash into the sea at the end of it.

As far as Luke was concerned, there were probably three options. Either he'd been left behind when the

Learjet took off; he had jumped with the others and was still being held hostage, or he'd been abandoned on the plane before it crashed, which meant that he was dead.

The only reassuring thing was that the hostage-taking had been planned from the start. McMorgan had been the original target, but after they found out that Peter had an important role in Europol, they'd taken Luke instead. So they were probably planning to keep him with them until they were safe. But what then?

Peter took several long, slow breaths. Then he grasped the microphone and prepared to speak to his team. The hijackers had to be found, quickly.

Luke unwrapped the piece of beef jerky that he'd managed to smuggle inside his belt... He thought of Rosita's dimples and her pink fingernails and her dark hair... He was pleased he'd been able to hide something from his captors. Chewing on the dry meat, Luke studied his prison, examining it with his hands as well as his eyes. Mercifully, a little light from the passage passed through the gaps between the timbers of the door. The walls of the ancient toilet were round. Opposite the door was a semi-circular wooden seat with a lidded round hole. Luke had already tried to prise off the lid, but it was nailed shut.

He went back to the seat and grabbed the wooden handle on the lid. It didn't even budge. Luke stroked his fingers along the edges of the lid, feeling for the shape of the massive long nails that had been bent over the lid to hold it in place. There was no way he could bend them back with his bare hands.

Luke remembered a story that Gran used to tell of how Gustavus Vasa, the great sixteenth-century King of Sweden, had slipped away from his Danish captors by escaping through a latrine.

What was she and everyone else back home thinking? Presumably they'd already heard that the Learjet had crashed. But surely they'd continue looking for him?

Part of him, a small part, felt angry at his parents for not having rescued him already, and for having let him get into this situation in the first place. They didn't like his independence or his car rides with Toni, but what was he supposed to do without any company all summer long? Well, Gran was company, but it wasn't the same thing. How he missed the old fishing trips and precious man-to-man discussions with Dad. Where had that Dad gone? And yet, Luke knew he could count on Dad to keep looking for him. Thoroughness was Dad's obsession.

Luke felt in his pockets but he had nothing that could have helped him attack the nails. He needed a tool of some sort. His Swiss Army knife would have been perfect for the job, but it was in his bedroom at Gran's house. He took his belt off again, but couldn't think of any sensible use for the fishing line. He decided to save the fructose tablets for later. He zipped up the secret compartment and put his belt back on. It was when he sat on the floor and crossed his hands behind his neck that he suddenly felt the leather cord and remembered the amulet that Rosita had given him.

He pressed the flat tip of the metal amulet under the rusty nail and twisted carefully, worried that the edge would simply break off. The nail moved fractionally, but then a piece got chipped off the amulet, just as he'd feared.

Even in this life and death situation, he felt guilty, treating Rosita's gift like this.

He turned the amulet in his hand and forced a slightly thicker edge under the nail, then prised. The amulet didn't break this time, but the nail rose up another fraction, so that Luke was able to twist it round. He quickly moved to the other side and managed to do the same to the other nail.

Within seconds, the lid of the wooden toilet seat had been lifted aside and Luke was staring down through a short chute leading to a sheer drop that continued well past the castle's foundations, into the ravine beside it. The end of the short chute was a glowing circle dimly lit by the light of dawn. No wonder the lid hadn't been secured properly: the chute hung over an abyss. It was too dark to see what the structure was like immediately below the box surrounding the wooden seat, but it was clear that there was no way up to the chute from below and that anyone attempting to climb down it would smash himself onto the rocks below, unless he had a long rope. King Gustavus Vasa had had to crawl through human excrement to escape, but on balance, he'd been a lucky man.

Luke put the wooden lid back on and sat on it, reeling with disappointment after his moment of hope. The only other exit was the door. It was locked and there were hijackers and cameras behind it. He lay down on the floor and curled up in the foetal position.

44

Back in Porvoo, Hanna was hunched over the kitchen table, in the dark, with a framed photo of her son before her. Her eyes were sore from weeping. An untouched glass of milk glowed in the moonlight. If she strained her ears, she could hear the rustling of the blackcurrant bushes, the tiny creaks of the old wooden house and the cosy sound of Gran snoring quietly in her little bedroom.

'Gran's right,' she whispered to Peter over the phone. 'We've neglected Luke. This would never have happened if we hadn't.'

'*I've thought that…*'

'It's so utterly unlike him, to do something so irresponsible!'

'*Be fair. He was only returning lost property.*'

Hanna paused to wipe her eyes. 'I've blamed Toni. But it's not his fault either.'

'*Have you slept?*'

'Not a single second since this nightmare began…'

'*You must try… Listen, I have to go… It will all be OK. I promise you.*'

'Take care, Peter…'

Hanna listened to the beeping line, then got wearily to her feet and opened the window. There was a hint of autumn in the smell of ripening apples outside. She thought she should go and turn off her laptop, but decided just to let it switch itself off. She was supposed to be submitting her article this week, but hadn't touched it since Luke had disappeared. She'd also cancelled her trip to a physics symposium in South Korea – the first time she'd ever pulled out of a professional engagement. No, work hadn't been on her mind much these past couple of days, spent sitting beside the phone and combing the internet for news of the hijacking…

Minutes after the *Ocean Emerald* had sunk, the media had been awash with information, including interviews with the survivors. It was unbearable. Just as the hijacking situation as a whole had reached a happy conclusion, Luke had been singled out as a hostage.

Hanna brushed a moth away from her cheek. Suddenly she saw something slip into the darkness under the wooden steps. A hedgehog! She reached into the dish cupboard, grabbed her glass and crept outside to pour a saucer of milk for the little visitor. As soon as she'd placed the saucer at the bottom of the steps, the creature sped off towards the blackcurrant bushes and curled itself into a tight ball, bristling. She waited, resting her head on her knees. The weather was surprisingly warm. A fresh breeze stroked her face.

She woke with a start, to find it was already light. She'd fallen asleep without realizing.

'Mrs Baron, are you all right?' said a hesitant voice beside her. 'Sorry, I didn't mean to give you a fright…'

'Toni…' Hanna stood up stiffly and stretched her arms. 'What time is it?'

'Six o'clock. I've been waiting here since five, then I realized you were sitting outside. Did you see the news? It's wild. They've released everyone!'

'Not everyone. They've still got Luke.'

'Oh no...' Toni shook his head, unable say any more.

'Toni, you should go home.'

'I'm not flavour of the month at home right now.'

Hanna saw the dented roof of Toni's Nissan behind the fence. Thudding music was drifting from the open window, but at least the volume was turned way down – a rare state of affairs. She didn't want to hear about Toni's family troubles, although a small voice inside her was saying, if Luke was a neglected child, what was Toni, with two jobless parents and a boozing mother?

Toni shuffled his feet and kept moving his hands from the pockets of his black fleece to the pockets of his jeans and back again. Hanna went to pick up the saucer, which had been licked clean while she slept.

'I spoke to Peter at around four. He still thinks everything will be OK.'

'He should know.'

The door opened and Gran appeared.

'Morning, darling,' Gran said in a bright voice and turned the packet of cigarettes in her knobbly hands, reluctant to light up in front of her disapproving daughter. 'Morning, Toni!'

'Good morning!' Toni said. 'How's the Norton running?'

'She purrs like a cat, thanks to you!'

'Quite a loud cat.'

Gran gave Toni a huge grin, and padded across the grass to the gate to fetch the morning newspaper from the tin letterbox. Hanna glanced at Gran's motorbike under its green tarpaulin beside the woodpile. For all his faults, the boy most certainly had a knack for fixing things. One year, when they'd been about to miss their flight back to Brussels, Toni had saved the day by simply changing a spark plug in the old family Volvo.

Hanna looked at the unattractive wispy hairs on Toni's chin and upper lip. His jeans could have done with a wash. So could his hair.

'Come in and have some breakfast, Toni,' she said. 'Frankly, you look awful.'

'Thanks,' Toni grinned. 'But I should get going.'

'That's fine,' Hanna said, secretly relieved.

Toni slouched to his car, swinging the keys round his forefinger, then turned to look at Hanna.

'Luke is my best friend,' he said suddenly. 'I know I'm older and that I should look out for him. If anything happens to him, I'll never forgive myself.'

The traffic at Kloten Airport near Zurich was picking up as dawn broke. Peter listened as one plane after another went screaming into the sky.

Once again, he turned to the map that showed the route taken by the hijackers. They'd cut across Switzerland along the spine of the Alps. Peter had drawn a circle over Dijon, near the Swiss border, the last known residence of Philippe Delacroix.

Was it significant, then, that the plane had passed just south of Dijon? One thing was certain: Delacroix wouldn't hide out at his own home address. After a heist like this, he had to disappear for ever. But he might feel most comfortable lying low in France first. Juliette du Pont, too, was almost certainly French, although her real identity hadn't been established so far.

Yet again, Peter skimmed through the thumbnail sketch of Delacroix that had been compiled on the basis of the information from the French police and Interpol. The man was thought to be an audacious professional criminal with exceptional patience and planning ability. He was also a sophisticated man, with a taste for high culture and history. It hadn't always been so. In his youth, he was thought to have committed violent bank robberies of a nasty, inelegant kind. Then he'd made a new career in art theft and become a big player on the black market for art, before going back to construction work and evening classes. The man was an enigma.

To penetrate some of the world's best guarded museums such as the Hermitage in St Petersburg, Delacroix, if it was him, had used intelligence and high-tech equipment. And he always covered his tracks. No evidence had ever stuck to him. A brute on the one hand, a cultivated intellectual on the other – it was a tough combination to fight.

45

Luke was roused from a short sleep by footsteps in the corridor outside his tiny prison cell. He leaped up as though he'd received an electric shock. Had they come for him already?

No – the person continued down the corridor outside and entered through one of the other doors. This time…

Trying not to give in to the panic swelling inside him, he took the lid off the toilet seat once more and placed it on the floor, then peered down into the chute. Dawn had broken outside, but as far as he could see, it wasn't day yet. Light filtered through into the timber structure beneath the seat, above and on either side of the chute.

He turned round and swung a leg through the hole, feeling around with his trainer. There was a gap between the chute and the structure around it. Thrusting his foot into this gap, he found what felt like a wooden beam. He pushed hard on it and it was solid. With a thudding heart, Luke swung his other leg into the hole, holding onto the wooden edges of the toilet seat with both hands.

Without looking down, he levered himself into the gap and found himself in a maze of timbers beneath the garderobe. The toilet was supported by a piece of stone jutting from the castle wall, but additional support had at some point been added by means of timbers joined to form a kind of scaffolding beneath it. Under the scaffolding was just air. If Luke fell, he knew he would fly for several seconds before hitting the stony ravine far below.

To his surprise, through the crossed timbers, he saw a row of Gothic windows to his left. Dim yellow light seeped through the drawn curtains. He could see there was a ledge the width of his palm under the windows, but how to get there? He had to try. He couldn't just wait for his captors to come and kill him. Besides, now was the time to act, when the hijackers were probably sleeping off their exhaustion.

He scrambled back up into the garderobe, took the fructose tablets from his belt and ate them. He put the fishing line and hooks into his back pocket – he couldn't imagine what he'd do with them, but he'd brought them this far. Then he stretched thoroughly, slapped his cheeks once or twice and took a few deep breaths before lowering himself back down, supporting himself with a foot pressed against an angled beam made of thick round timber.

As he let go of the toilet seat and grabbed a joist lower down, the timber beneath his foot simply came loose and plunged downwards. His whole weight was now supported by the joist alone. It was impossible to climb back with the beam gone. Hanging onto the joist, with just nothingness beneath him, he cast around for something else to stand on. There was a second beam, but he had no reason to think it was any stronger than the first. His hands were hurting already. He had to risk it.

Making the shift as gently as he could, he let go of the joist and hugged the slanting timber instead, gripping it with his legs and arms. There was a cracking sound, and the structure seemed to readjust itself, but it didn't collapse. Luke held his breath. The breeze caressed his sweaty skin. The windows glowed just a few metres away. He climbed along the scaffolding, until he could almost touch the wall. He kept his eyes well away from the void below.

The stone ledge was just wide enough for his feet and he was able to support himself by clutching at the mossy windowsills with his fingers. He recognized the amber windows of the hall with the paintings and the trestle table. It was best not to imagine who was behind the windows, or to wonder whether they could hear him rustling along outside.

When he was halfway across, Luke came to a slightly wider ledge. It was too narrow to sit on, but he was able to stand comfortably with his back against the wall. He decided to rest his feet and hands. He wasn't sure, but he thought he'd heard a car approaching somewhere down below.

He turned round and continued sidling across. The next stained-glass window was decorated with blue lozenges and bore the image of a face, probably a saint, judging by the halo and the aura around the bearded face. The next one along was larger than the others and had clear glass and a small ventilation hatch that was half-ajar. Heavy dark-green curtains hid the scene inside, but there was a small gap in the middle, from which a bright light shone.

Breathing heavily, Luke peered into the long, pillared hall where he'd seen the paintings and the removal boxes.

His sense of direction and space hadn't let him down: escaping from the garderobe, he'd climbed down to the level of the floor below. There were even fewer paintings on the wall now, and more removal crates on the floor, but the large vase was still in the middle of the long trestle table.

He'd been wrong to assume that the hijackers would be sleeping. He saw Delacroix, cigar in hand, speaking to someone standing behind the vase. The voices were muted, but by pressing his ear close to the ventilation hatch, Luke could make out the words, spoken in English.

'You got here faster than I expected,' Delacroix said. 'Where did you fly to?'

'I chartered a business jet from Kaliningrad to Zurich, where Bob was waiting with my Beamer. Great motorways round here.'

'That's not what we agreed!' Delacroix threw up his hands. 'I told you to take the back roads.'

'Yeah, yeah, but I Google-earthed you and I saw there was an easier route,' replied an American voice. 'I don't like off-roading.'

'And I don't like it when my orders are disobeyed.' Delacroix tapped the ash from his cigar as he spoke. 'So you prefer the easy route. Do you know what the other difference between us is?'

'What?' the American voice said with an exaggerated sigh.

'I have values, and you don't. For you, this is all just *assets*.' Delacroix gestured at the vase and the painting of the Crucifixion and the packed crates. 'Paintings, sculptures, tapestries...'

'Sure, it's pretty stuff,' the unseen man said. 'And that beauty has a value that can be measured – in cash.'

'Cash!' Delacroix shook his head. 'Cash is a means, not an end. Beauty is an end. Take this vase, lovingly hand-crafted in China during the early Ming dynasty, in the fourteenth century, when this castle was new.'

The other man let out a long cackle and as he did so, Luke realized he'd heard him before. But where? Just then, the man stepped forward into the light. Luke's eyes widened when he realized who Delacroix had been talking to.

It was Max Lownie Junior, a can of Coke in hand.

'At least we both enjoy a smoke,' Max said, reaching for the box of fat cigars. 'Mind if I help myself?'

46

The surprise of seeing Max was almost enough to send Luke plunging into the ravine behind him.

'If you were talking about music, I'd understand you. An original Mozart score, say.' Max hitched up his shorts and placed his plump hand on Delacroix's shoulder. 'These are just mouldy old pictures. What's the big deal?'

'History,' Delacroix said, with contempt in his voice. 'To have the chance to buy just *one* of these pieces in his life, a collector would have to be extremely lucky. The alabaster statue in that small crate, for example, is five and a half thousand years old. It's the Sumerian Mona Lisa.'

'You can thank our American forces for that. Ask Bob the bodyguard,' Max grunted, gesturing at a man with a military air standing to one side. 'Bob personally witnessed the looters getting their hands on the treasures in Baghdad.'

'That was a barbaric chapter in history.'

'Barbaric? We kicked ass! Usual story, American servicemen dying to make Europe a safer place.' Max was warming to his subject. 'You say we're different, but the only difference I see is that I take the risks and you take the profits. You get the funds to buy up looted Iraqi art, and I get to sink my dad's cruise ship for the insurance money.'

'Money which you'll now inherit, instead of inheriting a bankrupt shipping company,' Delacroix said.

Insurance money... In a flash, Luke understood why the *Ocean Emerald* had been sunk.

There was a knock. The man Max had referred to as Bob moved closer to the door. Juliette burst in, and handed a metal briefcase to Delacroix.

With some ceremony, Delacroix put out his cigar, placed the briefcase onto the trestle table and flicked open the combination locks. He drew out a bulging bag, loosened the string and dipped his hand inside. Light flashed on the contents of Delacroix's palm: diamonds.

'That concludes the transaction,' Delacroix said. 'You get the insurance and half the diamonds purchased with the ransom we collected, which has now been laundered via the Cayman Islands. Even *you* will need a long time to gamble away your share, but I've already invested mine in a collection of unique statues from Baghdad.'

'I've quit gambling,' Max said. 'And I'm going on a diet.'

'Sure you are,' Delacroix said, patting Max on the back.

'You can patronize me all you like,' Max said. 'As long as I get the last laugh.'

Luke saw Max nod at Bob. What happened next seemed completely unreal. Bob pulled out an Uzi sub-machine-gun and released a burst of automatic fire into the timber ceiling above Delacroix. Juliette threw herself onto the floor. Then Bob kicked over the table with his combat boot, tipping over the vase, which shattered on the floor.

Luke cowered on his ledge as the echoes of the deafening rounds died over the ravine. Max stepped across to Delacroix, who had also taken cover on the floor, and prodded him with the tip of his trainer.

'Hey! Cheese-eater! Sorry about the crockery,' he cackled. 'Winner takes all? Sound fair to you?'

Delacroix sat up. He was staring open-mouthed at the shards of blue-and-white porcelain, all that remained of the priceless vase.

'Where's your team?' Max taunted.

'Helmut! Eva! Emilio!' Delacroix roared. 'Get over here!'

'Oh, I forgot. They're locked in their bedrooms. You know what your problem is, Delacroix? You're too bossy.' Max took the bag of diamonds from the table. 'You lose friends that way. Bob, tie him up and get the others.'

Bob reached under his jacket and took a bunch of handcuffs from his belt. With practised movements, he swiftly handcuffed Delacroix and Juliette, then fetched Helmut and Eva, from their bedrooms upstairs.

'All that hard work for nothing!' Max smiled at Delacroix with mock-compassion. 'Never mind. Take it as a life experience.'

Out on the ledge, Luke could feel his legs trembling with shock. What would be the safest thing to do? Maybe he should wait until Max had gone. But then he'd be stuck here alone with the hijackers, who were likely to be even more furious than before.

'Hang on… where's Emilio?'

Bob shrugged his shoulders. 'There were only these two up there…'

'Go and find him.'

Before Bob could even move, automatic fire rattled and one side of the door leading into the main hall came flaking to the floor. Springing like a cat, Bob crouched under the window behind which Luke was standing. Max himself let out a frightened screech and took cover behind the collapsed trestle table.

Emilio saw the bodyguard under the window and fired without a moment's hesitation. The window next to Luke shattered and the torn green curtain billowed out through the empty pane, pulled to one side by the wind. He was now visible to anyone who cared to look.

The firing had stopped and clouds of dust settled in the silent room. Luke realized that everyone was staring at him.

'Morning,' he said, clearing his throat. His options were limited to one. He couldn't go back, but he could try for a surprise.

He leaped in through the window and bounded onto a sofa, whose springs sent him flying into the middle of the room. Without even thinking, he kicked the barrel of Emilio's sub-machine-gun, which flew out of his hands. Luke could almost feel the mental effort that was being made in the room, as everyone tried to make sense of his sudden appearance.

Bob saw his chance and seized the sub-machine-gun from Emilio's feet.

Luke scurried over to Max and snatched the heavy bag of diamonds from his hand – without encountering any resistance. He continued towards the door and found himself in the narrow passage outside.

'Bob, tie up Emilio!' Max's voice shouted behind him. 'I'll get the boy.'

Luke glanced back and saw the hulking, hippo-like figure of Max charging after him down the passage. He wasn't limping any more.

'Hey!' Max roared, panting hard. 'Give that back, or you're dead!'

Luke sprinted along the stone passage and up a long staircase, at the top of which was a massive door. Max had moved surprisingly fast and his heavy tread was already close. Luke lifted the latch and found himself on a walkway leading across the steep-gabled brick roof of the castle.

His heart missed a beat. He was at the very top of the tall building – unless you counted the tower that jutted over the ravine and the round cobbled terrace below. The early morning sky glowed a rosy pink between the dark mountains that soared up in every direction. The sun was appearing above the eastern horizon, its rays already touching the snow-capped summits in the west.

'Do you hear me?' Max's voice was right outside the door. 'Bob, is that you? I need a weapon here. We need to take the kid out.'

Luke had no head for heights and his self-preservation instinct was telling him to lie down flat on his stomach on the wooden walkway. Instead, he crossed it, clutching the skimpy railing that was provided on only one side, and passed into the narrow spiral staircase leading up into the tower. He began to climb even higher. By peeking through the narrow loopholes in the tower, he could see down onto the walkway below.

'Kid? The game's up...' Max came rushing onto the roof, giving a terrified start as he realized where he was. He grabbed hold of the railing and seemed to go white. 'Give me that bag, or else. You have nowhere to run.'

It was true. Luke knew he was cornered. All he could do was play for time. He bounded up the spiral stairs to the top of the tower, which was about ten metres high. There was a light morning breeze. Luke could sense the thinness of the air, a reminder of the altitude at which the monastery stood. On a school trip, he'd once skied at twenty-five hundred metres, and this felt much higher.

'Are you crazy? You'll break your neck.' Max's voice was a blend between a whine and an insult. 'You hear? You're trapped, sonny.'

Clutching the railing with both hands, Max proceeded gingerly across the walkway, towards the door leading into the tower. Then Bob appeared behind him on the walkway, sub-machine-gun in hand. He didn't relish the height of the castle roof, either, judging by the expression that spread over his face when he glanced down.

'Kid? It's two against one and we're both armed.' Max showed a pistol. He rubbed his glistening cheeks onto his shoulders, loath to let go of the railing. 'I'll give you one last chance.'

Lungs burning with the effort, Luke raced up the remaining steps and tried not to look at the plunging depths all around him. He leaned into a niche to look down through one of the loopholes and saw his pursuers still standing at opposite ends of the rickety walkway over the steep brick roof.

The diamond bag was heavy in Luke's hand. The immense ransom collected by the hijackers was all there –

and it was entirely worthless to someone in Luke's situation.

'Kid!' Max screamed. 'We're coming for you right now!'

His voice sounded even more quavery than usual in the thin Alpine air.

'You better stay right where you are,' Luke shouted back. His voice wasn't quite itself either.

'Why's that, kiddo?'

'Because if you come any closer, I'm throwing the diamonds down into the valley. They're worthless to me – what do I care?'

As he spoke these words, Luke was already at the summit of the tower. A circular platform no more than a couple of metres across, it was ringed with a crenellated parapet that only reached up to Luke's knees. The medieval bowmen must have knelt down to shoot at their besieging enemies from up here, Luke decided. Beyond the parapet was a sheer vertical drop of several hundred metres into the ravine on one side and an almost equally terrifying although much shorter drop to the circular cobbled terrace on the other. The frost and the wind had been at work on the masonry, loosening some of the stones of the parapet.

'Check this out.' Crouching behind the parapet, Luke dangled the bag over the ravine. 'If you try to catch me, or if you fire at me, you can kiss goodbye to your diamonds.'

'Let's talk.' Max squinted up at the tower. 'All I want is my own property.'

Luke reached into the bag of diamonds and threw one off the tower, into the depths of the ravine.

'What was that?'

'A stone.' He picked out another diamond, threw it. 'Pretty, isn't it, the way they flash in the sun?'

'Stop that right now, you idiot!'

'I want a mobile phone.'

'What?'

'A mobile phone, I said, or it will rain diamonds down there.'

'What am I? Your phone supplier?'

'Do it.'

Luke swung the bag in his hand. He sensed Max's hesitation and it gave him heart. He'd played the right card – the only card he had.

'Bob?' Max called to his bodyguard at the opposite end of the walkway. 'Bring me my phone. It's in the car.'

'Not so fast,' Luke said. 'I want *you* to bring it.'

'You think you can boss me around?'

'Yes, I do. And I want Bob to stay right where he is, so that I can see him. Get me that mobile, right now. You could do with some exercise.'

While Max was running back through the castle to his car, Luke took out the fishing line and tied a hook to one end. Then he shrugged off his jacket and inserted the hook in the collar, pulling to be sure that it held.

Luke glanced down over the parapet. The green Range Rover and Max's small white BMW convertible looked like rectangular gaming chips on a tiny round table formed by the cobbled terrace. Luke wondered how Max had managed to drive up the mountain in the sports car – then saw an asphalt road on the mountain ridge across the valley. The hijackers had taken a back route, but not Max. He grinned when he saw Max open the door of his

BMW, reach inside, then hasten back for the long climb up the tower. The sound of the car door, Max's footsteps and even his wheezing breaths were clearly audible in the silent mountain air.

As soon as he'd seen Max cross the walkway, Luke moved to the other side, where the outside wall of the tower drew a continuous line with the mountain face that fell straight down into the ravine below. He pulled back and sat down, pressing his palms against the stone to chase away the spinning sensation in his head. He was shivering in just his black T-shirt. At last he heard Max gasping his way to the top of the tower. A sweating, flushed face appeared at the top of the stairs and Max raised his hand, holding a mobile.

'Stop! One more step, and I drop these.'

'Come on,' Max panted, holding the mobile in front of him. 'You don't think I'm stupid enough to give you this, even if you give me my diamonds. You'll have the police up here in no time.'

'Shut up and listen. I'll offer you a deal. Are Delacroix and his gang definitely out of action?'

'Yes, Bob handcuffed them together in a nice little heap.'

'Good. Here's the deal. You give me the phone and I call the police and tell them everything I know.'

'No, you won't!'

'I will, but after the call, I'll give you the diamonds and that way Bob and you will have a chance to get away. I'll tell them you were behind all this, and once they know that, you have no reason to silence me. If you let me live, you'll also get a shorter prison sentence when ... I mean, *if* you're caught.'

Max, who'd been red before, now turned the colour of beetroot. 'Don't you get smart with me, kid, or I'll come and personally chuck you off this stupid tower...'

'Do we have a deal?' Luke grinned, swinging the bag of diamonds. 'My hand is getting tired.'

'You bet we don't have a deal.' Max fumbled for his pistol. 'You take me for an idiot.'

'I think the bag is slipping...'

'Wait!' Max threw up his hands. 'Run me through this deal again...'

'You have two options. Shoot me and escape without the diamonds, or let me make one call and escape *with* the diamonds.'

Max stared, mouth hanging, then spoke with a defeated voice. 'OK then. We have a deal.'

'Good.' Luke said. 'Now, where is this place exactly?'

'Switzerland, La Renard, near Sollard.'

'Lovely spot. Do you know any nice youth hostels nearby?'

'You know, I might just shoot you.'

'Climb down a few steps.'

Max did as he was told and Luke threw his jacket down the stairs.

'OK, now put the phone into my jacket pocket and button it up.'

'It's done.'

'Put your pistol into the other pocket.'

'Done.'

Luke hauled in his jacket and took the mobile out and checked that it was working. Then he made sure the pistol was in the other pocket. It was. He put on the jacket, leaving the pistol in its pocket.

'OK, you can go back down now. I'll call you back up when I'm done.'

'I'm not climbing those stairs again.'

'You are if you want your diamonds.'

'You know what will happen if you don't give me those diamonds right after your call?' Max hissed, wagging his fat forefinger. 'I'll personally drop-kick you off this tower, I swear I will.'

He began trudging down the spiral stairs once more.

Luke was already dialling Dad's mobile.

47

Peter's hand shot to his pocket when he felt his personal mobile vibrate. He was in the air-traffic control centre at Zurich airport. He glanced at the display and saw an unknown number. He hesitated for a fraction of a second, then took the call.

'Baron.'

'*Dad, it's me...*'

'Luke! Where are you?'

'*Listen. The hijacking was organized by Max Lownie Junior. I'm in Switzerland, in a place called La Renard, near Sollard. It's a castle. You'll need a chopper to get here...*'

Peter was scribbling down the place names on a sheet of paper. He beckoned a Swiss police officer closer.

'I've got that, Luke. What's happened? Can you talk?'

'*Sorry, I can't. I've got a diamond deal I need to clinch. See you later.*'

The line went dead.

The Swiss officer was already drawing circles onto the wall map.

'Let's go,' Peter said. There were dark rings around his eyes, but his face was beaming.

***

When he reached the top of the tower again, Max was too tired to stand. He knelt at the top of the stairs, hands extended towards Luke, like a beggar.

'Well?' Max shrieked, his voice whistling with the exertion. 'Are you as good as your word, or would you rather take a leap off this thing?'

'Here.' Luke swung the bag to safety. His arm was numb from holding it. Clutched in his other hand was Max's pistol.

Max crawled forward and eagerly clamped his fingers around the bag.

'I also want my phone back,' he said. 'Both phones, come to think of it.'

'Sorry, I threw the satellite phone into the sea,' Luke said. 'I didn't like the colour.'

Still pointing the pistol, Luke handed Max his phone.

Max laboured back down the stairs. Luke watched him reappear on the rooftop and cross to the other side of the walkway, where Bob was still waiting.

'Go and chuck the kid off the tower,' Max said. 'Then meet me at the car.'

A cold feeling spread itself through Luke's chest as he stared down over the parapet and saw Bob advancing gingerly across the walkway, towards the tower.

'Hey! I'm sending you a gift.' Max shouted, to make sure Luke knew what was in store for him. 'It's a flying lesson! Teach you some respect for your elders, you miserable little shrimp.'

Luke looked down. Bob was already halfway across the walkway. Luke met his eyes, in which he saw no trace of human feeling. Luke clutched the pistol – then put it away. If it came to a gun battle, he had no chance against a professional.

Peter went tearing towards the police helicopter at Zurich airport. The blades were already flogging the air.

The call from Luke had consoled him immensely, but he wouldn't believe his son was really safe until he held him in his arms. What could the boy have meant by the 'diamond deal' he had to 'clinch'?

Four members of the Swiss Special Police dressed in overalls were already climbing through the hatch. As he joined them inside, Peter quietly prayed that their services wouldn't be needed.

48

Luke braced himself, then stood to his full height on the tower and grabbed hold of one of the large blocks of stone that were half-dislodged from the parapet. He'd known all along he wasn't safe yet – he hadn't even tried to strip Bob and Max of all their weapons, as there was no way of knowing how many firearms they had access to. He'd counted on Max's haste to depart once he had the diamonds – and he'd been wrong. Faced now with the imminent danger of being shot or pushed to his death by Max's bodyguard, he found that he was suddenly able to look down into the narrow valley. He steadied himself, took a deep breath and heaved. The block came rasping towards him, but it was still a long way to the door of the spiral staircase, through which he could already hear the thud of Bob's climbing footsteps.

Luke changed position so that he was able to push the block with his legs and he eventually managed to slide it to the top of the stairs.

Luke waited until he thought he heard Bob's breathing, then launched the block down into the spiral stairs, pushing it as hard as he could with his legs. An image from childhood came to him suddenly: Tintin on the Black

Island, hurling stones from the tower of a Scottish castle.

The block went scooting and bouncing down the steep stairs.

'Nice one, kid,' Bob's voice echoed in the stairwell. 'You'll pay for that.'

Luke was already struggling with another block. It was even heavier, but he somehow managed to slide it to the edge. There were two more loose blocks after this one. Then he'd have nothing left.

Bob tried to sprint up to the top of the tower and Luke could already see the barrel of the man's weapon when he dispatched the second block. With a curse, Bob turned on his heels. Luke could feel the tower trembling a little as the weighty stone spun down the stairs.

There was a thud, a cry of pain, then silence.

Luke crept down a few steps with Max's pistol in his hand. Bob lay spread-eagled on the stairs, with his head against the wall in a position that looked uncomfortable for his neck. Was he dead? Or paralysed? Luke felt a wave of alarm rise through him, but then he thought of all the things that the hijackers had done on the cruise ship and the feeling passed.

He dropped to his knees beside the man and felt for a pulse. The heartbeat was vigorous and regular in Bob's strong wrist and Luke pulled his hand away in fright. The man was probably just knocked out.

Somewhere down below, an engine whirred into life. Luke hesitated, then raced back up the stairs to the top of the tower and peered down. The round, cobbled terrace where the cars were parked was clearly visible at the foot of the castle, a distance of about fifty metres. Squeezed beside the Range Rover in this narrow space was the white

BMW convertible that Max Lownie Junior was trying to reverse onto the small road.

Luke thought to himself for a moment. What guarantee did he have that Max would get caught? None. With the fortune he carried in his bag, he could easily start a new life somewhere under a new identity – no doubt he already had it planned. The thought made Luke feel physically sick. He studied the last block he had. It was the smallest of the three. It pulled loose quite easily. Luke edged it towards the gap he had made when he removed the other two blocks from the parapet. The hole was immediately above the cobbled terrace where the cars were parked. He sat on the floor, supporting his back against the doorway, and pushed the block into the void.

He sprang up just in time to see the small dot land on the bonnet of Max's car. It took a second before the sound – part crunch, part hammer-blow – made it up to the top of the tower. The engine stopped instantly.

The only sounds left were the morning breeze whistling on the battlements and the song of a distant bird. Then Max's car door opened with a painful creak.

Luke dived out of view and raced down the spiral stairs, supporting himself against the stone walls. He passed the unconscious Bob and continued towards the walkway.

'*Bob, where the hell are you?*' he heard Max's voice spluttering over the radiophone on Bob's belt. '*That little thief wrecked my car. Bring the keys to Delacroix's vehicle, or we'll never get out of here…*'

Luke hastened across the walkway, through the castle and down the stairs to the hall hung with paintings, moving as fast as his legs would carry him. He found a place to hide behind a heavy curtain and waited there until he heard Max go puffing into the room where Delacroix and his cronies lay handcuffed together.

The moment the door closed behind Max, Luke sprinted down the stairs leading to ground level. He thought they would never end. At last he was on the small round terrace. He took a moment to admire his handiwork. The block of stone from the parapet had survived its collision with Max's sports BMW almost unscathed, but the same could not be said of the car.

Then he fixed his attention on Delacroix's Range Rover.

'Bob? For the last time, where are you?' Max shouted, ignoring the enraged stares from Delacroix, Juliette, Emilio, Eva and Helmut. Fortunately, they all had a piece of wide insulation tape over their mouths – at least Bob had got part of his job right, Max thought to himself.

He crammed the radiophone into his loose-hanging shorts and began rifling through Delacroix's pockets. The Frenchman tensed his muscles. He was bursting with anger and frustration.

'Now then, cheese-eater,' Max hissed. 'I'll only ask you once. Where are the keys to the Range Rover?'

Outside, Luke had taken cover behind a mossy stone wall on the flank of the mountain and was keeping an eye on the green Range Rover on the cobbled terrace below. Max seemed to be taking ages.

At last he appeared – and he wasn't alone. He was leading Bob by the arm. The bodyguard was holding the back of his head and Max had to support him, which he did with an ill grace. The pair got into the front seats of the Range Rover and Max started the engine. Revving impatiently, he turned the vehicle round, giving his wrecked BMW an additional dent in the process.

The heavy Range Rover swung a turn onto the track leading back down the mountain. The brake lights flashed once, then the vehicle slipped out of view behind the trees.

Luke breathed in the mountain air and rubbed his cheeks. His hands were shaking slightly. They were still sore from the struggle with the stone blocks at the top of the tower. For the first time in forty-eight hours, he enjoyed a moment of mental peace.

He was still trying to get his mind round Max's involvement in the hijacking. It made a warped kind of sense that the hijackers should have had an inside accomplice at a high level – it was all a big insurance scam, the biggest ever. Luke now also understood why Max had been so relaxed during the hijacking itself.

The sun, which had climbed high over the valley, was beating down over the lovely Alpine scene. Behind the white snow of the sharply drawn summits, the sky was an intense pool of blue, with just a few wisps of cloud.

He felt like sitting down in the sun, but he picked up his jacket and padded back towards the stairs leading up into the monastery. The stairwell was silent. Luke felt the tension tighten up his stomach once more. Had Bob and Max really put the hijackers out of action? It seemed to be the case – there hadn't been a squeak from Delacroix and his team for about an hour.

Luke could nevertheless hear his own heartbeat thudding in his ears as he climbed on tired legs through the dimly lit building.

Nothing stirred. He stepped into the hall and listened behind the door of the room where the hijackers lay handcuffed. There was a faint moaning sound. Luke nudged at the door with his foot and saw the hijackers lying in a kind of star-formation on the floor, cuffed together wrist to wrist, ankle to ankle.

Luke stepped inside and looked down at Juliette and Delacroix. They looked strangely helpless with their limbs locked together. Every so often, one of the other members of the gang would wriggle and moan in frustration, but the leaders were motionless. Juliette's intense eyes, fixed on Delacroix, wore a look of adoration, and her sister Eva was gazing at him from the other direction. The leader and mastermind of the plot lay completely still. He looked older. The skin around the pink scar on the side of his neck was wrinkled and loose. His big, strong hands were bunched into huge fists, their knuckles bleeding from beating the floor.

'Checkmate,' Luke said, with a wink. Then he swung on his heel and left the room, locking the door behind him.

He went down to the round terrace and sat on the cobbles. It was sunny, but he was shivering.

Then Luke heard the rhythmic chopping sound of a helicopter. He stood in the middle of the terrace, took off his jacket and waved it like a flag.

Dust and leaves danced in the air whipped down by the police helicopter hovering above him. The terrace would have been an ideal place to land, but the wrecked

BMW was in the way. The side hatch slid open and Luke saw his father waving at him. The helicopter climbed a little higher, then a man in overalls came whirring down, suspended from a cable, landing between Luke and Max's squashed car. The man spun round, checking that the surroundings were secure, and with a gruff nod, put Luke in a harness that immediately winched him up to safety.

Feeling his tired, battered head begin to spin again as the terrace, the monastery and the ravine pulled away beneath him, Luke closed his eyes. He no longer had the energy to think. His ears hurt from the noise of the beating rotors.

He felt a strong pair of arms lifting him. He opened his eyes. A man wearing a helmet and overalls hoisted him into the cabin, where Dad rushed forward to embrace him. They exchanged a bone-crunching hug. Luke was brimming with happiness and some of that happiness found its way into his eyes.

'Greetings from Kaliningrad,' Dad said, raising his voice to be heard over the sound of the helicopter.

'Did everyone... survive?' Luke yelled.

'Yes. I understand one of the survivors is a particular fan of yours.'

Luke blushed – so Rosita had survived?

'I mean Mr Thomson,' Dad continued. 'He sends his greetings.'

'Coyote, sure.' Luke nodded. 'And what about... Rosita? The girl who worked in the kitchen...'

'Rosita's in hospital, but she'll be OK.'

Dad grabbed Luke by the shoulders and gave him a serious look. 'And what about the hijackers?'

'They're inside the monastery, handcuffed together.

But if you want to catch the brains behind this operation I suggest we fly *that* way.' Luke grinned as he pointed at the road below. 'We're looking for a Range Rover.'

'The brains being... Max Lownie Junior?'

'Yes. He plotted to sink his dad's ship for the insurance.'

Dad tapped the pilot on the shoulder and pointed down at the asphalt road. The chopper turned in a neat arc and began tracing the route of the road. Soon, they saw the Range Rover, its bonnet raised, and a portly figure in shorts beside it, staring up at the chopper.

'Oh dear.' Luke grinned at his Dad. 'I feared that might happen if you put sand in the petrol tank...'

'Where did you learn that trick?'

'From one of Toni's action films, as it happens.'

Dad laughed, shaking his head. 'Your life's been a bit of an action film, too, these past few days.'

'You can say that again.'

'You going fishing?' Dad said, pointing at the fish-hooks on the lapel of Luke's jacket.

'Who knows? How about it, actually? We used to fish every summer...'

'As soon as we get back, I promise.' Peter's face darkened, then brightened into a smile again. 'What about that diamond deal you mentioned. How did that work out for you?'

'Better than I thought. While Max was fetching the keys to the Range Rover, he left a bag of diamonds in his car. I swapped them for some honest Swiss gravel.'

Luke reached inside his pockets and produced a handful of small diamonds, which flashed like ice in the bright midday sun.

Dad's mouth dropped open.

'It's lucky I have so many pockets in these jeans.' Luke glanced down in the direction of the ravine. 'Can we come camping here some time? I dropped a couple of diamonds down there...'

'And which of the lucky ladies would you give them to?' Dad winked. 'Rosita or Emma?'

Luke blushed. 'What about one each?'

'You're looking for trouble, son.'

'You're right. Come to think of it, maybe I'd better just give them both to Gran.'

HACKING TIMBUKTU

STEPHEN DAVIES

Long ago in the ancient city of Timbuktu, a student pulled off the most daring heist in African history – the theft of 100 million pounds worth of gold. It was never recovered but now a cryptic map of its whereabouts has been discovered.

Danny Temple is a good traceur and a great computer hacker. When the map falls into his hands and he finds himself pursued by a bizarre group calling itself *The Knights of Akonio Dolo*, both of these skills are tested to the limit. From the streets of London to the sands of Timbuktu, this high-tech gold rush does not let up for a moment.

9781842708842 £5.99

THE CURSE OF
SNAKES

Christopher Fowler

'Something had been released into the night streets. It moved unnoticed and sucked the life from people. It caused slow painful death, but even those who could sense its presence were too scared to admit it was there.

And now, with quiet deliberation, it was heading for the street where I lived.'

Walking home from school one day, Red Hellion meets Max, who is trying to break in to the creepy, tightly locked park opposite Red's house. Soon Red finds himself sucked into Max's plans to discover the whereabouts of his father, who has disappeared under sinister circumstances. But neither Max nor Red realize that their investigations are about to lead them into horrific danger . . .

IISBN 9781849390569 £5.99

THE TRAP

JOHN SMELCER

Johnny pulled the fur-lined hood of his parka over his head and walked towards his own cabin with the sound of snow crunching beneath his boots.
'He should be back tomorrow,' he thought.

Johnny's grandfather is out checking trap lines, but he has been gone much too long. Proud, stubborn and determined to be independent he may be, but he has caught a foot in his own trap and hasn't the strength to free himself. As Johnny worries about him, he is menaced by wolves, plummeting temperatures and hunger. Does he have enough wilderness craft and survival instinct to stay alive? Will Johnny find him in time?

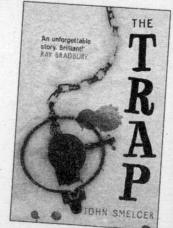

'An unforgettable story. Brilliant!' Ray Bradbury

9781842707395 £5.99